MacCallister:
The Eagles Legacy:
Kingdom Come

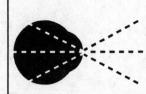

This Large Print Book carries the
Seal of Approval of N.A.V.H.

MacCallister: The Eagles Legacy: Kingdom Come

William W. Johnstone
with J.A. Johnstone

THORNDIKE PRESS
A part of Gale, Cengage Learning

GALE
CENGAGE Learning·

Farmington Hills, Mich • San Francisco • New York • Waterville, Maine
Meriden, Conn • Mason, Ohio • Chicago

GALE
CENGAGE Learning®

LIBRARY OF CONGRESS CATALOGING-IN-PUBLICATION DATA

Johnstone, William W.
  MacCallister : the Eagles legacy : kingdom come / by William W. Johnstone with J. A. Johnstone. — Large print edition.
    pages cm. — (Thorndike Press large print western)
    ISBN 978-1-4104-8218-1 (hardcover) — ISBN 1-4104-8218-9 (hardcover)
    1. Large type books. I. Johnstone, J. A. II. Title. III. Title: Eagles legacy : kingdom come. IV. Title: kingdom come.
PS3560.O415M335 2014
813'.54—dc23   2015017998

Published in 2015 by arrangement with Pinnacle Books, an imprint of Kensington Publishing Corp.

Printed in the United States of America
1 2 3 4 5 6 7 19 18 17 16 15

MacCallister:
The Eagles Legacy:
Kingdom Come

CHAPTER ONE

Carbon County, Wyoming

Riding along, minding his own business, Duff MacCallister crested the hill and was stopped by a man holding a pistol in one hand, the reins of his horse in the other.

"That's far enough, friend," growled the man.

"*Och,* it's friend that you call me, but you've a pistol in your hand. That would *nae* be the way to be greeting a friend now, would it?"

"It's only for a couple minutes, till we get our business done. We don't want anyone comin' along to interfere with what needs to be done."

It wasn't until then that Duff noticed four more men down at the bottom of the hill, some one hundred yards distant. One of them had his hands behind his back. One was holding a rope.

"And what business would that be, if you

don't mind the tellin'?"

The man nodded toward the base of the hill. "As you can see, we're about to hang someone."

"I take it he's *nae* been sentenced by a court, for I know of no court that would hang someone from a tree out in the middle of nowhere."

"Ha! You got that right. The only court this sumbitch has been to, is us."

"Who is *us*?"

"Us? That's me 'n my three friends. That's who *us* is."

"And would ye be for tellin' me what the lad's crime might be?"

"What's his crime? I'll tell you what his crime is. He's a Chinaman."

Duff frowned. "Is he now? Sure, and I wasn't aware it was against the law to be a Chinaman."

"It ain't only that. He's a Chinaman that don't know his place. He come into town drivin' a surrey 'n sittin' right there on the seat beside him was a white woman holdin' a baby."

Duff tipped his head to one side. "And was it his baby?"

"The baby didn't look Chinese, but that don't make no never mind. He had no business being with 'em."

8

"What did the white woman have to say about the situation?"

"We didn't give her no choice to say nothin' about it. It's more 'n likely that all she woulda done is just lie about it. Anyhow, she's done got hers." The man chuckled. "We laid the whip on her good. Now the Chinaman is about to get his."

Duff reached down to wrap his hand around his rifle. "I don't think so."

"What do you mean you don—"

That was as far as he got before Duff swung the rifle around, smashing it against the side of the man's head and sweeping him out of his saddle. He lay unconscious on the road as Duff slapped his legs against the sides of his horse, urging Sky into a gallop. As he approached the others, they looked around toward him. Not one of the men was holding a gun in his hand. Duff was holding a pistol, having slipped the rifle back into its sheath.

"Here, what is this?" one of the men asked.

"I'll be thanking you to let the gentleman go," Duff said, his Scottish brogue thick.

"Gentleman? What gentleman?"

"The gentleman whose hands you are about to untie."

"Mister, maybe you don't know, but this

here Chinaman was with a white woman. We can't just let him —"

Obscenities filled the air, coming from the man Duff had encountered moments earlier. Holding a rifle to his shoulder, he fired it, the bullet frying the air so close to Duff's head that he could hear it pop as it passed by.

Duff returned fire with his pistol, dropping his assailant with one shot. He turned back to the others. "Would you be so kind as to cut him loose now?" he asked in a calm voice.

"Mister, you've got no business interfering in this."

"Do you speak English?" Duff asked the Chinese man who, through it all, had been sitting quietly in the saddle, awaiting his fate.

"I speak English."

"What is your name?"

"I am Wang Chow."

"Wang, it seems like every Chinaman I've ever known is a good cook. Are you a good cook, Wang?"

"Here! What the hell is all this?" cried the man holding the rope. "We're about to hang this devil, and you want to know if he is a good cook?"

"Please, don't interrupt my interview with

this man."

"Huh? Your interview?"

Duff cocked the pistol and pointed it straight at the man's head. "I asked you nicely not to interrupt my interview."

The man put both hands up, palms facing out, fingers spread wide. "All right, all right, I ain't a-stoppin' you."

"Mr. Wang, I am thinking about hiring a cook. Are you a good cook?"

"I am very sorry, but I am not a good cook," Wang admitted.

"I admire your courage and your honesty. All you would have had to say is that you *are* a good cook, and that would save you from being hung. So, let me ask you this. If I hired you as my cook, would you be willing to learn?"

Wang, finally realizing what was going on, smiled broadly. "I will learn to be a very good cook."

"Mr. Wang, my name is MacCallister. Duff MacCallister. You're hired." He turned to the man who had been the spokesman for the group. "As you can see, sir, I do have a vested interest in the fate of this gentleman, as he is now one of my employees. I would be very disturbed if someone tried do something such as . . . well, let's just say, hang one of my employees. Now untie his hands."

"The hell we will!" shouted the third man. Jerking his gun from his holster, he snapped a shot toward Duff and missed.

Duff returned fire, and didn't miss. "So far this little encounter has cost you half your number," he said to the remaining two gunmen. "You can either untie Mr. Wang, *now,* or I will kill both of you and untie him myself."

"Untie him, Floyd, untie him!"

"That will not be necessary," Wang said, bringing both hands around front to show that they weren't tied.

"What the hell? How did you do that? It's impossible for you to get your hands free. I tied them myself," said the man with Floyd.

"Mr. Wang, if you would, sir, please collect their guns, including the guns from the man who is on the ground."

Wang dismounted.

"Wait a minute. I ain't about to give my guns to no Chinaman!" Floyd said.

"Oh, I think you will. You will either give them to him willingly, or I will arrange for him to take them from you just like he will be collecting them from your dead friend."

"Do it, Floyd, do it!" insisted his partner, his voice still animated by fear.

12

"This ain't right!" Floyd objected. "There ain't nothin' right about this!"

"Their rifles as well, Wang."

Grumbling, the men gave up their rifles.

"That horse you were sitting on. Is it yours?" Duff asked Wang.

"Hell no, that ain't his horse. It's mine," Floyd said. "We just brung it here for the hangin'."

"Can you read and write, Floyd?" Duff asked.

"Can I read and write? Hell yes, I can read 'n write."

"How much did you pay for that horse?"

"Mister, what the hell difference does it make to you how much I paid for that horse?"

"I plan to buy this horse from you, Floyd. I can't have Mr. Wang walking now, can I?"

"Buy it? You mean, with cash money?"

"Yes, of course I mean with cash money. It just so happens that I am returning from a trip where I sold some stock." Reaching into his saddlebag, Duff pulled out a piece of paper. "And by a fortuitous set of events, I also have a printed bill of sale here that is blank, left over from my business transactions. I'm going to give you one hundred dollars for the horse, and the saddle. And

13

you are going to sign this bill of sale over to me."

"What the hell? The saddle alone is worth a hunnert dollars," Floyd complained.

"You really aren't in a position to bargain right now," Duff pointed out as he began to fill in the blanks of the bill of sale. He turned to Floyd's partner. "You. What's your name?"

"What do you need my name for?"

"You're going to sign as a witness."

"It's Durant. John Durant."

"And his name? Beside Floyd, I mean."

"It's Russell. Floyd Russell," Durant said.

At the same time Durant said *Russell,* Russell said, *"Smith."* Realizing that Durant had spoken, he added, "Damn you, Durant, what for did you give him my real name?"

Duff secured the signatures of both men, then, putting the bill of sale in his pocket, he gave Russell five twenty-dollar bills. After that, he made the men dismount.

"What the hell? You only paid for one horse. You plannin' on takin' all of them?" Russell asked.

"Just to keep you two men alive," Duff said.

"How is leavin' us stranded goin' to keep us alive?" Durant asked.

"Because if I left the horses with you, no

doubt, you would try to come after us. And if you did that, I would have to kill you."

"You're a funny man, mister. You buy one horse, 'n you steal three," Russell said.

"I'm *nae* stealing the horses. About ten miles ahead, you'll come to the town of Le Bonte. I'll be leavin' the horses with the local constabulary, in your name. All you have to do is call for them and pay their keep."

"Le Bonte? That's where we come from. You show up in Le Bonte with that Chinaman on a stole horse, what do you think is goin' to happen to you?"

"*Och,* but the horse isn't stolen now, is it? Sure 'n I have a bill of sale confirming that I bought the horse from you."

Russell frowned. "You don't expect us to walk ten miles, do you?"

"Aye, you'll have to now, won't you? For 'tis a sure and certain thing that Le Bonte won't be coming to you."

"What about our guns?" Durant asked.

"They'll be with your horses. Mr. Wang, since you're having to keep up with the guns, I'll take charge of the three horses. Shall we go?"

"We go," Wang said.

Suddenly and unexpectedly, but in a coordinated move that the two men must have planned, Durant and Russell lunged

15

toward Wang Chow in an attempt to recover their guns.

Wang dropped the guns and pivoted on his left foot while driving his right foot into first Russell's, then Durant's face. Both men went down.

"Well now, that is a neat trick," Duff said. "It makes me wonder how they were able to capture you in the first place."

"They pointed guns at the woman," Wang said as he retrieved the weapons.

"They threatened to shoot a woman? What an unpleasant lot I stumbled into today."

"As you are now my employer, I ask your permission to check upon the woman."

"Of course we will. Is she your woman?"

"No," Wang said without further explanation.

"You've got too many guns to keep up with very easily. I'll take half of them. And, seeing as you aren't armed, perhaps you should strap on one of the holsters."

Wang shook his head. "I have no need for guns."

Duff chuckled. "After seeing you in action back there, I can almost believe you."

CHAPTER TWO

La Bonte, Wyoming

As Duff and Wang rode into town leading riderless horses, people on the street and board sidewalks stopped to stare.

"Ain't that the Chinaman Russell 'n the others had with them this mornin'?" a man asked his neighbor.

"Hey, mister. Who are you?" someone else shouted at Duff. "What are you doin' with that Chinaman? Where at is Russell, Mc-Gill, Alberson, and Durant?"

Neither MacCallister nor Wang answered the shouted question. They rode directly to the town marshal's office, tied off the horses, and went inside. Two badge-wearing men were drinking coffee and engaged in an animated conversation. They looked up, the expression on their faces showing their surprise at seeing the Chinaman.

"Which of you is the marshal?" Duff asked.

"We ain't neither one the marshal," said one. "We're deputies. The marshal has gone to Cheyenne to report on a lynchin'. Only this here Chinaman is the one we thought was lynched."

"You made no effort to stop it?"

"Hell, mister, half the town was in on it. They was only three of us. What was we s'posed to do?"

"Where are the woman and baby?" Wang asked.

"If I was you, Chinaman, I'd stay away from that woman, seein' as that's what got you into trouble in the first place," the short deputy said.

"Where are the woman and the child?" Duff asked.

"Well sir, after she got whupped, she got took down to Doctor Dunaway's office. More 'n likely that's where you'll find her now."

"Thank you. Oh, you will find four horses tied up out front. Eventually two men will call for them."

"Two men? What about the other two?"

"They are dead."

Duff and Wang found the woman in the doctor's office.

Her eyes opened wide and the expression

18

on her face was one of relief and joy when she saw Wang. "Oh! You are alive! Thank God, you are alive!"

Dr. Dunaway was just as surprised to see Wang. "What happened? I was told that the men who took you planned to hang you."

Wang nodded. "That was their plan, but this man stopped them."

"Oh, bless you," the woman said. "I have been feeling so bad about all this, knowing that it was my fault. How innocent we were. No one would listen, and this man's good deed was nearly repaid by him being murdered. Oh, Mister —" She stopped. "I never even learned your name."

"I am Wang Chow."

"Mr. Wang, you were nearly killed for your good deed. I can't thank you enough for what you did for my baby and me."

"How is the baby?" Wang asked the doctor.

"The baby will be just fine, thanks to you. He was very dehydrated when he got here, but I've been giving him water a little at a time. He's a strong little boy. It's Mrs. Harrison I've been worried about. I can't believe anyone could be so evil as to take a bullwhip to a defenseless woman."

"Has Mr. Wang told you what happened? I mean, how it was that we wound up together?" Mrs. Harrison asked Duff.

"I have not pried."

"He saved my life, that's what happened. He saved my life and the life of my baby. My husband, Lieutenant Harrison, was killed two weeks ago in a tragic accident at Fort Fetterman. I was on the way with my baby to Cheyenne to catch the train to go back home to Ohio. On the way here, the horse pulling the surrey stepped into a prairie dog hole and broke his leg. He suffered for a long time. I had not brought a gun with me so I had no way of putting the poor creature out of his misery.

"I kept hoping someone would come along who could help. I didn't think I could walk all the way to the next town, carrying a baby. By the end of the second day water and food were gone, and I knew we were going to have to try. By then, mercifully, the horse had died.

"On the morning of the third day, just as we were about to leave, this gentleman came along." She pointed to Wang. "He had water and food, which he shared, and he disconnected the surrey from poor Harry, connected his own horse to it, and drove us into town."

Dr. Dunaway took up the story. "Some of our seamier citizens took over then. They became incensed at seeing a white woman with a Chinaman. They pulled her down from the surrey and threatened to kill her if Mr. Wang didn't go with them. When Mrs. Harrison tried to protest, they took a bullwhip to her."

"Why didn't someone in the town try to intercede?" Duff questioned.

"Most were too frightened to do anything and some, I am sorry to say, agreed with what was happening."

"How long before Mrs. Harrison and the child will be able to travel?"

"Oh, they can travel now," Dr. Dunaway said. "I have put a lotion and bandages on her back to keep down the infection. And, as I said, the baby is strong as a horse."

Duff smiled at Mrs. Harrison. "Then I suggest we go down to the stagecoach depot and put you on the next coach to Cheyenne."

"Oh, I can't take the coach. If I do, I won't have enough money to buy the train ticket."

"Where is your surrey?"

"I don't know." Mrs. Harrison shrugged. "I don't know what happened to it or to my luggage. My baby and I have no clothes except for what I'm wearing."

Duff offered a suggestion. "You no longer have need of your surrey. Suppose I give you three hundred dollars for it? That will give you enough money for a coach ticket and for new clothes."

"Three hundred dollars? Why, even if I could find it, I don't know if it is worth that much."

"Don't worry about it. I'll find it."

Tears formed in Mrs. Harrison's eyes. She reached out to take first Duff's hand, then Wang's hand. "I thank you both, so much. I can't help but feel that Michael is in heaven, looking down on us, and that, somehow, he sent the two of you to me. God bless both of you."

Sky Meadow Ranch, Wyoming

Duff and Wang Chow reached the ranch and dismounted.

Elmer Gleason, Duff's foreman and friend, came out to greet them. "What's this Chinaman doin' here?"

"He has come to work for us."

"Really? Just what kind of work do you have in mind for 'im?"

"He's going to cook." Duff handed his reins to a cowboy and nodded to Wang to do the same.

"Well, Chinamen have been known to make pretty good cooks." Elmer glared at the young Chinese man.

Wang returned Elmer's gaze with an expression of trepidation.

Then Elmer smiled and stuck his hand out. *"Wei biao shi win hou. Huanying."*

Wang Chow's smile was broad as Elmer's, and he took the foreman's hand and shook it enthusiastically. *"Wei biao shi win hou."*

"Elmer, would you be for telling me what you and the young Celestial lad just said?"

"I just said hello, and I welcomed him. He said hello back to me."

"I had no idea you could speak Chinese."

"I made enough ports of call in China when I was a sailor to pick up some of the lingo." To Wang he said, *"Wo cunzai* Elmer." He pointed to himself.

"Elmer," Wang repeated, pointing to Elmer. He pointed to himself. *"Wo cunzai* Wang Chow."

Duff chuckled. "I see there's no need to introduce you, you've already done that." He motioned for them to walk toward the house.

"So he's going to be a cook, huh? That's a good idea of your'n, gettin' a cook instead of passin' it off among all the cowboys. Some of 'em is so bad it's a wonder we ain't none of us been pizened afore now."

"Wang can't cook."

"What? Whoever heard of a Chinaman

23

who can't cook? Is he tellin' the truth, Wang? You can't cook?"

"He tells the truth. I cannot cook."

"Then why in the Sam Hill did you hire him as a cook, if he can't cook?"

"It's a long story," Duff said. "I'm going to count on you to teach him."

Elmer smiled. "All right, I'll do it. As long as I don't have to teach him none o' that nasty stuff like neeps 'n haggis."

"Elmer, how is it that a man of your experience and world travel has never been able to cultivate an appreciation of such a delicacy?"

" 'Cause it ain't a delicacy is why. Neeps 'n haggis ain't worth feedin' to the hogs. Oh, by the way, Miss Megan said to tell you that her sister 'n brother-in-law is comin' to Chugwater soon. And they're bringin' her nephew with 'em."

"That's good to know," Duff said. "It will be nice meeting some of Megan's family."

Elmer chuckled. "It ain't just a meetin', you know."

"What do you mean?"

"It's more 'n likely she's brought 'em up here to check you out, to see iffen maybe you're a fit person for her to marry."

"There you go again, Elmer, tryin' to be a matchmaker. When the time comes, I'll make my own match, thank you."

Elmer laughed again. "If you say so. Come, Wang, let me introduce you to some of these critters you'll be cookin' for, oncet I learn you to cook."

Elmer led Wang into the barn where three cowboys were standing on a board stretched between two barrels. "Boys, I want you to meet our new cook. This here is Wang Chow." Elmer pointed to the cowboys one at a time as he introduced them to Wang.

"This here feller with his nose mashed up against his face 'cause he got into a fight with someone he ought not to have, is Tom Woodward, only don't never call him nothin' but Woodward."

"It warn't no fight. I got kicked in the face by a mule. You know that, Elmer."

Elmer ignored him. "And the feller that ain't hardly got no teeth to speak of is Martin. I don't know as I've even heard his first name spoke. And this long, tall, drink of water is Adam Dewey. He's the youngest, but he ain't the dumbest."

"And just what qualifies you to pick the dumbest?" Dewey asked.

"That's easy, 'cause there ain't nearly no one dumber 'n me," Elmer said good-naturedly, and the others laughed. "You fellers want to tell me why in Sam Hill you got a board lyin' twixt these two barrels?" He pointed at the board in question.

"We're plannin' on usin' it as a wedge under the corner of the waterin' trough," Woodward said. "But it's too long, 'n none of us wants to walk all the way back to the machine 'n toolshed just to get a saw. We was plannin' on breakin' it with a shovel, but so far there ain't none of us been able to do it."

"I've only had one or two tries," Dewey said. "Here, let me try again." He swung the shovel hard at the board, but it just bounced back up. After four or five tries he handed it to Martin, who tried, unsuccessfully, to break it.

"Let's see what our new cook can do," Martin said, handing the shovel to Wang. "Here, see if you can break this board."

Wang took the shovel from Martin, held it for just a moment, then handed it to Elmer.

"No, don't give it to me. I know damn well I can't break the board."

"You want the board broken here?" Wang pointed to the shovel marks on the board.

"Yes." Elmer tried to hand the shovel back to Wang, but he waved it off.

"I do not need shovel."

Wang put the knife edge of his hand on the board and held it there for a moment.

26

"Ha! What are you going to do? Break the board with your bare hand?" Dewey asked.

"Haiiiiiiiiiiiiiuh!" Wang shouted, quickly lifting his hand, bringing it down sharply against the board, and breaking it in two.

"I'll be damned!" Woodward said. "I ain't never seen nothin' like that."

"I have," Elmer said quietly. "Wang, you know *wu shu*?"

"Shi dey wo wancheng?"

"What the hell did he just say?" Woodward asked.

"I asked if he knew *wu shu,* and he said yes, he did."

"What the hell is *wu shu*?"

"Let's put it this way. I would advise none of you to ever get into a fight with Mr. Wang."

"Why would I want to fight a little feller like that in the first place?" Dewey asked.

Elmer laughed. "Yeah, why would you?"

"I ain't never seen nothin' like that," Woodward said again, the expression on his face reflecting his awe.

CHAPTER THREE

Chugwater, Wyoming

A banner was stretched across Clay Avenue.

CHUGWATER RIFLE MARKSMANSHIP CONTEST

The shooting had started at nine o'clock that morning, with thirty-five shooters. There were only five left, all five shooting Creedmoor Rifles. For the last four rounds of shooting, all five had hit their target at dead center. The target was now three hundred yards away.

"What are we going to do now, Mr. Guthrie?" one of the townspeople asked.

Normally, Bob Guthrie was the owner and proprietor of a building supply company, but today, he was the judge of the shooting contest. "We can move the target back another hundred yards."

"Or you could just go ahead and move it

on down to Cheyenne," one of the townspeople suggested, to the laughter of many.

"We may as well. We've got the target three hundred yards away now. Another hundred yards would be almost a quarter of a mile," Fred Matthews said.

"Yes, well, pretty soon it's not goin' to make that much difference anyway, 'cause the truth is, we're runnin' out of targets," Guthrie said.

One of the shooters was Duff MacCallister, and another was Duff's good friend, Biff Johnson, who owned the Fiddlers' Green Saloon. He had given the saloon that name because he was an old cavalryman who had ridden with Custer on his last fight. Cavalry legend held that anyone who had ever heard the bugle call "Boots and Saddles" would, when they died, go to a cool, shady place by a stream of sweet water called Fiddlers' Green. There, they would meet all the other cavalrymen who had gone before them, and they would greet those who come after them as they await the final judgment. Biff had managed to avoid Custer's fate because he was part of Reno's battalion.

The other three shooters still in the contest were not from Chugwater. Jason

Bowles was married to Megan Parker's sister, Melissa. Megan owned a dress shop in Chugwater, and Megan and Duff were — as the women of the town explained to anyone who might ask about their relationship — courting. Jason, Melissa, and their nine-year-old son, Timmy, lived in Eagle Pass, a small town in West Texas. Jason was the sheriff of Maverick County, and they had come to Chugwater to visit Megan.

The two remaining shooters, Louis Wilson and Roy Carter, had come to town specifically to participate in the shooting match. They were drawn there because of the award money. Seven hundred and fifty dollars were being offered for first place. Second place was worth five hundred dollars, and two hundred and fifty dollars was the prize for third place. That was a significant amount of money, and it made entering the contest worthwhile.

"You fellas ready to give up?" Carter asked. "If they move that wagon any farther back, I doubt any of you will even be able to see it, let alone hit the target."

The paper targets had been printed by the newspaper just for the occasion, and they were attached to a wooden frame that had been placed into the bed of a wagon.

"Ha! I seem to remember you sayin'

somethin' like that up in Soda Creek," Wilson said. "But I beat you up there, an' I'll damn sure beat you here."

"We'll see about that," Carter replied. Their bantering was good natured because the two had competed against each other many times before. They could be considered professional shooters, so many contests did they enter. As a result of their frequent head-to-head competition, they had become good friends.

"Mr. Guthrie," Duff said. "Would you be open to a suggestion as to how to solve this dilemma that has been created in the shooting match as it is currently constituted?"

"I would be open to anything that would put an end to a match that seems like it might be goin' on until this time next week."

"I would say move the wagon back another two hundred yards. Place it five hundred yards from here, and let us continue."

Gasps of surprise and disbelief came from those who had spent most of the day watching the contest, drawn by a demonstration of shooting such as had rarely been seen before.

"Nobody can put a bullet into a bull's-eye no bigger than a silver dollar at five hundred yards," Carter said. "This is ridiculous. This is a waste of time. We will all miss, then we'll

31

just have to reset the wagon in order to start over again. I say just move it another fifty yards and be done with it."

"I won't miss at five hundred yards," Duff said.

"What? Of course you will," Wilson said. "I'm telling you, nobody can hit the bull's-eye from that far out," Carter said. "What do you other fellas say?"

"I don't know," Biff said. "I've seen Duff shoot before. If anyone can do it, he can."

"Impossible."

"I have a suggestion," Duff offered. "If I don't hit the bull's-eye, no matter what the rest of you do, I'll drop out of the contest. Then you can pull the wagon back to whatever distance you want and resume shooting."

"You mean even if all of the rest of us also miss, you'd still be willin' to pull out?" Wilson asked.

"Yes."

Wilson grinned. "What do you say, Carter? If he misses, he's out?"

"Yeah, if he wants to do it that way, I don't see no problem with it."

Duff wasn't finished. "However, if I hit the bull, dead center, I'll be declared the winner."

"Dead center? You mean, not touchin' the

line anywhere?" Wilson clarified.

"Yes."

"Mister, you're on," Wilson said. Carter quickly concurred.

"Biff, Jason, what do you think?" Duff asked.

"Then the rest of us will be shootin' for second and third prize?" Biff asked.

"Yes."

"I don't have a problem with that, do you, Jason?" Biff asked.

"No problem," Jason said.

It wasn't until all four of the other shooters had agreed to Duff's proposal that four men went out, then half pulled and half pushed the wagon all the way down to the far end of Clay Avenue. From where the shooters stood, the entire target could barely be seen, let alone the bull's-eye. It looked like a tiny white patch.

Wilson turned to Duff. "You do understand, don't you, mister, that we're goin' to be holdin' you to your brag. Hittin' that little old piece of paper don't count for nothin'. You got to hit the bull's-eye dead center. How are you goin' to do that?"

Biff concurred. "Duff, I got to ask the same question. You can barely even see the bull's-eye from here. How are you going to hit it?"

"Mathematical calculation," Duff replied.

Biff frowned. "I know that in the artillery, the gun crews use geometry to find their targets, but I've never heard of anyone firing a rifle that way."

"It's simple," Duff said. "I know the size of the target paper because I'm the one that arranged to have 'em printed. The size of the target is twelve inches wide by fifteen inches tall. So, I just estimate my target point as seven and one half inches up from the bottom of the paper and six inches in from the left-hand side. If the target isn't a misprint, that is where the bull's-eye will be. All I have to do then is squeeze the trigger."

Everyone grew quiet expecting Duff to pause for a long time to control his breathing and lay in his sight picture. To the surprise of everyone who was holding their collective breath, Duff brought the rifle up to his shoulder smoothly, then pulled the trigger almost as if in the same fluid motion.

Some of the women let out a little startled reaction to the loud pop. It wasn't that the shot was unexpected; people had been shooting all day. What was unexpected was the fact they he had fired so quickly at his target.

Carter laughed out loud. "Ha! You missed. Are you going to just stay here and watch the rest of us shoot, or have you had enough for now?"

"I didn't miss," Duff said.

"How do you know? You can't even see the bull's-eye from here."

"Then how do you know I missed?"

"Because there can't nobody hit a target that small, from this far away."

"Duff can, and he did." Guthrie was staring through a pair of binoculars.

"Well? How far off the bull's-eye was he?" Carter asked.

"He wasn't off at all," Guthrie said in a matter-of-fact voice. "On the contrary, he put the bullet dead center."

"Mr. MacCallister," someone called. "Swede, Clovis, and Loomis is takin' off on your Chinaman. You'd better come get 'im, or they're goin' to beat him up bad."

"Where is he?"

"He's down in front of the grocery store."

"Oh, Duff, don't let them hurt Mr. Wang," Megan said. "He is so much smaller than they are."

Duff, Jason, Megan, and Elmer hurried down to the grocery store. Holding a bag filled with groceries, Wang stood in the road in front of the store, surrounded by three large men.

"I'm goin' to tell you one more time — put them groceries down and walk away. If you don't, we're goin' to beat the hell out of you 'n take 'em ourselves."

"Mr. Bloomington, what seems to be the trouble here?" Duff asked.

"Your Chinaman bought the last package of brown sugar I had in the store a moment before Swede came in, looking for the same thing. When the Chinaman wouldn't give the sugar up, Swede and the two who came in with him got mad."

"Wang, do we really need the brown sugar?" Duff asked.

"Yes," Wang said.

"Well, there you go, Swede. My cook says that he needs it."

"You takin' a hand in this fight, MacCallister?"

"Me? No. Wang says he needs the brown sugar, and you want it as well. My suggestion to you is, if you want it badly enough, go ahead and take it from him. That is, if you think you can."

"Look here, MacCallister. Are you sayin' you ain't goin' to take a hand in this?"

"That's what I'm saying."

"Duff!" Megan gasped. "What do you mean? How could you?"

36

"Watch," Duff said calmly.

"You hear that, Chinaman? MacCallister has done give us permission to take it from you."

"That's not quite what I said, Swede. I'm sure you heard me add, 'if you can.' "

"Oh, yeah, I heard you say that," Swede said, an evil smile spreading across his face as he raised his fists. "And we can. We damn sure can."

"Go ahead, Wang," Duff said.

Wang nodded and set the bag of groceries down, then he assumed a fighting position with his right arm bent at the elbow, his hand in front of his face, and his left arm stretched out before him. His hands were open and the fingers extended and joined.

"Ha! Look at him, Swede!" Clovis said. "I think he's going to slap us."

"I almost feel guilty about fightin' someone that fights like a woman," Loomis said.

"No need to feel guilty," Duff said. "Go ahead, teach this Chinaman a lesson."

"Duff, I can't believe what I'm hearing," Megan said with a gasp.

"Don't worry none, Miss Megan," Elmer said. "I've seen how these Chinamen fight before. It's different from anything anyone around here has ever seen, but Wang will be

37

all right." To Wang he said, *"Yìjue cíxiong, Wang, pengyou."*

"What did you say to him?" Megan asked.

"I told him to fight well."

Swede was the first to commit himself, using his size and strength in a bull-like charge.

Wang bent his knees, lowering himself so the roundhouse swing went over his head. He shot out his right arm and drove the point of his fingers deep into Swede's solar plexus. Swede, with a sudden expulsion of air, bent over trying to breathe, out of the fight.

Wang's right foot smashed into Clovis's face, taking him down, while he stopped Loomis with a knife-edged blow of his hand to the Adam's apple. All three of his attackers were immobilized in less than five seconds.

As everyone looked on in shock, Wang picked up the grocery bag. "I understand that you are having guests, Mr. MacCallister."

"I am."

"I will make something special for dinner."

"That's why you needed the brown sugar?"

"It is."

"I appreciate that."

Wang walked over to the buckboard, put his purchases in the back, then drove off.

"Did you see what that one little China-man did to them three big men? I ain't never seen nothin' like that in my livelong life," someone said.

"You knew he could fight like that?" Megan asked.

"I knew."

"And you knew as well," she said to Elmer.

"Yes, ma'am. I've seen the Chinese priests fight like that before."

"Priests. Good heavens, are you saying he is a priest?" Megan gasped.

"Yes, ma'am, but not like any priest you've ever heard of."

CHAPTER FOUR

Sky Meadow Ranch

That night, Duff hosted a dinner for Megan, her sister Melissa, her brother-in-law Jason, and her nephew Timmy. Elmer was there with his "personal" friend, Vi Winslow. Biff Johnson and his wife Rose came, too. Rose was a first-generation American, the daughter of Scottish immigrants. Duff was a Scottish immigrant, which had helped establish an immediate friendship with Biff.

"This is absolutely delicious," Duff said. "What is it called?"

"Tian Suan Rou," Wang replied.

"Sweet-and-sour pork," Elmer translated. "That's why he needed the brown sugar."

"When I hired you, you told me you couldn't cook."

"I can cook Mandarin. I cannot cook American," Wang replied.

"I'll have 'im cookin' American in no time atall," Elmer said. "But I had almost forgot how much I liked Chinese food."

"I've had it in San Francisco," Biff said. "But I've never had it any better than this."

For the next several minutes all the diners enjoyed their food, especially Elmer, who enjoyed showing off by eating his meal with chopsticks.

Vi Winslow, a widow in her mid-forties and still quite attractive, owned Vi's Pies, and she had brought a couple pies for dessert.

After dessert, they moved into the parlor, where they enjoyed a glass of scotch, which was Biff's contribution to the evening seeing as he owned a saloon.

"Well, 'tis a happy occasion for us all, what with the three of us, Duff, myself, and Sheriff Bowles winning prizes as we did at the shooting match today," Biff said.

"I'm Sheriff Bowles when I am at work in Texas. Here, among friends and family, the name is Jason." He smiled.

"Jason it is then," Biff continued. "And you know what I liked best about winning? It was sending Mr. Carter and Mr. Wilson home with nothing to show for their efforts but a handful of spent cartridge casings."

"You were magnificent, all of you," Megan said.

"And shouldn't we be drinkin' to that?"

Elmer asked, holding up his glass.

"Why should you be drinking?" Vi asked. "You didn't have anything to do with it."

"Why sure I did," Elmer insisted. "Who was cheerin' for 'em the loudest, I ask?"

"Aye," Duff said with a chuckle. "There can be no denying but that Elmer was vocal in his support, and 'tis for sure and certain that he deserves to be drinking this toast with us."

"Duff, give us an appropriate Scottish toast, would you?" Jason asked.

Duff lifted his glass. "Here's to the heath, the hill, and the heather, the bonnet, the plaid, the kilt, and the feather!"

"And while goin' up the hill of fortune, may we never meet a friend comin' down," Biff replied.

The others laughed.

"What a great toast!" Jason said.

"Elmer, here's something you will appreciate," Megan said. "I'll bet you didn't know that, for several years, Jason was a sailor, like you."

"You sailed before the mast, did you?" Elmer asked. The term referred to serving as one of the crewmen, because the crew billets were ahead of the foremast.

Jason chuckled. "You won't hold it against

me if I was one of the ship's officers, will you?"

"Nah," Elmer smiled. "You never laid a cat across my back, so I got nothin' ag'in you."

"I never laid, nor did I ever order, a cat-o-nine against the back of any man," Jason said.

"It would-a been a pleasure to sail with you, then," Elmer said.

"I'm afraid all of my voyages were on the Atlantic," Jason said. "I never got the opportunity to visit China, and I admire you for picking up the language as you did."

"I don't know all that much of the lingo," Elmer replied. "Mostly I knew just enough to get around in the seaports."

"I've never seen fighting like the kind Wang Chow did today," Jason said. "Have you?"

"I've seen it a couple times."

Timmy had not seen Wang Chow's fight, but he had heard about it. He was listening with his full attention. "Do you think Mr. Wang could teach me how to fight like that?"

"Wang can't teach you," Elmer said.

"Why not? Is it because I'm too young?"

"No, that has nothing to do with it. In fact, people who learn *wu shu* generally start when they are your age or even younger."

"*Wu shu?*"

"That's what it's called."

"Well, if I'm not too young, how come he can't teach me?"

"I tried to get someone to teach it to me once," Elmer said. "But it's a secret that they learn from some temple, and word I've heard is, if they teach it to anyone outside the temple, why, they could be kilt. You wouldn't want Wang to be kilt, would you?"

"No," Timmy said. "I wouldn't want that."

"You say it's learned in a temple?" Duff asked. "Does that mean Wang Chow learned it in a temple?"

"More 'n likely he did. But it won't be somethin' he'll talk about."

"I wonder what he is doing here, in America?" Biff asked.

Elmer shook his head. "I don't know, and it ain't my place to ask."

"You are a wealth of information, Mr. Gleason. Even if you did sail before the mast, I would almost be willing to change places with you," Jason said. "I'm afraid I have no experiences to match yours."

"I never did get into the Atlantic, so I ain't never been to places like London or Paris, Rome, or anyplace like that."

"Rome was the most fascinating," Jason

said. "Though London and Paris were very interesting, as well."

For the next several minutes Elmer, Jason, and even Duff entertained the others with their tales of the sea and foreign places. After a series of misadventures back in Scotland, Duff wound up coming to America as an able-bodied seaman onboard the *Hiawatha,* a merchant ship plying the Atlantic trade. But his sailing adventures differed from those of Elmer and Jason, both of whom had spent a few years at sea. Duff's maritime experience was due to a set of circumstances, and he left the sea as soon as he reached America.

Biff shared stories of riding with Custer, and, after much prodding, Duff even told a few stories of his own service where he took part in the battle of Tel-el-Kebir in Egypt.

"What Duff left out was that he was awarded the Victoria Cross," Biff said. "That's like our Medal of Honor."

Wang Chow overheard some of the conversation, especially the part of the conversation that had referred to him. He could understand English better than he could speak it, and he heard someone ask why he had come to America.

He'd had no choice in the matter. It was

come to America or be killed. He thought back to four years ago in Shishou, Hubei Province, China.

The town was on the Yangtze River. Carp jerked and flopped as Wang Chow drew in his nets.

"You have had much luck today, Wang Chow." The speaker was Ching Ji, a member of the warrior society Taiyang. Although the town had a *shizhang* — mayor — and city government, Taiyang and another warrior society, Yuequi, actually ruled the city, levying heavy taxes, which they called, "tributes for protection."

"We will be good to you and take only one half of what you have caught. You may put our half in these baskets." Ching Ji nodded to another man and he brought four straw baskets down to the river and lined them up along the river's edge.

"We will return for the fish when the baskets are full."

Ching Ji and the man left. Wang Chow recovered all his fish and put none in the baskets Kwan Li had left.

"It is good that you paid no tribute to the Taiyang," Chen Mai, a member of the Yuequi, told him that evening. "Come, be a warrior for the Yuequi, and you will not have to labor.

46

You can live on the tributes given by the others."

"I do not wish to join a warrior group," Wang said. "I want only peace."

"Then you will have to pay tribute."

"I will not pay tribute," Wang insisted.

What no one in town, except Wang's family, knew, was that he was a priest of the Shaolin Temple of Changlin. He had entered the temple as a boy of nine, and left when he was twenty-eight years old, a master of the Chinese martial art of *wu shu.*

When Wang Chow returned to the river to cast his nets the next day, the Taiyang went to the fish market to kill Wang's father. The Yuequi went to the house to kill Wang's mother and sister. In both incidents, they left their mark, a red card representing Taiyang, and a black stone for Yuequi.

Wang buried his family, then went to the Changlin Temple to burn incense in their honor.

"Seek no revenge," he was told.

"But Master Tse, am I to do nothing to honor my family?"

"Changlin is your family. If you spill blood, you will bring dishonor to the temple."

After leaving the temple, Wang cut the topknot to his hair, which was his spiritual connection to Changlin. Then, donning a changshan and arming himself with a sword, he went to the tong of the Taiyang.

"Stop. You cannot enter," said the guard at the door.

One quick slice of his sword opened the stomach of the guard, killing him before he could call out a warning.

Wang went into the hall where six men were drinking wine and laughing about having killed the father of the fisherman Wang.

"Arm yourselves," Wang said calmly.

The men looked at each other in surprise, shocked that a mere fisherman would challenge any of them, let alone all of them.

Within less than a minute, all six were dead.

A visit to the tong of Yuequi left nine dead, though he gave all nine the opportunity to arm themselves, then form into a group for their battle with him.

Upon hearing about the carnage caused by Wang, the Changlin Temple expelled him from their order, and the Empress Dowager Ci'an issued a decree ordering his death.

Disguised, Wang left China with a group of laborers who were going to America to work on the railroad.

When the railroad was completed, Wang supported himself in a number of menial tasks, never disclosing to anyone that he was a Shaolin priest.

Now he was cooking for the man who had saved his life. Still lost in thought, Wang made a personal vow to be ever loyal to the man who had saved his life and, if required, to give his life in defense of *Xiansheng* MacCallister.

"Wang?" Duff's call interrupted Wang's rumination.

The Chinaman stepped out of the kitchen and through the door into the dining room.

Duff held up his glass of wine. "Join us, Wang. Someone who could cook a meal such as the one we have just enjoyed should be able to bask in the compliments of appreciative diners."

Wang put his hands in a prayer-like position and dipped his head slightly. "I thank you a thousand times, Xiansheng."

"What does that mean?" Rose asked Elmer.

"I think it's either sir, or mister, or something like that."

"Yes," Wang replied. "It is a word of respect."

Later, as Biff and Timmy were playing a spirited game of chess, Duff stepped out onto the porch and watched the last rays of light play on the Laramie Mountain Range.

As he expected she would, and as he hoped she would, Megan came out onto the porch a moment later to join him.

"It was very sweet of you to host a dinner for my sister and her family."

"Sure 'n twas glad I was to do it, lass. Your sister is nearly as pretty as you are, 'n Jason is a fine man." Duff chuckled. "And Timmy is a fine young lad as well, though he should have more manners than to beat his elders in chess."

"Timmy is a very smart boy." Megan smiled. "Who knows, he might be president of the United States, someday."

"And if he is, will he be forgetting the friends he made here in Wyoming?"

"*Och,* but 'tis more than a friend I am, Duff MacCallister. 'Tis the aunt of the president I'll be."

"*Och? Och?*" Duff said, laughing as he spoke the words. "Sure now Megan Parker, 'tis mocking the brogue you can do, but there could be heather flowers in your hair, 'n ye would still *nae* be Scots lass, would ye?"

"Maybe not, but you have taught me to love the pipes, and I promised Melissa that you'd play for us before they go back. Now would be the best time."

"All right. You talked me into it."

Megan laughed. "I didn't have to talk much. You're always ready to play the pipes, with but the slightest suggestion that you do so."

"Aye, lass, but 'tis my mission, don't you see?"

"Your mission?"

"Aye. 'Tis honor bound I am, to teach the rest of the world to enjoy the music of the pipes."

"Duff . . . and in your kilts?"

CHAPTER FIVE

A short while later, Duff came into the parlor wearing his kilts and carrying the bagpipes. The kilt of the Black Watch was a plaid of dark green and blue. The tunic was blue with brass buttons, a gold braided loop over his left shoulder, and the Victoria Cross pinned to his chest. The uniform was completed with a black cockade, and the *sgian dubh,* a small, ceremonial knife stuck down in one of his knee-high socks.

"Megan." Melissa then leaned closer to say something to her sister, speaking so quietly that nobody could hear her.

Duff saw her asking the question, and from the humorous expression on both sisters' faces, knew what it was.

"Would ye be wantin' Megan to check for herself if 'tis true what they say about the wearin' o' kilts?" he asked in a jocular voice.

Melissa gasped, then blushed as the others laughed. By Duff's comment, and

Melissa's reaction, they all knew she had just asked if men wore anything under their kilts.

Duff played "Scotland the Brave" and as he did so, Timmy, with a broad smile, marched around the room.

Duff finished playing the pipes to polite applause, then Wang Chow came into the room bearing a platter of Nian Gao coconut rolls. Everyone, especially Timmy, enjoyed them.

After the rolls and coffee, Jason, Melissa, Timmy, and Megan returned to town in one four-passenger trap. Biff, Rose, and Vi followed them in another. Duff and Elmer stood out on the front porch to tell them good-bye and to watch them drive away.

"It was a fine evenin', Duff," Elmer said. "As fine as I've enjoyed in a long time."

"Aye, 'twas that," Duff agreed. "And due in no small part to Wang Chow. What was that he served us tonight?"

"Tian suan rou," Elmer said. "Sweet-and-sour pork."

"I never knew I could like Chinese food so much."

The Drew farm, southeast New Mexico Territory
Mickey Drew held his head under the spout

and worked the pump handle as cold, deep-well water cascaded over him. The water washed away the dirt and sweat from an afternoon of hard work in the field. Although he was only fifteen, he did a man's work around the place, and he swelled with pride when his father bragged on him to the neighbors.

He reached for the towel he had draped across the split-rail fence, but drew his hand back, empty, when he couldn't find it. He heard a girl's giggle.

"What are you lookin' for?" the girl asked.

"Jean Marie," he said angrily. "What are you doing? Give me that towel."

"What towel?" she asked.

Mickey rubbed the water out of his eyes and saw her holding the towel behind her back. She was smiling at him.

"What towel? That towel." He pointed to the towel she was holding.

She pulled the towel from behind her back. "Oh, you mean this towel? Why didn't you say so? I wasn't sure what towel you were talking about." She passed the towel over to him.

Mickey took the towel and began drying his face. "You're not funny, Jean Marie. Unlike you, I've been working hard in the field all day. What have you done?"

"Nothing much. I just made some corn-bread for supper is all."

"Big deal."

"And a cherry pie," she added.

Mickey pulled the towel down and looked at her. "You made a cherry pie?"

"Yes, and I did it just for you. Mama wanted to do an apple pie, but I reminded her that you liked cherry pie better."

"Just for me, huh?"

"Yes, just for you."

"Why?"

"Why? Because you're my big brother, that's why."

"No, that's not the only reason. You want something."

"What makes you think I want something?"

"This is your brother you're talking to, Jean Marie. Remember? Now, what do you want?"

Jean Marie grinned. "Well, there is one thing."

"I thought so. What is it?"

"I want you to talk to Papa for me."

"Talk to Papa? What about?"

"About the barn dance in town Saturday night."

"What about it? He already said I could take you with me."

"I don't want to go to the dance with you."

"You don't? What do you mean, you don't? I thought you were wanting to go to the dance," Mickey said. "Girl, you need to make up your mind, one way or the other."

"I do want to go to the dance. I just don't want to go with *you*. I mean, how do you think it is going to look to all my friends if my own brother takes me to the dance? They'll think nobody but my brother wants anything to do with me."

"You do want to go to the dance?"

"Yes."

"Well, tell me this, Jean Marie. How do you plan to get there, if I don't take you?"

Jean Marie smiled. "With Danny Dunnigan."

"You want to go to the dance with Danny Dunnigan?"

"Yes, but Papa won't let me go with Danny. He says I'm too young to go to the dance with anyone but a member of my own family."

"You are too young," Mickey said easily.

"Too young? I'm only one year younger than you are, Mickey Drew."

"That don't make no difference. You're a girl. It's different with girls."

"I'm not a girl. I'm a woman . . . near 'bout." Jean Marie leaned against the split-rail fence and thrust her hip out, proudly displaying the developing curves of her young body. "Mickey, please tell Papa to let me go to the dance with Danny. Papa will listen to you."

"Not about something like this, he won't. Come on. Let's go have supper. You made the cornbread and the pie, did you?"

"Yes. Mickey, please talk to Papa."

"Maybe if we all three went together," Mickey suggested. "That way it would look to your friends like you were going with Danny, and I was just tagging along. And to Papa it would look like Danny was just tagging along with us."

"Oh, Mickey! You think so?" Jean Marie said excitedly. She threw her arms around his neck. "You are the best brother in the whole world!"

"I can't be that much, if you don't want to go with just me," Mickey said, laughing."

As the two walked back up the path to the house, they saw two horses tied to the fence in front.

"Who's visiting?" Mickey asked.

"I don't know. There wasn't anyone here when I left the house."

Mickey pushed the door open, then came to a complete halt, his eyes wide with confusion.

Two strange men were in the kitchen, and both were holding guns in their hand. Marvin Drew was lying on the floor with blood pooling beside his head. Mickey didn't know whether his father was dead or unconscious. His mother was standing to one side, her face contorted by confusion, fear, and grief.

"Mama?" Jean Marie asked, barely able to get the word out.

"Who are you?" Mickey asked angrily. "What are you doing here?"

Neither of the men replied. The one with swarthy skin and dark eyes turned his gun toward Mickey and pulled the trigger. When the bullet struck him, Mickey felt as if he had been kicked in the stomach by a mule. He fell facedown onto the floor.

"Mickey!" Jean Marie screamed.

"Murderers!" Mickey's mother yelled.

"Which one of these two women do you want, Jaco?" one of the men asked.

"Hell, Putt, it don't make that much difference to me. They's two of them, 'n two of us. I reckon we can just start out on one, then trade. That way, we can have 'em both."

"Yeah," Putt said with an almost insane giggle. "Yeah, that's a damn good idea."

Mickey could hear the conversation, but

there was nothing he could do about it. Try as he might, he was unable to move. Just before he passed out, he heard a scream. Whether it was from his mother or his sister, he didn't know.

Chaperito, New Mexico Territory

When Mickey came to he was lying in bed, with bandages wound completely around his stomach. Dr. Pinkstaff was standing alongside the bed, looking down at him.

"Where am I?" Mickey asked.

"You're in my office. You gave us quite a scare, Mickey. I didn't know if you were going to make it or not."

"Mom, Dad, Jean Marie! Where are they?"

Dr. Pinkstaff reached out to touch his hand to Mickey's shoulder. He shook his head. "I'm sorry, son. They're —" he paused in mid-sentence.

"They're dead, aren't they? Those men killed them."

"I'm afraid so. I'm sorry."

"I know who it was that did it," Mickey said. "I heard 'em talkin', and I heard 'em call each other by name."

"Sheriff Baxter was hoping it would be something like that. He wanted to talk to you as soon as you woke up. I'll go get hm."

Mickey lay in bed after the doctor left,

replaying the event in his mind. He had, indeed, heard them call each other by name, or at least, by something. Whether or not that was their real names, he had no way of knowing.

"You're sure those are the names you heard?" Sheriff Baxter asked a few minutes later, after Mickey shared them with him. "Jaco and Putt?"

"Yes, sir. I mean, I know they're kind of dumb soundin', and I don't know if that's their real names, but that's what I heard 'em callin' each other."

"Was one dark, almost Mexican or Indian lookin'? And was the other one an albino?"

"Yeah, one of 'em did look like a Mexican. The other one . . . what's an albino?"

"Someone that's so pale that his skin is almost white."

"He had funny-lookin' eyes, too. Like they was pink, or somethin'."

"Yes. The descriptions fit, and that's their names, all right. One is A. M. Jaco, and the other 'n is Blue Putt."

"You know these men?" Mickey asked.

"I don't think there is a sheriff or city marshal in all of New Mexico who doesn't know them. Or at least, know of them. You were real smart, Mickey, by pretending to be dead. That not only kept you alive, it

60

means we're going to get these outlaws for this."

Mickey didn't tell him that he wasn't purposely pretending to be dead. He wanted to get up, wanted to do something to help his mother and sister. But though he had tried hard, he had been totally unable to move.

"Will they hang for killin' Ma, and Papa, and Jean Marie?"

"Oh, they'll hang all right," the sheriff replied.

With the butt of his rifle resting on his hip, Sheriff Harold Baxter stood out on the front porch of his office, talking to a group of about twenty men. All were armed with various weapons from pistols to shotguns to rifles. "All right, you men raise up your hands," he shouted.

The men did so.

"Do you swear to uphold the law, and to do what I tell you to do, and not to get drunk while you're part of the posse?"

"Damn, Harold, that's askin' an awful lot of Keith," one of the men said, and the others laughed.

"This ain't no laughin' matter," Sheriff Baxter said. "Now I'm goin' to ask you again. Do you swear to uphold the law, and to do what I tell you to do, so help you God? Say I do."

"I do," the men of the posse replied.

"Those of you that's got good ridin' horses, get mounted. If you ain't got a good horse, go down to Finley's Stable and pick one out. Better get a saddle too, if you need one. Tell Finley you're in the posse, and he'll charge it to the county."

As the posse broke up to get their mounts, a man with white hair and a long white beard called out. "When you catch them that kilt the Drew family, don't bother to bring 'em back. Just hang 'em where you find 'em." He'd been watching the swearing-in from the front porch of the feed store next door to the sheriff's office,

"Enough of that, Bowman," Sheriff Baxter said, pointing toward the man. "When we find them, we're goin' to bring 'em back, 'n they're goin' to stand trial. Then we'll hang 'em."

Those who were close enough to overhear the exchange laughed.

CHAPTER SIX

Mescalero Valley, New Mexico Territory

Jaco and Putt stopped just below a butte, then dismounted. Jaco handed the reins of his horse to Putt. "Hold the horses. I'm goin' to climb up here 'n see if there's anyone a-followin' us."

Putt frowned. "What are you worried about? It's been four days 'n there ain't nobody that's been a-followin' us yet. Besides which, we kilt ever'one in the house, so there ain't nobody that can say we was the ones that done it."

"It's better to be safe than sorry," Jaco said as he started up the side of the butte.

Reaching the top, he shielded his eyes and studied the terrain all around them. He wished he had a spyglass, and thought it might be a good idea to steal one, if he could find one. Seeing nothing, he climbed back down. "I didn't see nobody, so I reckon it'll be all right to spend the night here."

"What about the bottle of whiskey we bought back at that store we stopped at? Reckon we could break it out 'n drink it now?" Putt asked.

Jaco chuckled. "What the hell did we buy it for, iffen we didn't plan to drink it? Let's fry us up some bacon first, 'n maybe open up a can of beans."

"All right. I'll get us a fire started."

The owner of Jim's Yes I Have It Store, looked up with some trepidation when he saw so many riders stop in front of his place. He stepped behind his counter and reached down to wrap his hand around the shotgun that lay on the shelf. It was a foolish gesture — he knew he couldn't fight off all of them.

When he saw the star on the shirt of the man who came into the store, he took his hand off the gun and breathed easier.

"I saw the name of the store. Would you be Jim?"

"Yes, sir, the name is Jim Ponder. Can I help you?" he asked, putting both hands on the counter so the sheriff would know that he represented no threat.

"Mr. Ponder, I'm Sheriff Baxter, and I'm looking for two men, one named Jaco and the other Putt."

Ponder shook his head. "No, sir, them names don't mean nothin' to me."

"One of 'em is kinda dark, like an Injun or a Mexican, or maybe he's a breed. The other 'n is an albino, skin real white, and with —"

"Pink eyes?" Ponder asked, completing the sheriff's sentence. "Yes, sir, I seen 'em. I seen 'em both."

"When did you see 'em?"

"I seen 'em this very afternoon. They bought some bacon, beans, 'n a bottle of whiskey."

"Which way did they go from here? North or south?"

Ponder smiled. "They didn't go either way. If you're a' trackin' 'em, it shouldn't be all that hard. They left the road and headed east toward Round Mountain over in the Mescalero Valley."

"Thanks. You've been a big help."

"Sheriff?" Ponder called as the sheriff turned to leave.

Baxter stopped and looked back toward him.

"What did them two boys do?"

"They murdered a farmer, his wife, and their little girl. And they raped the wife and the little girl."

"Damn," Ponder said. "I hope you find them."

"Don't worry, Mr. Ponder. We will," Baxter said resolutely.

Just before dawn the next morning, A. M. Jaco was awakened from a sound sleep by a stream of water splashing on his face. He coughed, sputtered, and spat. Where was the water coming from?

Jaco opened his eyes and saw Sheriff Baxter standing over him and buttoning up his pants.

"Sorry to have to wake you that way," Baxter said. "But I didn't have any other water handy."

"You . . . you pissed on me?" Jaco shouted angrily.

"Yeah, I did. Oh, by the way, Jaco, you and Putt are under arrest."

Jaco sat up quickly. Looking around, he saw as many as twenty armed men surrounding the place where he and Putt had bedded down for the night.

Cheyenne, Wyoming

"See here, my good man. I was told that the railroad did not run to a place called Chugwater. Is that correct?"

"Yes, sir, that's right," the ticket agent

66

said. "If you want to go on to Chugwater, you'll have to go by coach."

"How long of a trip will that be?"

"About five hours."

"And, may I inquire as to where I might obtain passage?"

"Right here."

"Really? I would not have expected that. I thought that the railroad and the coach lines would be competitive."

"Only when we're goin' to the same place." The ticket agent picked up a printed booklet. "What is your name, sir?"

"It is Hanson. Sir Calvin . . . ," he stopped in mid-sentence and chuckled in embarrassment. "I beg your pardon. My name, sir, is Calvin Hanson."

The clerk wrote out the ticket, then stamped it, and handed it to Hanson. "An Englishman, are you?"

Hanson smiled. "My accent always gives me away."

"Well, yes sir, that, but I could also tell by the hat you are wearing that you are English."

"I am an Englishman by birth, but I have chosen to live in this wonderful country and hope, soon, to acquire citizenship."

"And an American hat?"

"Indeed, sir, and an American hat." Hanson removed his hat and examined it thoroughly, turning it in his hands. "Though I must say, this hat is still in as good a shape as it was the day I bought it at Locke and Company Hatters on St. James Street in London."

"I'm sure it is a fine hat, Mr. Hanson. And welcome to America."

"Thank you, sir."

After receiving directions as to the location, Hanson left the railroad depot and walked the two blocks to the stagecoach station. He much preferred to travel by train, where he could secure first-class accommodations. Stagecoaches were the great equalizer of travel — all passengers rode in the same general discomfort.

Hanson carried a suitcase in one hand and a briefcase in the other. When he reached the station, he checked his suitcase in to be carried in the boot.

"We can put your briefcase back there as well, if you'd like," the station manager said.

"I appreciate your kindness sir, but I prefer to keep it on my person."

"I understand. You're a drummer, aren't you? You've got your samples in there. Notions and such?"

"Yes, you are most astute, sir," Hanson said.

"Well, Mr. Hanson, you're all checked in, so you may as well have a seat out there in the waiting room. The coach will be leaving in" — the manager pulled a watch from his pocket, opened the cover with his thumb, and looked at it — "another twenty minutes."

Hanson took a seat and, with his hat on top of the briefcase that was lying on his lap, began his wait for the coach.

Nine other people waited in the room, and he began calculating how uncomfortable the coach ride would be. Some coaches had a third seat in the middle, and three on each seat would enable the coach to accommodate nine. He thought of the other passengers he would be riding with, and wondered what they would think if they realized that he had thirty thousand dollars in cash in the briefcase he was holding. Almost subconsciously, he tightened his grip on the case.

At almost exactly twenty minutes after he took his seat, a man carrying a shotgun stepped into the waiting room. "Folks, my name is Brody Pierce. I'm the shotgun guard. Hodge Weatherly will be your driver this mornin'. The team is hitched, 'n we're ready to get started. Anyone holdin' a ticket to Chugwater, come climb aboard."

To Hanson's great relief, only three people responded to the call. A woman and two children got up, and Hanson hurried to reach the door first so he could hold it open for her.

"Thank you, sir," the woman said with a broad smile.

"My pleasure, madam."

Chugwater

Duff had come into town to visit with Megan's brother-in-law. He met Jason at Megan's Dress Emporium, where Megan, Melissa, and Timmy were also inside.

"I swear, when you get Melissa into a store, it's almost impossible to get her out," Jason complained. "You could stick hot needles under my fingernails, or you could make me spend time in a store with Melissa. It's the same thing."

Duff laughed. His own personal feelings about being in a store, any store anywhere, pretty much mirrored those expressed by Jason. "There's always a good conversation going on in Fiddlers' Green. What do you say we spend some time there?"

The two men walked next door to the saloon.

As a surprise for her sister, Megan had

made a new dress of dark green silk for her, selecting a pattern from *Harper's Bazaar.* With a bustle in the back and a frilled front, it was quite stylish. She held it up for Melissa to see.

"Oh, it's beautiful!" Melissa said. "But where am I going to find a place to wear it in Eagle Pass?"

"I'm sure Jason will find some excuse for you to wear it," Megan said. "You'll look so pretty in it, he'll have to. In the meantime, we'll find some reason for you to wear it here. I want to see you in it, anyway."

While the two sisters were talking, Timmy was sitting on the shelf at the front window, looking out onto the street. He saw the stagecoach roll by, then watched as the passengers disembarked. He laughed at one of them. "Mama, come over here and look at that man's funny hat," he said, pointing to the man, who, unlike the other passengers, was wearing a suit.

He was also wearing a hat that was considerably different from all the other hats that could be seen on the street.

"Why, that's called a bowler hat, Timmy," Megan said. "It's the kind of hat that's worn by gentlemen from the East. I expect he is a salesman of some sort, from the case he is carrying. No doubt he will be calling on me soon, trying to sell needles and pins, ribbons, and the like."

"Do you buy such things from traveling salesmen?" Melissa asked.

"From time to time, I do. Often they will have just what I need, and I can order without having to leave town."

Nate Hanson stepped down from the coach, squared the hat on his head, then went into the station. "I say, I wonder if it would be possible for me to leave my luggage here for a while."

"Sure, we can keep it for you. Is it on the coach?"

"Yes. If you'll come out with me, I'll show you which piece is mine."

"What about that little pouch thing you're a-carryin'? Do you want to leave that here, as well?"

"No, thank you. I'll take care of it myself."

After making the arrangements for his luggage, Hanson went to the bank, and, stepping up to the teller's cage, put the briefcase on the counter beside him. "My good man, I just arrived on the afternoon coach, and would like to open an account."

"Very well sir. We'll be glad to oblige." The teller opened a book, entered Nathan Hanson's name, then had him sign it. "All right, Mr. Hanson, how much do you wish to put in your account? Fifty dollars? One hundred?"

"Thirty thousand," Hanson said.

The bank teller gasped. "How much did you say?"

"Thirty thousand," Hanson repeated. "I have it right here."

Hanson loosened the straps on the briefcase, then opened it. When he did so, it exposed several stacks of money.

"Good Lord, man! Are you telling me that you had all that money with you on the stagecoach?"

"Yes. I thought it would be more convenient for me to bring the money with me."

"I don't know that it was such a good idea for you to have so much money on your person. You were wise to say nothing about it."

"Yes, I thought that would be the better part of discretion."

The teller chuckled. "You're a foreigner, aren't you?"

"How could you tell?" Hanson asked, though the teller didn't pick up on his sarcasm.

"I can tell by the way you talk. Don't get me wrong, we've got nothing against foreigners in this town. One of our leading citizens is a foreigner." The bank teller offered no further information. He was busy recording the deposit.

The money Hanson deposited wasn't his alone. Though he was the majority investor, the consortium consisted of English investors who had bought a ranch in Texas. Hanson was going to manage it for them. After doing a little research, he'd decided that, instead of longhorns or Herefords, it would be more profitable to raise Black Angus. The others agreed with him, and gave him carte blanche to do whatever he felt was necessary.

That same research had led him to Chugwater, where he planned to buy Black Angus cattle from a man named Duff MacCallister. He'd decided that, under the circumstances, the transaction could be better facilitated if he paid in cash, rather than waiting for a bank draft to be enacted.

Hanson had not met with Duff, nor had he communicated with him. But he was sure that two honest men could make a business arrangement that would be satisfactory to both sides. From what he had learned about Duff MacCallister, he was certain he was an honest man.

Even if he was a Scotsman.

CHAPTER SEVEN

With the money safely deposited, Hanson left the bank, and seeing Fiddlers' Green, he decided to go there. One of the first things he had learned since arriving in this country was that, in America, just as it was in England, a pub is where you went if you wanted to find out what was going on in the local community.

Removing his hat, he went into the saloon and stepped up to the bar.

"Yes sir, mister, what can I get for you?" the bartender asked.

"I wonder if I might trouble you for a pint."

"A pint? A pint of what?"

Duff heard the man order, and noticing his accent, he chuckled, and turned toward the bar. "Sure now, Willie, and if Biff were here, he would be for knowin' what that is. Give him a mug of beer and put it on my tab." He turned toward the stranger. "If I'm

75

right, you'd be an Englishman."

"I am, sir, and I can tell that you are Scottish by your brogue. Might I also presume that you are Duff MacCallister?"

"Aye, ye can presume that, and 'tis right ye are in your presumption. Bring your pint to the table. I'll introduce you to my friend and you can tell us who you might be, and how it is that you know my name."

The bartender drew a mug of beer and handed it to the Englishman, who carried it over to the table.

"The name is Hanson, sir. Cal Hanson. I represent a group of businessmen from my country who have invested in land in Texas. We intend to build a cattle ranch there, and I am to manage the operation. I know who you are because I've come to do business with you. That is, if you have some Black Angus cattle you would be willing to sell."

"Aye, I've cattle, and my business is selling them."

"Good, good. I'm sure we'll be able to do some business then. I thought it would take me a few days to find you. It was most fortuitous that I happened upon you in the first pub I visited."

"You didn't just happen on me, Mr. Hanson, for Fiddlers' Green is the only pub I frequent. The owner is a good friend of mine. And this is my friend, Jason Bowles. By coincidence, he is a sheriff in Texas."

"Mr. Hanson, Texas is a very big state, so I know that the chances of this are quite remote," Jason said, "but I've heard that a group of Englishmen are starting a ranch in Maverick County."

"Maverick County," Hanson said. "Indeed, sir, that is where Regency Ranch is to be located. Would that be the county where you are sheriff?"

"Yes, it is," Jason replied.

"Texas may be large, but the world is small. It would appear, Sheriff, that we shall be neighbors, sir. I will endeavor to be a good neighbor."

Hanson reached across the table and he and Jason shook hands.

"Regency Ranch, you say? That's quite a classy name for a ranch," Jason said.

"Yes, but it is appropriate, as I am but a regent of the consortium that is financing the operation."

"Do you have autonomy?" Duff asked.

"Yes." Hanson smiled. "It helps, somewhat, to be the majority stockholder of the consortium.

Jason chuckled. "I would say so."

Hanson finished his beer. "And now, gentlemen, if you would allow me, I would like to buy the next round of drinks."

"If we would allow you? Here, 'n what Scotsman would turn down an offer to take an Englishman's money?"

"Or anyone's money if you are a true Scotsman," Hanson teased.

Robbins, New Mexico Territory

"Oyez, oyez, oyez, this here court of Lincoln County, Robbins, New Mexico, will now come to order, the Honorable Earl Nesbit presiding. All rise."

There was a scrape of chairs, a rustle of pants, petticoats, and skirts as the spectators in the courtroom, which wasn't really a courtroom, but a schoolhouse, rose at the bailiff's decree.

The two defendants were A. M. Jaco and Blue Putt. Jaco had a swarthy complexion and it was known that he was a half-breed. What wasn't known was what breed he was half of. He didn't actually have a first name. He had only the initials A. M. and since he didn't like that, he had always been called Jaco. Blue Putt was an albino, with chalk white skin, white hair, and pink eyes.

The two men were being charged with the murder of Marvin Drew and his wife and daughter. There was no question as to who did it. Having survived his gunshot wound, young Mickey Drew was present, and was prepared to stand up in court and identify them again, this time for the judge and jury.

Judge Nesbit was a big man, with a square face and piercing blue eyes, so his presence was immediately felt. He moved quickly to the bench, then sat down. "Be seated."

The gallery sat, then watched as the two defendants were brought in.

"Your Honor, I'm going to make this case quick and simple," prosecutor Bill Gillespie said. "These two men killed Marvin Drew, his wife Zelda, and his daughter, Jean Marie. They tried to kill Mr. Drew's son, Mickey, as well, but he survived a gunshot wound to the stomach and provided the law with the information necessary to make the arrest."

"Is this eyewitness in the courtroom today?" Judge Nesbit asked.

"He is, Your Honor."

"And will he testify?"

"He will, Your Honor. I call him to the stand now."

Gillespie walked over to help Mickey stand, then stepped back as he was sworn in.

"Now Mickey, you were an eyewitness to the murder of your father, mother, and sister, is that correct?"

"No, sir."

There was a gasp of surprise from the gallery.

"I didn't see my pa get killed," Mickey said. "He was already dead when me 'n Jean Marie went into the house."

"But you did see two men standing over the body, did you not?" the prosecutor asked.

"Yes, sir."

"Are those men present in this courtroom?"

"Yes, sir."

"Would you point them out, please?"

"It's them two over there." Mickey pointed to Jaco and Putt.

"And would those also be the same men who shot you?"

"He's the one that shot me." Mickey pointed to Jaco.

"And did you see these men kill your mother and your sister?"

"Yes, sir."

"No further questions, Your Honor."

Ethan Poindexter was the court-appointed defense counsel. "Young man, were you shot before or after your mother and sister were killed?"

"I was shot before," Mickey said.

"Then how is it you can testify that you

saw these two men kill your mother and sister?"

"On account of I wasn't kilt," Mickey replied. "I was just playin' like I was dead, but all the time I was lyin' there, I was watchin' what was happenin'."

"No further questions," Poindexter said, realizing that by asking that question he had only made the situation worse for his clients.

Gillespie rested his case, and Poindexter called a witness for the defense, a man named Benton, who claimed that he had come by the Drew ranch just before noon and that when he left, Jaco and Putt left with him.

"I don't know who shot the boy and kilt his folks, but it wasn't Jaco and Putt, seein' as they was both with me," Benton said.

Poindexter surrendered his witness to Gillespie.

"Mr. Benton, what is your mother's name?" Gillespie asked.

Poindexter stood and shouted, "Objection, Your Honor. Irrelevant."

"Your Honor, I will establish relevancy," Gillespie promised.

The judge nodded. "You may continue. Witness is directed to answer the question."

"What is your mother's name, Mr. Benton?" the prosecutor repeated.

"She don't have the same last name as me," Benton said. "Her name is Miz Pittman."

"Would her first name be Althea?"

Benton mumbled the answer.

Gillespie took a step forward. "I'm sorry, Mr. Benton. I didn't hear that answer."

"Yeah, her first name is Althea."

"Your Honor, if it please the court, I would like to read a court document, dated two years previous. 'Question: 'What is your mother's name? Answer: Althea Pittman.' The person responding to the questions in this case, Your Honor, was A. M. Jaco. Benton and Jaco are brothers, and I submit that Benton has just committed perjury in order to help his brother."

"That ain't true!" Benton said.

Gillespie faced the witness. "Mr. Benton, you can go to prison for five years for lying or you can recant your statement now, and I won't prosecute you. It is your decision."

Benton looked over at Jaco. "Brother or not, I ain't goin' to jail for you!"

"So, Mr. Benton, I'm going to ask you again. Did you stop by the Drew ranch, and were Mr. and Mrs. Drew still alive when you left with your brother and Putt?"

"I didn't go out to the ranch," Benton said. "I don't know what they done."

"Thank you, Mr. Benton, you have done the right thing."

In his instructions to the jury, Judge Nesbit reminded them that they were to disregard any exculpatory evidence that may have been supplied by Benton as being unreliable. On the other hand, the witness for the prosecution was a young man known to be of good character, and his very willingness to testify, despite his wound, could only add to his credibility.

To no one's surprise, the jury found Jaco and Putt guilty.

"Bailiff, would you position the prisoners before the bench for sentencing, please?" Judge Nesbit asked.

"Yes, Your Honor."

The two men were brought before the bench.

Jaco stared defiantly at the judge. "Get it over with, old man. I don't plan to be standin' here all day."

"A. M. Jaco and Blue Putt, I hereby remand you to the New Mexico Territorial Prison, where you will remain until such time as all the paperwork can be attended to, pertaining disposition of the sentence I am about to administer.

"My sentence is this. I am instructing the

warden at the territorial prison to lead you two men, one at a time, to the gallows, which will be permanently positioned within the prison grounds. There, after having a knotted rope placed around your neck, you will be dropped through a trapdoor where life will be yanked from your bodies, either by a broken neck or by strangulation.

"It is not within my authority to dispatch your worthless souls to Hell, but I have no doubt but that He who is the final judge will take care of that task for me. After all life has been extinguished, your worthless bodies will be cut down and placed without ceremony or fanfare into a crude pine box, then buried six feet underground. There, as food for worms and maggots, they will rot away until nothing is left that will indicate that you worthless persons ever walked on the face of this earth."

Territorial Prison of New Mexico, Santa Fe
The people of New Mexico were justifiably proud of their prison. On the evening of August 6, 1885, Warden Gregg hosted a "gala house warming" at the nearly completed penitentiary. The guest list read like a who's who of New Mexico society. The Santa Fe *Daily New Mexican* reported more than a hundred carriages and wagons

of all types and sizes "charged about the streets of the ancient capital city" bringing guests to view the new building.

The festivities began officially with a grand march led by Territorial Physician J. H. Sloan and Miss Rose Keller of Las Vegas. Music was provided by the 13th United States Infantry band from Fort Marcy, strategically positioned on an elevated platform at one end of a large room which was to be the prison chapel. As ladies in brightly colored dresses danced with gentlemen in formal attire among a vast arrangement of flowers, they created what one observer described as an enchanting, "ever changing variety of kaleidoscope views."

At midnight, dancing was halted for dinner on formally set tables. The menu is not on record, but the meal reportedly consisted of a variety of "edibles and drinkables," served in "the most approved manner" by a cadre of waiters in white aprons. After dinner, dancing resumed in the chapel and continued until two in the morning.

Neither Jaco nor Putt were aware of the activities which had so recently opened the prison. They arrived wearing their prison garb of black-and-white-striped uniforms, and were placed immediately in Death Row. Because they had been sentenced to hang, they were kept separated, not only from the general population, but also from each other.

They were able to communicate with each other only during their one-hour exercise time out in the yard. And though they were together, they were still separated from everyone else, except for a few trusties who were normally given very light work details and had freedom to move about the prison, going anywhere they wished.

"When do you think they'll build the gallows?" Putt asked.

"It don't matter when they build it. We won't be usin' it," Jaco said.

"What do you mean?"

"I'm goin' to get us out of here."

"How?"

"I'm goin' to get us out of here," Jaco repeated, without being specific.

CHAPTER EIGHT

Veigo, Texas

The town was small enough that almost everyone knew each other. Sitting in the Texas Republic Saloon, when they looked up to see who had pushed in through the batwing doors, it was with the expectation of seeing one of their own.

The man they saw wasn't one of their own. He was a relatively small man dressed all in black, with a narrow, hooked nose and close-set, very dark eyes. His face was pockmarked and one ear was missing an earlobe. A red feather protruded from the silver band wound around his low-crowned hat.

"Would you look at that?" murmured one of the saloon patrons. "You ever seen anyone that ugly?"

"I'd be careful if I was you, Jeb. Don't let 'im hear you? Don't you know who that is?" another asked.

"I ain't got a idea in hell who it is. Should I know?" Jeb asked.

"That's Manny Dingo," the first said, speaking the name quietly and in great awe.

At Jeb's pronouncement the others grew quiet, as well. Manny Dingo had the reputation of being of quick temper and even quicker with a gun. Nobody knew how many men he had killed. Stories gave him credit for as few as twelve to as many as thirty.

Dingo looked around the saloon, then stepped up to the bar. "Whiskey."

The bartender turned the bottle up over the glass, but his hand was shaking so that Dingo reached up to steady it. "In the glass. I don't plan on lickin' it up from the bar."

"Y-y-yes sir, Mr. Dingo."

"You know who I am?"

"Yes, sir."

"Well, don't be afraid of me. I ain't kilt no bartenders yet." Dingo laughed at his own joke.

Two young cowboys came into the saloon then, laughing and talking loudly. Both were wearing pistols, the holsters low, and tied down. They stepped up to the bar.

"Willie, two beers," one of them said.

"And I'll have the same," the other said, and the two men laughed.

"Hey, Standish, did you see the way Clemmons acted, when I told him if he said anything like that again about Sue Ann, that I was goin' to whip his ass? He damn near peed in his pants."

"If you don't shoot 'im I will," Standish said. "A man like him don't have no business around a girl like Sue Ann. So, tell me, Kenny, when are you goin' to get around to askin' her to marry you?"

"Schoolteachers can't get married, you know that. Besides, a nice girl like Sue Ann, what could I do for her?" Kenny replied.

"Who is this Sue Ann that you boys is a-talkin' about?" Dingo asked.

"Miss Pittman, the schoolteacher," Kenny replied.

"What did you answer him for, Kenny?" Standish asked. "Look at 'im. A fella like that don't have no need to know anythin' about a lady like Sue Ann."

"Oh, I know all I need to know about Sue Ann Kennedy," Dingo said with a smirking smile. "I know what she used to do over in Brackettville."

"What?" Kenny literally shouted. "Mister, you had better take that back if you know what is good for you!"

"She's a harlot," Dingo said. "And she ain't even a very good one. I heard she give a bunch of men the clap back in Dallas. That's how come she had to leave."

"Mister, you watch your filthy mouth!" Kenny shouted, so angry that spittle was flying from his lips.

"Oh?" Dingo replied. "And if I don't watch my mouth, what are you going to do."

"I'm goin' to beat the hell out of your scrawny little ass," Kenny said.

"You want to fight, do you?"

"Damn right, I want to fight," Kenny said as he began to unbuckle his gun belt.

"Uh-uh," Dingo said. "If we're goin' to fight, let's make this permanent."

"What do you mean?"

"You're wearin' a gun. Use it."

"Wait a minute, mister. There ain't no reason to get into a shootin' match over this," Standish said.

"You mean you don't want to defend Sue Ann's honor?"

"She ain't what you called her!" Loomis said.

"And I say she is. And the two of you are damn fools if you don't know it."

"Mister, you've about pushed this too far," Standish said. "You want to turn this into a shootin'? Well, you go ahead. Only think about this. There's two of us 'n only one of you."

"So, you're willin' to die for your friend's lover, are you?" Dingo asked. "All right, I'm goin' to kill you first."

"Mr. Dingo," the bartender said. "This don't need to go no further. I know both these boys. They ride for the Double R Ranch. I'm sure if you asked them, they would apologize to you. Tell you what, why don't the three of you have a drink together and you can work this out. I'll provide the free drinks."

"I ain't apologizin'," Kenny said. "Not after what he said about Sue Ann."

"Kenny, are you sure you don't want to apologize to Mr. Dingo? *Manny* Dingo?" the bartender asked, emphasizing the name.

"Dingo?" Kenny said. "You . . . mean Manny Dingo . . . the gunfighter?"

"Yes, Manny Dingo the gunfighter."

"Oh." Kenny looked back toward Dingo, who had turned to face him and was holding his hand near his pistol.

Kenny forced a smile. "Mr. Dingo, seems like me 'n you got off on the wrong foot. Why don't we start over? We can have them drinks Willie mentioned."

"It's too late," Dingo said. "You two boys has done got me riled. Now the only way you can keep me from shootin' both of you is if you two get down on your hands 'n knees, crawl over here, 'n kiss my boots."

"What?" Loomis exclaimed. "Mister, there ain't no way in hell I'm goin' to do somethin' like that."

"Me neither," Kenny said. "And I ain't goin' to draw on you neither — which means there ain't goin' to be no gunfight."

Dingo smiled, but it wasn't a smile of humor. "You don't understand, do you boys? There don't have to be a gunfight."

"Good. I thought you might see it my way," Kenny said.

"I'm goin' to count to three, then I'm goin' to kill you whether you draw on me or not."

"You can't do that! That would be pure murder!" Loomis said.

"Yeah, wouldn't it?" The smile didn't leave Dingo's lips. "One."

"Damn, he means it, Kenny! We ain't goin' to let 'im just kill us, are we?"

"Two."

Both Kenny and Standish went for their guns, but before either of them were able to clear their holster, Dingo had drawn, fired two times, and returned his gun to his holster, doing it so fast that most in the room hadn't even seen him draw.

Kenny and Loomis went down, both dead before they hit the floor.

Dingo turned to the others in the room. "I expect the law will be here in a couple minutes. You all seen that they drew first, right?"

"You made them draw," Willie said. "They would never have drawn on you if you hadn't made 'em do it."

"You think I would've really shot 'em, if they hadn't drawed on me?"

"I don't know," Willie said. "It's clear they thought you would."

"I wouldn't have. What would be the fun of just shooting them down?"

"Fun? You call this fun?"

"Yeah. Think about it. Ever'one who seen this can tell their children 'n their grand-children that they seen Manny Dingo shoot down two men in a fair fight. Now, how 'bout them drinks you promised?"

From the *Chugwater Gazette:*

ENGLISH BUSINESSMAN MAKES LARGE DEPOSIT

To Buy Cattle from Local Rancher

All who live here in the enchanting Chug-water Valley know that our fair garden spot is blessed not only with nature's beauty, but also with bountiful water and grass which makes this area ideal for cattle ranching.

And now we have gained world-wide attention due to the business dealings of Mr. Calvin Hanson. Mr. Hanson, an Englishman, is but recently arrived in America. He left behind in his native country a group of English investors who, in starting a ranch in America, sought out our own Duff MacCallister. Mr. MacCallister is well-known throughout the entire West as being particularly successful in raising the specific breed of Black Angus.

To facilitate his purchase of the cattle needed to start his ranch, Mr. Hanson has placed on deposit with the Bank of Chugwater the exceptionally large sum of thirty thousand dollars. As a way of celebrating this milestone in the history of the Chugwater Bank, Mr. Montgomery, president of the bank, will be sponsoring a reception for Mr. Hanson at the Knights of Pythias Hall this very evening.

The hall was located over the bank and accessed by an outside stairway. Megan had been accurate in her prediction that there would be an event in Chugwater that would enable Melissa to wear the new dress Megan had made for her. But Melissa wasn't the only one to wear an original Megan creation. The dinner could well have been an advertisement for Megan's Dress Emporium, as almost every lady present was wearing one of her dresses.

When everyone was seated, but before the food was served, C. D. Montgomery stood and banged his spoon against the glass to get everyone's attention. "Ladies and gentlemen, I want to welcome you to this special reception tonight, given in honor of a visitor from England, who has arrived with cash in hand to bring business to our fair community. Mr. Hanson has come to buy cattle from our own Duff MacCallister."

"A Scotsman and an Englishman doing business together," Biff Johnson shouted, interrupting Montgomery. "That's reason enough for a celebration right there!"

The others laughed.

"Perhaps it is," Montgomery agreed, "but I hasten to add, it is to the Scotsman that we owe our thanks for the steaks we'll be eating tonight. For they were carved from one of MacCallister's own Black Angus steers."

"I thank ye for the kind words, Mr. Montgomery, but I want the Englishman to be aware that the animal that's being served here tonight will be tallied against those that Mr. Hanson buys."

"To be sure sir, understanding the penurious nature of the Scottish, I would be disappointed if it were any other way," Hanson said in good-natured response.

The next morning, Duff stood at the stagecoach depot with Megan, as they told Melissa, Jason, and Timmy good-bye. The Bowles family was taking the coach to Cheyenne, where they would board the train for the long trip back home.

"You will have to come visit us soon," Melissa said to Duff. "You have been most hospitable, and I would like to return the favor."

"Perhaps I will after I conclude my business with the Englishman," Duff said. "It might be necessary to help him get the cattle settled on his ranch."

"And he won't come alone, for I shall not allow that," Megan said.

"Good, then it's all settled," Melissa said with a happy smile.

"When you come, will you teach me to shoot as good as you do?" Timmy asked.

"Why, Timmy, whatever do you mean?" Duff asked. "Your father shot neck and neck with me for the whole time."

"But you beat 'im," Timmy said.

Jason Bowles laughed. "My goodness, Timmy, you're going to have to spend a lot of time learning things, aren't you? You want Duff to teach you how to shoot, and you want Mr. Wang to teach you how to fight. Are you sure you don't want your aunt Megan to teach you how to make dresses?"

"What? No! I don't want to learn how to make dresses!" Timmy said resolutely.

Jason laughed, and reached out to run his hand through his son's hair. "I'm just teasin' you."

"Stagecoach is a-comin'," someone called.

At the call, a couple men came out of the stable behind the station leading a six-team hitch, already in harness. They had the team changed out in the amount of time it took the passengers and their luggage to be loaded.

With the team hitched and the passengers loaded, the driver cracked his whip, and the coach got underway at a rapid trot.

"Did you mean it when you said you would go to Texas?" Megan asked as they watched the coach roll swiftly out of town, trailed by a long, billowing, rooster tail of dust behind it.

"Yes, I meant it."

Megan took Duff's arm in both her hands.

97

"Good."

"What do you mean, good?"

"Just good," she said, smiling at him.

"Before I go back out to the ranch, I think I would like to stop by Vi's Pies, and have a piece of black and blue pie. Would you be for joining me?"

"I would love to join you, Duff MacCallister," Megan said. "As long as I can choose my own pie."

"Aye, that you can do. But why anyone would want anything other than black and blue pie is beyond me. 'Tis no better pie in the world."

Vi Winslow greeted Duff and Megan effusively as they stepped into her establishment. The place was redolent with the aroma of freshly baked pies, which, except for coffee, tea, and milk, was the only thing she served. She did, however, serve a variety of pies, listing on her board twelve different kinds.

Upon arriving in Chugwater and stepping into Vi's Pies for the first time, Duff made the announcement that he was going to go through the entire list, one pie at a time. He started with apple, then apricot, then black and blue, which was a combination of blackberries and blueberries. He never got beyond that one, and now, he ordered black and blue every time he visited.

"Elmer didn't come into town with you?" Vi asked, the disappointment evident in her voice.

"Someone has to run the ranch," Duff replied.

"You work him too hard. He's getting on in years, you know."

"Be truthful with me, Vi. Do you honestly think I could make Elmer slow down?"

Vi chuckled. "I don't think you can. I've never known anyone who enjoys working as much as Elmer does."

"I just came into town to see Megan's sister and her family off on the stagecoach, and I thought I'd stop by for —"

Vi slid a piece of black and blue across the counter before Duff could finish his order.

Megan ordered peach pie.

CHAPTER NINE

Onboard the coach

"When you were with Duff, just the two of you, did he talk any about Megan?" Melissa asked.

"Sure," Jason replied. "He talked a lot about her."

"What did he say?"

"Oh, I don't know as I can remember anything specifically. Like I said, he talked a lot about her. And I know that he really likes her."

"Did he say anything about getting married?"

"I don't know."

"You don't know? What do you mean, you don't know? How can you not know whether or not he said anything about getting married?" Melissa asked in a tone of voice that showed her frustration over the lack of information Jason was supplying.

"We talked about a lot of things. I just

don't remember whether or not the subject came up. What about Megan? Did she say anything about getting married?"

"Not directly. But I'm pretty sure she would marry him if he asked her. They said they're coming to Texas soon. You heard them say that, didn't you?"

"I heard."

"Maybe if you —"

"Melissa, it's best to stay out of other people's business."

"But you know how they feel about each other. Maybe all they need is a nudge."

"Like I said, Melissa, it's —"

"Best to stay out of other people's business, I know. Still," she said, letting the word hang there without response.

The coach moved on at a rapid clip.

"Good, then it's all settled."

Ten miles ahead of the Cheyenne-bound coach, two men, Lenny and Larry Israel were waiting at Horse Creek crossing. Half an hour earlier, they had put a tree limb across the bridge so that the coach coming from Cheyenne would have to stop.

Larry was standing on the creek bank, urinating into the water.

"What the hell you pissin' in the creek for?" Lenny asked. "Hell, I just filled my canteen from there."

"If you've already filled your canteen, what do you care?"

Lenny chuckled. "Yeah, I guess you're right."

"Besides, fish piss in the water all the time. You ever thought of that?

"What do you mean fish piss in it?"

"Well, you tell me, brother. You don't think they get out of the water to take a leak, do you? They pee in the creek." Larry was buttoning his pants as he spoke.

"Damn, I never thought of that."

"Listen," Larry said holding up his hand. "You hear that? The coach is a-comin'."

Lenny nodded. "Yeah, I hear it."

"Get ready."

The two men got into position behind a rock. Cocking their rifles, they stared south, waiting for the appearance of the coach.

Before they could see it, they could hear it, the clopping of hoofbeats, and the clank and rattle of the coach itself. By the time the two highwaymen could see the coach, the driver and guard could see that there was a tree limb across the bridge. The driver called out to his team, bringing them to a halt.

"What the hell?" the driver said. "How the hell did that get there?"

"You want me to pull it out of the way?" asked the guard.

"Yeah, thanks."

"You shoot the lead offside horse, I'll take care of the guard," Larry said quietly.

The two men raised their rifles and fired, the shots so close together that they sounded as one.

The lead horse went down. The other horses whinnied and reared up in fear, but the dead horse kept the coach from going anywhere.

The shotgun guard went down as well.

"Danny!" the driver shouted, but it was the last word he spoke. He was the next target, with both Larry and Lenny shooting him.

"You people in the coach, come out now," Larry shouted.

When nobody came out, Larry fired into the coach. They heard a woman cry out.

"We're goin' to just keep a-firin' into the coach till you all come out," Larry called.

Two men, a woman, and a young boy stepped down from the coach. One of the men was holding his hand over a shoulder wound. His face was contorted with pain, and blood was oozing through his fingers.

"Turn around and face the coach," Larry

said as he and Lenny approached with drawn pistols.

The passengers complied and Larry nodded at Lenny. They shot the two men in the back of the head, then the woman and the young boy.

"I don't reckon any of these folks will be identifyin' us," Larry said. "Climb up there and throw down the box."

Lenny climbed up to the driver's seat. The driver was slumped over, dead. Lenny pulled the box out and threw it down, where Larry shot off the lock.

"A hunnert and fifty dollars?" Larry said a moment later. "That's all that was in the damn box?"

"Maybe some of the passengers is carryin' money," Lenny suggested.

After rifling through the bodies they came up with another thirty dollars, plus two men's pocket watches.

"Damn," Lenny said. "I can't believe how slim the pickins has become."

"You know what I think?" Larry asked.

"What's that?"

"I think we should go south to do our next job."

"I thought we was goin' to go up into Montana. Besides, we already done one in Colorado."

"I'm talkin' a lot farther south. Maybe all the way to Texas. There for sure ain't nobody ever heard of us down there. And from all that I have heard, folks has got a lot more money in Texas than almost anywhere else. The pickins won't be quite so slim."

"All right. Let's go," Lenny said.

Splitting the one hundred and eighty dollars, each of them took a watch. The two brothers rode away as buzzards began to circle over the dead they were leaving behind.

Fifteen minutes later the southbound coach crested a small rise in the road. Ahead of them they saw dozens of circling buzzards.

"Damn, Muley, what do you make of that?" the shotgun guard asked.

The driver stroked the stubble on his chin as he studied the scene, which was about three hundred yards in front of them. "I don't know, they's too many of 'em for it to just be a dead coyote or somethin'. I don't like the looks of it. Not one bit."

"I don't, either," his shotgun guard said.

"Hey, Jack, ain't one of our passengers a sheriff?"

"Yeah, I think so. But I don't know where at he's the sheriff."

"It don't matter. Call him out here." Muley pulled hard on the reins.

Inside the coach, the passengers were unable to hear the conversation between the driver and the guard.

"Why did we stop, Papa?" Timmy asked.

"I don't know, son. Maybe there's somethin' in the road."

A man's face appeared in the window. "Ain't you a sheriff?" the man asked.

"Yes, in Texas. I have no authority here."

"Yes, sir, I know that. But me 'n the driver have somethin' we'd like you to take a look at, anyhow."

"Jason, what is it?" Melissa asked, reaching across to put her hand on his leg apprehensively.

"I don't know, but I guess I'm about to find out." Sheriff Jason Bowles climbed out of the coach, then stepped up to the front.

"I got the sheriff, Muley," the shotgun guard said.

"Sheriff, what do you think about that?" Muley asked, pointing ahead.

Jason didn't have to ask him what he was talking about. The subject of the driver's concern was obvious. About a mile ahead of them he could see a swarm of buzzards, some circling, others diving down to the ground to feast upon whatever carrion they had found.

"That's more than just a dead critter," Jason replied.

"Yeah, that's what me 'n Jack was a-thinkin' too," Muley replied. "Thing is, we shoulda met Hodge and Brody by now, only we ain't met 'em."

"Hodge and Brody?"

"They drive the coach from Cheyenne to Ft. Laramie while we're comin' from Ft. Laramie to Cheyenne. Then the next day we each change directions. An' like I said, normally we woulda met before now."

"You think somethin' has happened to 'em, Muley?" Jack asked.

"I don't know, but I got me an awful bad feelin' about it."

"Do you have an extra rifle?" Jason asked.

"Yeah, we got one right up here."

"Why don't I climb up on top of the coach with the rifle. You can drive ahead real slow, and we'll be on the lookout for anything that looks unusual."

"Jason, is everything all right?" Melissa asked, stepping out of the coach.

"I don't know," Jason answered truthfully. "You get back inside with Timmy. I'm going to ride on top for a while."

They drove quickly to cover the mile, and

soon the stagecoach came into view.

"Why is it just sittin' there?" Muley asked.

"Look, there's a horse down in the team," Jason said.

"Looks like someone coulda just cut him out and —" Jack stopped in mid-sentence. "Damn, look there. There's people lyin' on the ground."

"That's your missus and the boy in the coach, ain't it, Sheriff?" Muley asked. "You might not want them to see this."

"I don't see how I'm going to be able to prevent it."

After some discussion as to how best to handle the situation, they decided to cut the dead horse loose from the coach, then they loaded all the bodies aboard the ill-fated coach. The shotgun guard, Jack, took the reins of what had been the northbound stage, turned it around, and drove it back to Cheyenne, following Muley. Jason rode as shotgun guard in case whoever hit the first stage might return.

Cheyenne

Seeing two coaches rolling into town at the same time was strange enough. Several people noticed that the team pulling the trailing coach was short by one horse, then the more discerning saw that it was being driven by Jack Cumbie, who wasn't a driver, but a shotgun guard.

Curiosity caused more than one person to follow the two coaches to the depot to get to the bottom of the mystery. By the time the two coaches stopped, at least two dozen people had gathered.

"Good Lord in heaven!" one of the men in the crowd shouted. "That coach is filled with dead people!"

"Will, get the sheriff down here!" Muley called to the manager of the depot as soon as the two coaches rolled to a stop."

"You didn't hear a thing?" the sheriff asked.

"Not a thing," Muley said. "But I wouldn't expect to. It happened a good two hours before we arrived."

"How do you know when it happened?"

"Sheriff, I drive this route every day. I know how long it takes to get to Horse Creek Crossing from Cheyenne, and that's where it happened. More 'n likely they got there by nine o'clock. We got there at eleven and found this."

"The shotgun guard and the driver were shot from ambush by a .44-.40 rifle," Jason said. "I found these shell casings at the site. But the passengers," Jason paused to take a breath. "The passengers were shot from behind at point-blank range."

The sheriff examined the shell casings. "Good job of investigating."

"This feller is a sheriff from Texas," Muley explained.

"I appreciate your help, Sheriff."

"Do you have any idea who might have done this?" Jason asked.

"I heard about something like this happening over in Nebraska, and down in Colorado, where someone robbed a coach and killed everyone. And now he's done it here in Wyoming. I'm sure it's the same person, but nobody seems to have the slightest idea who it is that's doin' all this."

"According to the signs back at the scene, it's two people, not one person, doing this," Jason said.

"Yeah, well that makes more sense, anyway. I think it would be hard for one person to do this all alone. I guess I'd better get a couple messages off to Montana and Idaho to be on the lookout for these people. Seems like they only do one, then they move on."

CHAPTER TEN

Sky Meadow Ranch

Duff MacCallister had left Scotland after killing the men who had killed his fiancée. Shortly after arriving in the United States, he'd moved to Wyoming, where by homesteading and purchasing the adjacent land, he'd started his ranch, which he'd named after Skye McGregor, the woman he had intended to marry. Since leaving Scotland, Duff had been exceptionally successful. Over the years, his ranch had spread out to some 100,000 acres of prime rangeland lying between the Little Bear and Big Bear creeks.

Little and Big Bear creeks were year-round sources of water, and that, plus the good natural grazing land, allowed Duff to try an experiment — introducing Black Angus cattle. He was well familiar with the breed, for he had worked with them in Scotland. His experiment was successful, and today he was running 30,000 head of Black Angus cattle, making his ranch one of the most profitable in all of Wyoming.

Duff's operation was large enough to employ fourteen men, principal of whom was Elmer Gleason, his ranch foreman. Cowboys had to be jacks of all trades, part carpenter to keep the buildings in shape, part wheelwright to keep the wagons repaired, part blacksmith, and even part veterinarian and doctor, so as to be able to tend to wounds and illnesses of animal and man.

A couple of the cowboys, Woodward and Martin, were replacing shingles on the roof of the barn. The job was hot, and the slant of the roof made it not only uncomfortable, but a little hazardous as well, but it needed to be done.

"How you boys doin'?" Elmer asked.

When the two men looked toward the sound of his voice, they saw that he was standing on the ladder, with just his head and shoulders above the eaves of the roof.

"We're doin' fine, Elmer," Martin said. "Why don't you crawl on up here 'n look for yourself if you are of a mind?"

"No need," Elmer said. "I can see it just fine from here. Ain't no call for me to be crawlin' around on some roof."

The two cowboys laughed. "Didn't think you'd much want to come up," Martin said.

"Hey, Elmer, once we get this here roof done, what you got 'n mind for us to do next?" Woodward asked.

"What do you mean, what do I have in mind? You two boys is both full growed. Why don't you just look around and see if you can't find somethin' that you know needs a-doin'? You don't need me to tell you ever'thing that needs done, do you?"

"No, there ain't no need for you to have to find somethin' else for us. We can do it our ownself," Woodward said. "But after we're done, you don't mind if we run into town, do you?"

"No, if all your work is done, you can go into town. I don't mind," Elmer said. "But try 'n stay out of trouble."

"What makes you think we'd get into trouble?" Martin asked.

"I don't know. Maybe it's because a couple weeks ago Duff had to bail the two of you out of jail."

"Now wait a minute. That warn't none of our fault," Woodward said. "Them two boys from the Runnin' J is the ones that started it."

"They ain't the ones that wound up in jail. You two was. If Duff wasn't such good friends with Marshal Ferrell, more 'n likely you'd both still be there."

"Yeah, well, you don't have to worry none 'bout us 'cause we're not goin' to do nothin' that'll cause any trouble a-tall," Martin said.

"You better not. If you wind up in jail again, I'm goin' to tell Duff to just leave you there."

Elmer climbed back down the ladder and was walking away from the barn when he saw one of the other cowboys coming toward him. There was a worried expression on his face.

"What's up, Dewey? Why you got such a sour look on your face?" Elmer laughed. "I reckon that's a sour look. You're so damn ugly, I can't always tell."

"Yeah, like you're so handsome," Dewey teased. But the smile left his face rather quickly, and the frown returned. "I was just comin' to tell you that I found two beeves that has been mostly et by wolves."

"Damn. Well, I'm not surprised. We've had trouble with 'em before."

"I woulda shot 'em, but they was too damn far off, 'n I couldn't get no closer without 'em hearin' me, or smellin' me, or somethin'."

"How close could you get?"

"I couldn't get no closer 'n three hunnert

yards away. And hell, you can barely see 'em from that far, let alone shoot one of 'em."

"All right. Thanks for tellin' me about it. I'll let Duff know."

"Well, yeah, Duff needs to know," Dewey said. "But other 'n puttin' out poison, I sure as hell don't know what he can do about it."

"Nah, we don't want to put out poison. Problem with that is, you'll wind up killin' critters you don't have no intention, or need of killin'. Like I said, we've had trouble with 'em before, and Duff has shot 'em before."

"How's he goin' to do that? I tol' you, you can't get close enough to 'em to shoot."

"Dewey, you was in town for the shootin' match last month, same as the rest of us, wasn't you? You seen Duff hit a bull's-eye, no bigger 'n a half dollar, from five hunnert yards away, didn't you?"

Dewey chuckled. "I sure as hell did. And I won me ten bucks, too, bettin' Wendell Forbis that Duff could do it."

"And you really think he can't hit a wolf from three hundred yards?"

"Now that I think about it, I reckon he can."

Half an hour after Elmer had informed Duff of the wolf problem, he pulled his horse Sky to a halt. Sitting still in the saddle for a moment, he perused the range before him. Except for roundup and cattle drives when he would drive a herd down to the loading pens and railhead in Cheyenne, the cattle were never in one, large herd. Rather, they tended to break off into smaller groups, bound to each other within those groups as if they were family units.

Duff saw one such group gathered near the water and standing together under the shade of a cottonwood tree.

With a pair of binoculars hanging around his neck, Duff dismounted, then walked out onto a flat rock overhang. Lifting the binoculars to his eyes, he studied the open range below him. He spotted the pack of wolves at least 500 yards away, sneaking up on the cattle. Had he not been specifically looking for them, he wouldn't have even seen them.

Duff walked back to his horse, then pulled out the same Creedmoor rifle he had used during the shooting contest in town last month. He had attached a telescopic sight to the weapon.

Returning to the point he had chosen as the lookout, he lay on his stomach and wet his finger to check the windage. Using the scope, he sighted in on the lead wolf.

Duff squeezed the trigger, and the gun boomed and kicked back against his shoulder. One second later the lead wolf was sent sprawling by the impact of the heavy bullet. A tenth of a second after the strike of the bullet, the sound of the shot reached the remaining pack, but it was so far away that they were unable to connect that sound to what happened to the leader of the pack.

A second shot killed a second wolf, and the pack turned and ran away. Duff remounted and started toward the retreating wolves. The advantage was his. He was so far away the wolves didn't even know he was after them. He urged Sky into a ground-eating gallop, and after a few minutes the wolves were once again within range. He didn't even dismount, but shot from the saddle, killing two more.

It took him less than half an hour to kill every wolf in the pack. When he started back, he saw that the buzzards had already started on the first ones he had killed. He would send some men out to take care of the carcasses, but there were enough buzzards that he knew there would be little left for them to bury.

"I told you," Martin said when Duff came

riding back. "I told you Mr. MacCallister would take care of 'em."

"How do you know he did?"

"He's back, ain't he?"

"I've got somethin' to ask you," Elmer said later that same afternoon, as the two of them were having drinks at Fiddlers' Green. "Are you ever goin' to marry, Miss Parker?"

"Now why do you ask, Elmer? Are you Megan's father?"

Elmer chuckled. "No, I ain't her father, though I'd be proud to be. She's one fine woman, one of the finest women I've ever knowed. I was just wonderin' 'bout whether or not you're goin' to marry her, is all."

"Well, you can just keep on wondering, because the truth is, I am still wondering myself."

"Wonderin' what? If she'll have you?"

"Among other things."

"Ha! She'll have you all right."

"How do you know that? It seems to me like she is pretty satisfied running her own business. Why would she want to get hooked up with me?"

Elmer chuckled. "Well, now, you got me on that one, Duff. I don't have no idea in the world why she, or any woman, would be wantin' to marry up with someone like you.

But Vi tells me that she thinks Miss Parker would marry you iffen you was to ever ask her. And I put a lot of store in what Vi says 'cause she's one smart woman."

"Yes, she is. And that brings up my question. Why haven't you married Vi?"

"I ain't never asked her. In my case, it ain't somethin' I wonder about. I know she won't have me," Elmer replied. "I'm too damn old and too set in my ways. Besides which, if I was ever goin' to get married, other than Injun married, I woulda married Janey Jensen."

"Jensen?"

"Yeah. Most of the time I knowed her, she told me her name was Abbigail Fontaine. It warn't until we was just about to part company that she told me her real name was Janey Jensen. Turned out she was sister to a feller I rode some with, back durin' the war. Someone you know."

"Elmer, are you talking about Smoke Jensen?"

"Yeah, Smoke Jensen is exactly who I'm talkin' about. Abbigail Fontaine, whose real name I done told you was Janey Jensen, was Smoke's sister. All the time I knowed her, she was a fancy woman, but that don't make no never mind to me. I always thought she was a good woman."

"If she was Smoke's sister, then she came from good stock. I can see how you might have felt so about her."

Biff Johnson came over to join them at the table. "Did you hear what happened to the Cheyenne stage?"

"The Cheyenne stage? No, I ain't heard nothin'. What about it?" Elmer asked.

"It was held up and everyone was killed; driver, shotgun guard, and all the passengers, including the woman and child."

"Biff!" Duff said anxiously. "Megan's sister was on that coach. And Jason and the young lad!"

"No, no," Biff said, holding out his hand reassuringly. "I'm sorry, I didn't mean to get you all concerned. It wasn't the coach they were on. It happened on the northbound coach. But it was the southbound coach that came upon them, all dead."

" 'Tis bad enough to rob a coach, to take the hard-earned money of decent people," Duff said. "But what kind of brigand would do such a thing as kill everyone on the coach?"

"I don't know the answer to that, Duff. All I know is that there are some incredibly evil people in this world. And for some reason a lot of them have decided to come west."

CHAPTER ELEVEN

Territorial Prison of New Mexico

"One thousand dollars," A. M. Jaco said to Lou Miller, who was standing in the corridor, separated by the bars of Jaco's cell.

"Where are you going to get one thousand dollars?" Miller was a trusty due to be released in one more week. At the moment, he was supposed to be sweeping the corridor in front of the row of cells.

"I've got a thousand dollars put away in a secret stash. Actually, I've got more than that," Jaco said. "All you have to do is get me a key. I know you can do that. I've seen you come in 'n out when you're cleanin' and such."

"Why should I take a chance on doing anything like that? I'm gettin' out in a week. I'd be crazy to risk such a thing."

"What are you goin' to do for money when you get out?" Jaco asked. "Wouldn't you like to have a thousand dollars? Why, with that much money you could go somewhere new 'n start all over again. Nobody would ever have to know you was once in prison."

"A thousand dollars would be good to have," Miller said. "Where is it hidden?"

"You get me a key so's I can get out of here, then meet me in Seven Rivers. I'll give you the money then."

"Is that where you got the money hid? In Seven Rivers?" Miller asked.

"No, it ain't where I got it hid, 'n I ain't goin' to tell you where I got it hid. But I will have the money when you meet me there."

Miller nodded. "All right. It's a deal."

The next day Miller was mopping the corridor out in front of the jail cells. When he got in front of Jaco's cell, he knocked the pail over, causing the dirty water to splash into the cell.

"You clumsy pig! Watch what you're doin'!" Jaco shouted loudly. Going up to the bars, he saw a key lying in the water that had been splashed into his cell, and he put his foot on it.

"What's goin' on in there?" the guard called.

"This oaf spilled his dirty water into my

cell," Jaco called.

"Did he?" The guard chuckled. "Miller, if it was up to me, I'd let you out a day earlier just for makin' Jaco a little more uncomfortable."

"I didn't think you would mind all that much," Miller replied to the guard. Very quietly he said to Jaco, "Seven Rivers, two weeks from today."

"I'll be there," Jaco promised.

Jaco took the key back into his cell and slipped it into a cut he had made in his mattress. Then he resumed working on his dummy.

Three days later, Jaco lay on his bunk with his hands laced behind his head waiting for the guard to complete his ten o'clock rounds. He and Blue Putt were scheduled to be hanged at nine o'clock the next morning.

He heard the door open at the far end of the corridor.

"What do you think, Putt?" Jaco heard the guard say. "This is your last night. You won't have to put up with me anymore after tonight." The guard giggled. "Just think about it. This time tomorrow night, you'll be dead."

Jaco heard some sort of response from

Putt, but it wasn't loud enough or clear enough for him to understand.

Footfalls signaled that the guard was coming up the corridor to Jaco's cell. He held his lantern up to the bars and, with the reflector, cast a beam of light into the shadowed cell. Playing the light through the dark cell, it fell upon Jaco's bunk. Jaco's eyes were open.

"Hell, Jaco, it's ten o'clock. You're most always asleep by now. What's the matter? Can't you sleep any tonight?"

"No," Jaco replied.

"Well, I can't say as I blame you," the guard said. "I mean, thinkin' about gettin' hung tomorrow would just about keep anyone awake. Who would want to sleep on their last night alive? I mean, no more hours than you got left to live, I can understand how you'd want to be awake for 'em." The guard chuckled, but Jaco didn't answer.

"Well, one good thing. Fellas like you 'n Putt are bound to have lots of friends when you get to hell. And when you stop to think of it, you know that's where all the bad women wind up, too. Why, I wouldn't be none surprised a-tall if, by this time tomorrow night, you won't be partyin' with the likes o' Sam Bass, Curly Bill Brocus, Jesse James, and purt nigh' ever bad girl there

125

ever was. Yes, sir, you just go look those fellas up. I'm sure they'll be glad to show you around."

"That's right, Lucas. Me 'n Putt will be partyin' with liquor 'n women, 'n you'll still be workin' in this prison."

"What do you think, Jaco? You want to trade places with me?" Lucas asked.

"What? And miss out on all that?"

Lucas laughed loudly, and was still laughing as he walked away.

Once the guard left, taking his lantern with him, the cell was again plunged into darkness. Jaco continued to lie on his bunk, perfectly still, listening to the receding clomp of the guard's footsteps and the echoing rattle of the door being closed.

Not until there was one full minute of silence did Jaco hop out of bed. He stepped up to the bars, where he looked and listened until he was satisfied the guard was no longer present. Then he reached down into the chamber pot and extracted something wrapped in a towel. The towel was wet with urine, and soiled with offal. When he unwrapped the towel, it proved to be a gourd, but not just any gourd. This gourd had hair and eyebrows, so that it resembled a man's face. Jaco put the gourd on the small, thin pillow, then draped the blanket in such a way as to make it look as if a man was sleeping peacefully in the bunk.

That done, he dug around in the padding of his mattress until he found the key.

Stepping up to the cell door, Jaco stuck his arm through the bars, inserted the key carefully, then turned it. He was rewarded with the satisfying click as the key tripped the tumblers in the lock. Pushing the door open quietly, he stuck his head out and looked up and down the center corridor. Lucas, the guard who had checked on him but a moment earlier, was truly gone, and the coast was clear.

Jaco closed the door and locked it behind him, then he looked through the door back into his cell. He was satisfied with what he saw. From the corridor and in the reduced light, to a no more than cursory inspection, it would appear as if he were still in bed.

Jaco moved quickly down to a cell on the other side and at the opposite end of the corridor, where he knew he would find Blue Putt. The prison officials had purposely separated them as far as they could, so that they wouldn't be able to "come up with any mischief."

Jaco stepped up to Blue Putt's cell. "Putt," he whispered. "Are you ready?"

"Damn! You done it! I didn't believe you'd

be able to actual do it."

"I told you we was goin' to get out of here, didn't I?"

For purposes of economics, rather than have all the doors keyed differently, the territorial prison of New Mexico was arranged so that one key would fit every cell door. That made it simpler for the guards to move the prisoners around. It also made it simpler for Jaco to open the door to Putt's cell.

Just as Jaco had done, so too had Blue Putt prepared a dummy head, and though it wasn't as good as the one Jaco had made, it did serve its purpose. If someone didn't look too closely, they could easily believe that Putt was sleeping in his bed.

Moving quietly through the dark, they walked down to the far end of the corridor, the end with the door that opened into a hallway connecting two buildings. Jaco knew that the key he had would fit that door, as well.

It helped that, for the moment, Jaco and Putt were the only two prisoners on death row. There was little chance of their escape being compromised, at least at this stage of the operation.

Jaco opened that door that led into the hallway, then closed it behind him. The hallway was not part of the confinement area, so the windows had no bars and could be easily opened. He raised the nearest window, and he and Putt climbed through, then dropped down into the prison yard.

They were free of the cell, but not out of prison, for the prison yard was surrounded by a high wall with guard towers at every corner.

"Damn! Look at that." Putt pointed toward a gallows. This was the first time either of them had seen it. "They was gettin' ready for us, wasn't they?"

"Yeah, well, it ain't our worry now, is it?" Jaco replied. "Come on."

Moving swiftly through the dark, they hurried across the open yard to the prison kitchen. This, too, was a part of their escape plan. Every Monday and Friday night, a garbage wagon would come into the prison grounds to carry away the kitchen slop. The prison paid to have the garbage hauled off, and the garbageman made more money by selling the edible slop to the pig farmers. Jaco got the key on Tuesday, which meant he missed the opportunity to try his plan on Monday. He had to wait until Friday. It was not only the next opportunity to take advantage of the garbage wagon, it was positively the last opportunity to incorporate the garbage wagon into his escape. And without the wagon, he knew there was no way they would be able to get outside the walls.

Jaco and Putt hid under the kitchen porch where they waited until the wagon was loaded and the driver had gone back inside to conduct his business.

"Now," Jaco said.

The two men moved from the porch to the wagon, where they lifted up the canvas then crawled under it to hide in the slop that was being carried away from the prison. The canvas was used to help contain the smell so the wagon wouldn't be so offensive when it passed through residential areas. It did an excellent job of containing the smell. Inside, the stench was so strong as to be almost unbearable. They could barely breathe.

As they waited for the driver to conclude his business and return to the wagon, Jaco lifted enough of the canvas to glance back toward the big, dimly lit blockhouse from which he and Putt had just come. The guard would have already made another round, but so far, there had been no escape alarm given. So far, the guard had been fooled into thinking they were both asleep in their bunks, and the dummies that he and Putt had made were doing their job

Five minutes later, the back door to the kitchen opened and a wedge of orange lantern light spilled out onto the same porch under which Jaco and Putt had been hiding earlier.

Two men came outside.

"What gets me is how they can call garbage edible, and nonedible," the prison official was saying. "Ain't none of it edible at all, far as I can tell."

"If pigs will eat it, that means it's edible . . . at least to pigs," the wagon driver said.

"Yeah, well, if you charged us by the stink, we'd have to pay you more money just to have you haul it off tonight," the prison official said, laughing.

"Fish heads 'n guts do have a way of stinkin'. But it seems like the more the slop stinks, the more them pigs seem to liken it," the driver said with a chuckle.

"When you think about it, I suppose there ain't nobody that's ever said that pigs got 'ny sense." The prison official waved as the garbageman drove the wagon away.

A moment later, the wagon started toward the front gate. As they passed the kennel, the dogs started barking.

One of the dogs managed to leap over the kennel fence and came rushing toward the wagon, growling viciously, his fangs bared. He darted toward the wagon and jumped at it, barking and growling.

"Get the hell out of here!" cried the driver of the garbage wagon. He banged against the side of the wagon with his whip.

"What's going on?" one of the guards asked as the wagon stopped at the gate.

"What's going on? I'll tell you what's going on. Your damn dog has gone crazy," the driver answered. "Call him off."

The guard yelled at the dog, who stood crouching, his head lowered, as he continued to growl. Finally one of the dog handlers arrived.

"What's got into him?" the guard asked.

The handler smiled. "More 'n likely he's wantin' some of what you're haulin'."

"Yeah? Well he can have it, if you're willin' to pay for it. Pig farmers pay me for this."

"Smells like fish," the handler said.

"That's most what it is."

"Yeah, well, I don't want my dogs eatin' fish. They'll get bones in their throat."

"Well, open the gate then," the wagon driver said. "I'd like to get out of here before he takes it in his mind to attack me."

The guard nodded at someone up on the wall and the gate, assisted by swinging weights, opened. The driver snapped his reins and the team moved forward through the open space.

"Let's get out of this here wagon," Putt said quietly. "I'm damn near to suffocatin'."

"Not yet," Jaco replied. "Not till I'm sure we're far enough away from the prison that we ain't likely to be seen."

Jaco waited until *he* reached the point where he couldn't wait any longer. Surely, he thought, they were far enough away to take a chance. "All right. Get out of the back and off the road quick as you can."

Dropping down onto the road, they scrambled quickly into the drainage ditch that paralleled the road, then lay there for two minutes, breathing deeply, gulping in the fresh, clean air.

Finally, Jaco stood up. "Let's get goin'."

"Which way?"

Jaco looked up at the night sky, found the Big Dipper, then located the North Star. "That way is Texas," he said, pointing east. "I want to get the hell out of New Mexico."

CHAPTER TWELVE

The two men walked through the rest of the night, finally stopping for a rest just as the sun was coming up.

"Jaco, I done walked my legs off near 'bout up to my knees. How much longer are we goin' to be a-walkin'?"

"What are you complainin' about, Putt? Would you rather be back there, gettin' ready to be hung this mornin'?"

"No."

"Then don't be complainin' so much about —" Jaco paused in mid-sentence, then smiled. "Smell that?" He held up his finger.

"Smell what? I still got nothin' but the smell of fish in my nose."

"That's 'cause you ain't tryin'. I can smell our horses right now."

"What do you mean you can smell our horses?"

"Take a deep whiff, and tell me what you

smell," Jaco said.

Putt responded. Then smiled. "I don't smell no horses, but seems like I can smell bacon a-cookin'."

"You think bacon can cook itself?" Jaco asked.

"Cook itself? Jaco, what are you talkin' about?"

"Just what I said. Bacon don't cook itself. That means someone is cookin' it and it's more 'n likely that whoever is cookin' the bacon has got hisself a horse. If there's more 'n one of 'em, there will be more 'n one horse."

"Yeah," Putt said with an understanding smile.

"I'd say that the polite thing to do would be to pay 'em a visit."

The two men moved toward the aroma of cooking bacon until they got close enough to see two people squatting by a camp fire. Two horses were ground hobbled nearby. An iron skillet was sitting on an iron grate stretched out over the fire.

"Hello, the camp!" Jaco called.

Not until the people turned did Jaco and Putt see that one of them was just a boy, probably no older than thirteen or fourteen.

"Who are you?" the man asked.

Jaco assumed, though he had no way of

135

knowing for certain, that the older man was the boy's father.

"What kind of clothes is them that you're a-wearin'?" the boy asked.

Jaco and Putt were still wearing the striped shirt and trousers of a prisoner's garb.

"Well, son, it's the kind of clothes you wear in a penitentiary," Jaco said easily.

"A penitentiary? You mean you two is prisoners?" the man asked.

"We *was* prisoners, but not no more," Jaco said. "My name is Jones, this here feller is Smith. Truth is, me 'n Smith done served our time, and we was being took to Santa Fe where we was goin to be set free, give a set of new clothes, 'n ten dollars apiece so's we could start all over again, an' go straight. But we got attacked by some renegade Injuns, and the driver that was takin' us back got kilt. Not havin' no guns to fight back, the onliest thing me 'n Smith could do was get away from the Injuns the best way we could. What we are a-doin' now is lookin' to go to the nearest town where we could turn ourselves in to the sheriff."

"If you're bein' let out, why would you want to turn yourself in to the sheriff?"

"Why not turn ourselves in? We ain't 'n no trouble now, and this way the sheriff can take us to Santa Fe where we'll get our new clothes 'n the ten dollars that's owed us. We ain't got nothin'. No clothes, no money. Truth to tell, mister, we don't even have anything to eat, 'n that bacon is smellin' awful good to us. That's what brung us over here in the first place."

The man smiled. "Well, Mr. Jones, my name is Foster. This here is my boy, Ira. If food is all you're worryin' about, we'd be real pleased to have you share breakfast with us. I'll just throw on another few pieces of bacon, and we'll be just fine. I was makin' some extra biscuits anyway, just to carry along with us."

"Mr. Foster, that's just real generous of you," Jaco said.

"Whooee. How come it is that you two men is stinkin' so?" the boy asked.

"Ira!" Foster said sharply. "That's no way to talk to a person."

"But Pa, they both stink," Ira said. "For sure you can smell 'em, can't you?"

Jaco laughed. "Don't be angry with the boy, Mr. Foster. I reckon we do stink at that, seein' as the wagon we was havin' to ride in was also the wagon that hauls away the slop from the kitchen. They don't give us freed prisoners our own carriage. No sir, we got to take a ride on whatever wagon it is that's a-leavin' the prison at the time. This here wagon was carryin' fish scraps. I reckon we'll have to take us a bath a-fore we put on any new clothes."

"I suppose so. But again, let me apologize for my son," Foster said.

As the four ate their breakfast, Foster told Jaco and Putt how he and the boy were on the way back home from having been in Santa Fe for the last few days.

"Is that far from here? Your home, I mean," Jaco asked.

"It isn't too terrible far. I reckon we'll be back by late tomorrow, sometime." Foster looked over at his son and smiled. "We drove ten head of beeves to Santa Fe and sold 'em."

"One of 'em was mine," Ira said proudly. "And I got thirty-five dollars for it."

"The boy's right. He raised 'im his own-self from when it was a calf. I figure it ain't never too early to learn the power of hard work," Foster said.

"You got that right, Mr. Foster. Iffen I'da had someone like you to keep me straight, more 'n likely I woulda never got myself in trouble in the first place. It ain't never too late to learn, neither. I mean, look at me 'n Jones. Yesterday we was in prison. Today we're free men."

"I thought you said his name was Smith."

"It is Smith. Bein' so excited 'bout bein' free again, I reckon I just got a little too excited, and misspoke. If you'll excuse me for a minute, I'm just goin' to step over there 'n take a leak. I don't want to be piss-in' in a man's camp.

"Smith, why don't you tell 'em that funny story about Lewis, 'n how when he was bein' hung, he asked them to tie the noose real tight so's he wouldn't fall, seein' as he was a-scared o' heights."

Putt, as if not realizing that Jaco had already given away his punch line, started the story. That did exactly what Jaco wanted it to do; it kept the attention of Foster and his son, allowing Jaco to step up behind them with a large stone. It took only two blows with the rock, and both Foster and Jimmy were dead.

"You're smaller 'n I am, and the boy was right big for his age," Jaco said. "See if you can fit into his clothes."

"Damn," Putt said. "There ain't neither one of 'em carryin' a gun. What kind of man would go off on a trip like this 'n not even have no gun with 'im?"

"Looks like there's a shotgun in one o' the saddle sheaths," Jaco said.

Rifling through the saddlebags of Foster and his son Ira, they found an extra change of clothes, then the two outlaws bathed in the nearby stream.

Half an hour later, cleaned up, wearing different clothes, armed with a shotgun, and riding horses, Jaco and Putt were heading east. They also had three hundred and fifty dollars, the money Foster and Ira had made from selling their cattle.

"What are we goin' to do now?" Putt asked.

"First, I'm goin' to take care of some business," Jaco said.

"What kind of business?"

"Killin' a sheriff kind of business."

Putt smiled. "You're talkin' about killin' Baxter, ain't you?"

"Yeah. I'm talkin' about killin' Baxter. After that's done, I aim to put together a gang of men that we can trust, and make up for some of that time we lost while we was in prison."

"Yeah!" Putt said. "Yeah, that sounds like a fine idea."

Chaperito

At three o'clock in the morning, the two men rode into the small, quiet town. The only sounds were night-singing crickets and frogs and the gentle squeak of a sign moving slightly in the breeze.

"Stop here," Jaco said. "If we ride all the way up to the jail, we'll more 'n likely be heard."

They tied the horses off in front of the feed store. Jaco pulled the double-barreled gun from the saddle holster, broke it open to check the loads, then snapped it shut. He and Putt moved quietly, staying in the shadows until they reached the jail. A soft golden glow shined through the window. Creeping up to the window, they looked inside and saw a deputy leaning back in his chair with his feet on the desk, his arms folded across his chest, and a hat tipped down over his eyes.

Opening the front door of the jail, they stepped in quietly. Holding the shotgun so as to be able to use it in a butt stroke, Jaco walked toward the deputy.

Something awakened him and he pushed his hat back and looked up just in time for his eyes to register fear. Jaco slammed the butt of the shotgun between his eyes before the deputy could make a sound.

Rifling quickly through the desk, Jaco found a pistol and holster and handed it to Putt. With that one and the one Jaco took off the dead deputy, they were now armed.

They went into the apartment attached to the back of the jail where Sheriff Baxter lived with his wife and his elderly mother-in-law. Loud snoring was coming from one of the two bedrooms.

"Go in there and kill whoever you find," Jaco ordered, pointing to one of the rooms. "I'll take this one." He indicated the room from which the loud snoring was coming.

Jaco had chosen the right room for his personal wish for vengeance. Sheriff Baxter was lying on his back, his mouth open, snoring loudly. Jaco held the end of the pistol one inch from the sheriff's forehead and pulled the trigger.

The sheriff's wife sat up with a start, but Jaco killed her before she could make a sound. He heard a gunshot coming from the other room.

"Let's get out of here," Putt said, meeting Jaco in the living room.

"Not until we let the prisoners go," Jaco said.

"Why should we let the prisoners go? What the hell do we care about them?"

"We don't care," Jaco said. "But, if the deputy and the sheriff are both dead, and the prisoners escaped, who are people going to blame for the killing?"

Putt laughed. "Yeah. Yeah, that's a great idea!"

A minute later, Jaco and Putt hurried back

into the jail, where they unlocked the cell doors to let out the two prisoners.

"What's happening?" one of the prisoners asked.

"You're free," Jaco said. "But you'd better get out of here fast."

"Gee, thanks, mister!"

"I'd go down the alley if I was you," Jaco said.

The two men ran out back as Jaco and Putt went out front, then moved quickly back to their horses. Dogs were barking and they could hear some shouting.

"What is it?" a man carrying a shotgun asked. "What was the shooting?"

"Jailbreak," Jaco said. "They killed the deputy, the sheriff, and his entire family. They're runnin' north down the alley."

"Tom!" the man shouted down the street toward another man. "Jailbreak! They killed the sheriff and his family. In the alley!"

Other armed men had appeared outside, and they started running toward the north end of town. Jaco and Putt mounted their horses as they heard shooting.

"There they are!" someone shouted. "They've run into the stable!"

"Don't let 'em get away!" another voice called. "Good Lord, they just kilt the sheriff 'n his whole family!"

"They ain't goin' to get away. I know exactly where they are."

As Jaco and Putt rode out of town, they heard shouts and more shooting.

"We got 'em, by God!" someone yelled. "We kilt both of 'em!"

"I got to hand it to you, Jaco," Putt said. "That was real smart, what you done."

CHAPTER THIRTEEN

Chugwater

"There's that English feller," Elmer said, pointing to Cal Hanson. Duff and Elmer had just taken a table at Fiddlers' Green. Hanson was sitting at a table with Biff and Fred Matthews.

"Ain't he s'posed to be buyin' some cows from you?"

"Aye."

"Well, how come it is that he ain't bought 'em yet?"

"He sent a message to his backers in England. I think they are waiting to decide how many head they want."

"You woulda thought he'd have that all figured out by now. I know he's got the money. I seen the story about it in the newspaper."

"Oh, yes, he has the money all right," Duff replied.

Biff said something which neither Duff

nor Elmer were able to hear, but whatever it was, it made everyone laugh.

"Duff," Biff called, waving to him. "Why don't you 'n Elmer bring your drinks and come on over. We're havin' a fine conversation, and Mr. Hanson is a-fixin' to tell us a joke."

"An Englishman is going to tell a joke, is he? Well, that would be most interesting. Sure now, and I was nae aware the English even had a sense of humor. But do give it a try." Although Duff had lost much of his Scottish brogue in the years he had been in America, he purposely let the words roll from his tongue as he spoke to the Englishman.

"I know a joke or two, but it will require a bit of intelligence to comprehend, and you, being a Scotsman, may have some difficulty in seeing the humor."

"Here now, and would you tell the joke and not bang your gums so and apologizing before you even tell it, for it not being funny," Duff said. Though they were deriding each other, it was obvious to their friends that it was all in good fun.

"All right," Hanson said. "A Scotsman and an Englishman met in a posh pub in London, in order to do some business. I expect it would be much like us, meeting here in this posh pub," he continued, taking in Fiddlers' Green with a sweep of his hand.

"A waiter approaches. 'May I get you something?' he asks. 'Aye, I'll have scotch,' the Scotsman replies. The waiter pours the drink, then turns to the Englishman. 'And will it be a scotch for you as well?' he asks.

"The Englishman glares at the waiter. 'Never!' the Englishman says. 'Why, I'd rather be raped and ravished by bad women than drink scotch whisky!'

"The Scotsman hands the drink back to the waiter. *'Och,'* he says. 'I *didnae ken* there wuz a choice!' "

The others, including Duff, laughed.

"Duff, my boy, it looks like the Englishman got you with that one. Do you have one for the English?"

"Aye, 'n 'tis one you might enjoy, Biff, being as you're an old soldier. This one is about the English army in Egypt. I can speak from experience, as I served in the Sahara alongside Englishmen."

"Careful now, I was with the Sussex Regiment in Egypt," Hanson said.

"Aye, and 'tis just a coincidence, I'm sure, that the story I'm about to tell is about the Sussex Regiment." Duff settled in his chair for the telling. "The Sussex Regiment had a large pile of discards in the middle of the

Sahara. An English brigadier, with a monocle stuck in his eye" — he made a circle of his thumb and forefinger and held it up to his eye, to the enjoyment of the others — "performed an inspection and gave his report. 'Improper Security,' he said. 'I strongly recommend four guards to be utilized so that the discards can be watched over, day and night.'

"So, because the Sussex listens to their brigadiers, they appointed four guards to watch over the trash heap. Then the brigadier said, 'there are no written orders for the guards to follow.'

"So, the Sussex Regiment created a planning section and staffed it with two corporals to write a set of orders and guidelines.

"The brigadier then pointed out that there were no supervisors to make certain that the guards and the two corporals were doing their jobs properly, so the regiment assigned two sergeants to look over the corporals and the guards.

"The general then pointed out that there was no company of soldiers provided to maintain the facility, so the army provided an entire infantry company with a captain in command, a leftenant as executive officer, a sergeant major, a first sergeant, five sergeants, and five corporals, along with one hundred privates.

"When that was done the brigadier said that the unit was now overstaffed and should cut back on some of its personnel. So, the army eliminated the four guard positions."

The others laughed.

"Upon my word," Hanson said. "I do believe that I was the commanding officer of that company."

After the exchange of a few more stories, Hanson excused himself, explaining that he had some business to take care of at the bank before it closed for the day.

"He seems like a good enough feller," Elmer said after Hanson left.

"Aye, he does," Duff agreed.

"What is it with the English and the Scots?" Elmer asked. "Why don't y'all like each other?"

"What is it between the group you call Yankees and your Rebels?" Duff replied.

"Damn. You mean y'all fought a war agin one another?"

"Aye," Duff said. "What the Battle of Gettysburg was to the American Confederacy, the Battle of Flodden was to Scotland."

"Who won?"

"King James of Scotland was killed. And now, Scotland is part of Great Britain."

"Sorta like the South is still part of the Union?" Elmer asked.

"You might say that, aye."

"But you and that feller seem to be gettin' on, all right."

"Are there any Yankees that you like?"

"Well, yeah, sure. Biff is a Yankee, 'n I like him."

"The idea of nationality might separate England from Scotland, but individual Englishmen and Scotsmen can transcend that separation to become friends, much like you and Biff."

"I'll be damned," Elmer said. "You sure got a way of explainin' things so that folks can understand."

At that moment someone came running into the saloon. "There's somethin' goin' on down at the bank!" he shouted.

"What is it?" Biff asked.

"It's a bank robbery. Or at least that's how it started out. Only now it's a standoff between Marshal Ferrell and the bank robber, an' that English feller is right in the middle of it."

"Are you for telling us, lad, that Mr. Hanson is one of the bank robbers?" Duff asked.

"No, he ain't the robber. He's the

hostage."

Several of the patrons of Fiddlers' Green, including Duff and Elmer, rushed out front to see what was going on. At the far end of the block Bill Ferrell, the city marshal, and Hanson were standing in the street in the front of the bank. A man was standing behind Hanson, holding a pistol against the back of his head.

Marshal Ferrell was also holding his pistol, but there was nothing he could do with it under the circumstances. "You may as well put down that gun and give yourself up. You can't get to your horse, and you sure as hell can't walk out of here."

"You think that was smart, runnin' my horse off, do you? You'd better get me another horse right now, or I'm goin' to kill this here foreign fella," the bank robber said.

"Then what?" Marshal Ferrell asked.

"What do you mean, then what? He'll be dead."

"You won't have the advantage anymore, will you?" Ferrell asked calmly. "If you kill him, I'll kill you."

As Ferrell continued to argue with the bank robber, Duff stepped out to his horse and pulled the Creedmoor rifle from its sheath. He was standing on the side of Sky opposite the three people in the street. Even

151

if the would-be bank robber happened to glance toward Duff, he was far enough away and blocked by his horse. The bank robber wouldn't be able to see what Duff was doing.

He slipped a shell into the chamber, then, using the saddle as a rest, aimed at the bank robber. He put the crosshairs of the scope, not on the bank robber himself, but on the gun the robber was holding, and pulled the trigger.

The loud bang of the rifle rushed down the street at the speed of sound, but the bullet was even faster. It struck the pistol, knocking it out of the bank robber's hand with a spray of blood at the point of impact. The bullet had traumatically amputated two fingers.

The bank robber let out a howl of pain and, grabbing his mutilated right hand with his left, bent over on the street. Hanson moved fast to get out of the way, and Ferrell closed the distance between himself and the would-be thief just as quickly.

Duff, his movement slow and casual, put the rifle back into the saddle holster. Not until then did he walk down to join Marshal Ferrell and the man who, but a moment earlier, had been holding Hanson hostage.

"Nice shot," Ferrell said.

Duff nodded toward the man holding his bloody left hand over the bleeding stubs of the two fingers that had been shot away. "Better get those fingers bandaged before you lose too much blood."

"What were you thinkin' shootin' from that far away?" the outlaw shouted. "You coulda kilt me."

"Nae, if I had wanted to kill you, I would have killed you," Duff said.

"I want to thank you for this, Mr. MacCallister," Hanson said, and although he had been terribly frightened a few minutes earlier, he was able to summon a smile. "I say, I shall never speak harshly of a Scotsman again."

"*Och,* you'll *nae* be holding me to the same standard, would ye now, Mr. Hanson? For 'tis one of a Scotsman's dearest pleasures to speak ill o' the English."

Hanson chuckled. "After what you did here today, Mr. MacCallister, you may say anything about the English you want. I may even join you."

"Sure now 'n dinnae ye be doing that, for what fun would it be to bedevil the English, if an Englishman agrees with me?"

Several had gathered at the scene, including the banker, and they laughed at the banter, as much from relief as from the actual humor.

"Mr. Montgomery, you'll be wanting to take that back into the bank with you, I suppose," Marshal Ferrell said, pointing to a cloth bag the bank robber had been carrying."

"Yes, thank you," the banker replied.

"Come along, you," the marshal said to the outlaw. "I've got a nice jail cell waiting for you."

"Jail? What about a doctor?" the bank robber complained. "You heard what this feller said. I got to get my hand looked after."

"I'll bring the doctor to the jail."

"Mr. MacCallister, you'll be dining on me tonight. Anywhere you want to go, and anything you want to eat," Hanson said.

"I think ye kindly for the invitation," Duff said. "But I've promised a lady friend I would be dining with her."

"I'll pay for her meal as well," Hanson said.

Duff smiled. "Well now, as a Scotsman, how can I not be pleased to accept something for free?"

Albuquerque, New Mexico Territory
Johnny Dane started killing when he was fourteen. He'd killed a thirteen-year-old girl

154

because she wouldn't dance with him. He killed another girl a year later because she looked away from him when he spoke to her. He had killed six others since then, four women and two men. He had gotten away with it because nobody believed that someone that young could be that evil. But someone had seen him shoot a man in the back when he was seventeen, so he'd had to leave Denver.

A few minutes earlier, he had gone upstairs with one of the saloon girls who worked at the Tiffany House of Pleasure.

"Honey, you don't look old enough to be with a real woman," Bella said.

"I'm old enough," Dane said.

"We'll see." Bella patted the bed she was sitting on.

Fifteen minutes later, a frustrated Dane got up from the bed. "That ain't never happened to me before."

"Don't worry about it, honey. It happens to lots of men."

"With you? It happens with you?"

"Yes, lots of times." With her back to him, Bella sat up on the side of the bed and reached for her camisole. She didn't see him kneel on the bed behind her or pull a knife from his belt. "If you want to try again in a few minutes, you're going to have to pay me for it, because I've got other custo—"

Dane reached around to cup his left hand over her mouth. With the knife in his right hand, he slit her throat, the knife going so deep it sliced through her windpipe. Her warm blood began spilling down over his hand, and he jerked it away so he could look at the terror in her eyes as she died.

"I'm glad to hear you say that it happens with a lot of men who are with you. It just proves that it's your fault, don't it?"

CHAPTER FOURTEEN

Chugwater

It was early morning, and though most self-respecting roosters had announced the fact long ago, half-a-dozen cocks were still trying to stake a claim on the day. The disc was still hidden by the mountains in the east. The light had already turned from red to white and here and there were signs the people of Chugwater were rising.

A pump creaked as a housewife began pumping water for her morning chores, and somewhere a carpenter had already begun hammering.

After the dinner last night, Duff had decided it was too late to ride back to the ranch, so he had spent the night in town. Awakened by the early morning sounds, he got out of bed and poured a basin of water for his shave.

That finished, he moved over to stand by the open window and looked out onto Clay

Street. He heard the clumping of hoofbeats and the rumble and rattle of a couple freight wagons as they rolled slowly down the street, just beginning what would be a day-long journey to Cheyenne. On the wooden porches and boardwalks, shopkeepers were busy sweeping them clean, the better to attract potential customers. A cowboy who had just awakened from a drunken night on the street was wetting his head in a watering trough.

There was a knock on his door. "Duff?"

It was Megan's voice. "Duff, are you awake yet?" she called through the door.

"I'm up." Without bothering to put on his shirt, he stepped across the room to open the door.

Megan smiled when she saw him. "I'm glad you didn't feel you had to dress for me."

"You've seen me without a shirt before."

"And without your pants," Megan said, her smile broadening.

"*Och,* lass, hush now, for 'tis embarrassing me you are, and yourself, too."

"Duff MacCallister, I am not in the least embarrassed," Megan said.

He stuck his head out in the hallway, then pulled her in quickly, and shut the door behind her. "Such talk for a public place."

"It didn't have to be public. You know you could have spent the night with me."

"And have it be known, not only by the Englishman, but by everyone in town who would see me stepping out of your place in the morning?"

"You mean, as opposed to people seeing me come out of your hotel room, this morning?"

"Och!" Duff said. "I hadn't thought of that. Woman, have ye no shame?"

"No shame at all," Megan said as she leaned into him for a kiss.

Standing on the front porch of the hotel when Duff and Megan came down was Hanson. He stretched, then took a deep breath. "Beautiful morning, isn't it?"

"Yes, it's quite a lovely morning," Megan said.

"I hadn't expected to see you here, Miss Parker, but one can never complain about the company of a beautiful woman. Will you be taking breakfast with us?"

"I will indeed, since we will be discussing the sale of our cattle this morning."

"I beg your pardon? *Our* cattle?"

"Miss Parker has long been a business partner in the cattle I raise at Sky Meadow," Duff explained.

"Oh, my. What a delightful surprise to know that I will be doing business, not only with the man who saved my life, but his beautiful lady friend as well."

Duff, Megan, and Hanson started toward the Tacky Mack Café. As they passed the general store they saw a woman picking through the fruits and vegetables on display on the front porch of the store.

"Good morning, Joanne," Megan called cheerily.

"Good morning, Megan," the woman replied. "Oh, I must tell you, when Frank and I went to Cheyenne last week everyone was talking about how beautiful the dress was that you made for me. I just love it so."

"I'm glad you do," Megan replied.

"Megan, is there anyone in town you haven't made a dress for?" Duff asked as they continued on up the street.

"I haven't made a dress for everyone," Megan replied. Then she added, "Yet."

"You appear to be a most enterprising young lady, Miss Parker," Hanson said. "You are involved in the cattle business and a seamstress, as well?"

"Oh, Megan is much more than a seamstress," Duff said. "She owns her own shop and she designs the creations she sells."

"That's quite impressive," Hanson said.

Duff smiled. "I got that right, didn't I, Megan? They aren't just dresses, they are *creations*."

Megan chuckled. "I'm proud of you."

"Nae, lass, 'tis proud of you, I am."

Stepping into the Tacky Mack Café, they were met by Rudy York, the proprietor.

"Hello, Duff, Miss Megan. I heard about savin' that foreign fella yesterday. I'll bet he's pretty thankful today."

"Indeed I am, sir, indeed I am," Hanson replied.

York looked surprised. "It was you?"

"It was."

"Sorry. I didn't mean nothin' by that 'foreign fella' comment."

"As I am a foreign fellow, there is absolutely nothing offensive in your remark, and no apology is necessary."

"Rudy, this is Cal Hanson. Mr. Hanson, this is Rudy York. If you don't like the food this morning, he is the one you must blame."

"Ha!" Megan said. "I've never seen you offer any complaints about Rudy's food."

"You've got me there, lass," Duff agreed with a smile.

"Let me escort you to a table," York offered.

Fifteen minutes later, Megan and Hanson were having a second cup of coffee, and Duff was having another batch of pancakes when two men approached the table. Both of them were wearing suits, and neither of them was wearing a gun. The short, bald-headed man was Charley Blanton, editor of the *Chugwater Defender.* The taller of the two men was Joe Cravens, the mayor of the town.

"Mr. Hanson, as mayor of this town, I would like to officially welcome you to Chugwater, and I thank you for choosing to do business here."

"And, my Lord Mayor, I would like to express my appreciation for the treatment I have received since arriving in your fair city."

The mayor chuckled. "Would that include being taken hostage in the attempted bank robbery?"

Hanson chuckled. "I must confess that there were moments when I was concerned as to my future, but thanks to the unerring marksmanship of the Scottish gentlemen here, no harm was done, and it but added to the excitement of the visit."

"Mr. Hanson, I'm Charles Blanton, editor

162

of our local newspaper. I wonder if you would consent to an interview," the shorter of the two men asked, extending his hand.

"I would be happy to," Hanson replied, taking the offered hand.

"Good. If you would, then, just drop by my office when you have finished breakfast. Duff can show you where it is."

"Would you two be for joining us?" Duff asked.

"No, I thank you kindly for the invitation, but I've city business to attend to," Mayor Cravens said.

"And I must check on the layout of today's edition," Blanton said. "We'll leave now, and let you good people enjoy your breakfast in peace."

"Mr. Hanson and I have had our breakfast, Charley," Megan said. "You may have noticed that the only thing we're doing now is seeing just how many pancakes Duff can actually eat."

Blanton, Cravens, and Hanson laughed.

"Here now, 'n I've had no more than eight," Duff said.

They laughed again.

"They seem to be a couple very nice gentlemen," Hanson said after the two men left.

"They are interesting men as well," Duff

said. "Joe Cravens, the mayor, is a graduate of West Point."

"Ah, yes. I am familiar with West Point," Hanson said. "We learned about it when I attended the Royal Military Academy at Sandhurst."

"Mayor Cravens reached the rank of brigadier, and performed with gallantry in the Civil War."

"Dare I ask for which side?"

"Aye, for 'tis a good question. Like many other graduates of West Point, Mayor Cravens resigned his commission in the U.S. Army and fought for the South."

"Charley Blanton owns the newspaper. He was a journalist for the *New York Times,* but he grew weary of city life and came west. We have a mutual connection in New York. He was a very good friend of my kinfolk, Andrew and Rosanna MacCallister, who are quite well-known thespians."

Finished with pancakes, Duff, Megan, and Hanson stopped by the newspaper office where Hanson would be interviewed by Blanton. Duff had a great deal of respect for the press, and he could almost believe there was something sacrosanct about a newspaper office. He looked around, taking in the editorial bay where Blanton had his desk, the composing room with its tables and drawers of type, and the press room where reposed the steam-powered rotary press, recently purchased to replace the Washington hand press, which for many years had been the backbone of western newspapers.

"Oh, Miss Parker, I beg your pardon," Blanton said. "I had no idea you would be stopping by my establishment. Had I known that, I would have swept the place out and cleaned it up a bit."

Megan laughed. "Why go to all that trouble? You never have before when I have brought advertising copy by for you. By the way, have you set my latest ad, yet?"

"I have indeed. Would you like to see it?"

"Oh, I wouldn't want to take up your valuable time. I know you want to interview Mr. Hanson."

"No problem at all. It's over there on the composing table," Blanton said.

Megan stepped over to look at it.

☞ LADIES
FINEST DRESSES

~

Made to Order at
MEGAN'S DRESS EMPORIUM

On either side of the copy was a cut of a dress.

"Yes, Mr. Blanton, that looks very nice," Megan said.

"It will run in the next five issues," Blanton said. Then he turned his attention to Cal Hanson.

Although the main part of the interview dealt with the business Hanson was transacting, Blanton also asked him how he felt when he was being held hostage by the would-be bank robber, who was in jail, recovering from his hand wound.

"Well, I would be lying if I didn't say that I was frightened," Hanson said. "I quite didn't expect the outcome that transpired, that is, to have the gun shot from the hand of the brigand who was holding me captive. The gunshot was from what had to be a considerable distance."

"We walked it off," Blanton said. "And we believe that it was about two hundred and fifty yards."

"An amazing shot. Especially considering that the gun was being held to my head."

"That was nothing," Blanton said. "You should have been here for the shooting contest."

"I expect Mr. MacCallister won."

"Oh, yes."

Blanton went on to describe in some detail the shooting contest.

"Tell me, Mr. Hanson, what made you decide to leave England and come to America to raise cattle?"

"You will think me foolish."

"Now, how could I ever think that an English gentleman like you would be foolish?"

Hanson laughed. "You are aware, I'm sure, of the novels of the American West, the dime novels. I'm sure the stories are all fiction, but some of them have stirred my imagination. One character I have found particularly intriguing is Smoke Jensen. I know he doesn't exist but —"

"He most certainly does exist," Blanton said.

"Really? How fascinating. At any rate, such stories stirred my interest, so I wrote up a prospectus for a cattle ranch in Texas, put up as much money as I had, and secured the necessary investment for the rest I needed to bring that to fruition. And, that done, here I am."

"Well, sir, you have started in the right place. All evidence points to the Angus cattle as being the most productive, and I can vouch for the fact that you are doing business, not only with the most knowledgeable of the breed, but also one of the most honest and sincere men in the business."

"I am not surprised to hear such accolades about Duff MacCallister," Hanson replied.

"Well, Mr. Hanson, I thank you very much for consenting to the interview. And Duff, thank you for bringing him by."

"I always want to stay on the good side of the press," Duff said.

"Well, where to now?" Hanson asked when he stepped back out into the street with Duff and Sally.

"Would you care to come out to the ranch and examine the cattle you'll be buying?" Duff asked.

"I would be delighted to. Have you a carriage of some sort? I have no means of transportation."

"You do ride, don't you?"

"Yes, I ride."

"Then there is no problem. We'll stop by the stable and rent a horse for you."

"I'm going as well," Megan said. "Just give me time to put a closed sign on the door."

CHAPTER FIFTEEN

Sky Meadow Ranch

"Oh, what a beautiful estate," Hanson said when they crested a little rise in the road, and the ranch came into view. "I hope, one day, to make Regency as beautiful and as attractive."

As they rode down the long road that led to the ranch, a rabbit jumped up from the dusty grass alongside, then bounded quickly ahead of them, its long strides kicking up little clumps of dirt before it left the road and disappeared into the bushes.

A welcoming gate arched over the road, bearing in wrought iron the words *Sky Meadow.* Beyond the gate was a spreading, two-story house, its mansard roof bracketed by chimneys. The porch stretched all the way across the front of the house. This was what the cowboys called the "Big House."

Set between the Big House and the bunkhouse was the ranch office, a small wood frame building painted red. The bunkhouse was a long, low structure, which was also painted red. A smaller, but quite functional house was behind the bunkhouse. It was where Elmer lived. Indoor plumbing had been installed in all the living structures, which meant no outhouses.

In addition to the living quarters, a barn, a granary, a machine shed, and a smokehouse were on the property.

A large paddock around the barn enclosed at least two dozen horses, all belonging to Duff, and used by the cowboys in operating the ranch.

They were met by Elmer just as they reached the house.

"What would be the cow to bull ratio?" Hanson asked.

Elmer answered the question. "Twenty bulls, three hundred and eighty heifers, along with two hundred one-year-old steers. The steers will put on weight and increase their value, and also, help to keep the bulls calm."

"Would you like to ride out and see the cattle?" Duff asked.

"Oh, yes. I would very much like to see them."

Duff, Megan, Hanson, and Elmer rode out to the east pasture to take a look at some of the cattle. Their black coats shining in the sun, they moved around quietly nibbling at the grass and drinking from Big Creek.

"I say, they are magnificent looking!" Hanson said enthusiastically.

After a ride through the herd, moving close enough so that all the animals could be checked for soundness, Hanson announced that he was ready to close the deal.

They returned to the office, where Duff made out a bill of sale.

We, Duff MacCallister and Megan Parker, owners of the Black Angus cattle raised on Sky Meadow Ranch in Laramie County, Wyoming, do by these presents, transfer ownership of 600 head of mixed cattle to Cal Hanson, the purchaser.

In response for this transfer of ownership, we hereto affix our signatures, acknowledging the receipt of fourteen thousand two hundred dollars and zero cents ($14,200.00).

"Here you are, Mr. Hanson. You are now the owner of six hundred head of the finest cattle in America."

"Thank you. By the by, since we have done business, and you have, in fact, saved my life, do you not think you could call me *Cal*? And might I not call you *Duff*?"

"Aye, 'tis." Duff chuckled. "A Scotsman and an Englishman on first-name basis. Who knows? It could lead to a rapprochement between our two homelands."

"Indeed it could," Hanson replied. "Tell me, Duff, how will we get my cattle home?"

"We will drive the herd from here to Cheyenne. There we will ship them to Texas by rail."

"Will we be able to get all six hundred on a single train?"

"No, it'll take two trains. You can go with the first shipment; I'll come with the second."

"Thank you. I appreciate that."

Business concluded, Duff, Hanson, and Megan were standing out on the porch of the office building when Duff saw someone coming toward them. "Ah, here comes Wang Chow."

Wang paused when he was about ten feet away, put his hands in a prayer position, and nodded his head.

"Cal, this is my cook, my valet, and my friend Wang Chow."

"A Chinaman," Hanson said. "I have often heard the virtues of Chinamen extolled, but I never expected to find one in the middle of the American West."

"Actually, there are several men and women from China all over the West," Duff said. "Thousands of them came to work on the railroad, and when the railroad was completed, they stayed to take on other jobs."

"And Mr. Wang found you," Hanson said.

"No, you are wrong, sir," Wang said. "Mr. MacCallister found me."

"Oh, I see. You went looking, specifically, for a Chinaman."

"I wasn't looking for anyone in particular. But when I encountered Wang, the situation was such that I couldn't just walk away."

"I was about to be hanged, and Mr. MacCallister saved me," Wang said.

"What? You were about to be hanged?"

Quickly, Duff told the story of how he had happened upon a lynching in progress.

"Ah, yes, lynching. Terrible thing, that."

"Wang, tell me, my friend, how long until lunch? I'm starved."

"Wang, you must get some food into this poor man," Megan said with a laugh. "Why, he practically starved himself at breakfast. He had only eight pancakes, four eggs, and no more than six or seven pieces of bacon."

"Aye, but that was four hours ago," Duff said.

"The meal has been prepared, Mister MacCallister."

"Good, let's go eat. As it so happens, Cal, the Chinese can do marvelous things with beef, and I have asked Wang Chow to prepare something special."

"If the beef is as good as it was at the reception given by Mr. Montgomery, I shall gladly sacrifice another of my animals," Hanson said.

Duff chuckled. "No need, Cal. To show you what a fine fellow I can be, I want you to know that this beef is from one of my own cows."

"Then I shall enjoy it all the more," Hanson insisted.

After dinner, Wang put on a show of knife throwing, successfully sticking the knife into various targets, not only from a considerable distance, but from many different body positions. He threw knives from under his legs, with his back to the target, and over his shoulder. He did it while leaping, and once, even as he turned a flip in midair.

"Oh, my, that is most impressive," Hanson said, amazed by the demonstration. "How did you come by such skills?"

"From Master Tse," Wang replied.

"And who, might I ask, is Master Tse?"

"I will clean the table now, Mr. MacCallister."

"Thank you, Wang, for the great dinner and the entertaining show."

Wang put his hands together and dipped his head as in a partial bow, then returned to the dining room.

"Your Mr. Wang seems to be a most unusual man. And quite accomplished," Hanson said.

Duff smiled. "You don't have any idea how unusual or how accomplished he is."

"I'm sure I don't. I noticed that the inscrutable Mr. Wang didn't answer my question when I asked about Master Tse."

"No, he didn't."

"Do you know who this mysterious Master Tse is?"

"Wang has never told me, and I've never asked. I'm sure he has a reason for being inscrutable."

"Quite so. Tell me, my good man, how soon will we be leaving for Texas?"

"It will take a week or so to get the cattle gathered up," Duff said.

"I'll be leaving for Texas tomorrow," Megan said.

"Tomorrow?"

"If Duff is going to take a herd down to the same place where my sister lives, then

I'm going down there as well. I'll be there to meet you when you arrive."

"Well, I shall look forward to that," Hanson said.

West Texas

Although the word had gone out about Jaco and Putt escaping from prison just before they were to be hanged, eastern New Mexico and western Texas were remote enough areas that the two men had been able to travel from small town to small town without fear of being recognized.

Sitting in the Red Dog Saloon, in Shumla, Texas, they were surprised when a woman approached their table and called them by name.

"Jaco and Putt. The last word I heard on you two boys was that you was both hung."

It was hard to judge the age of the woman who spoke. She could have been anywhere from her mid-forties to the mid-fifties. Many years of being on the line had taken their toll. She was overweight, her hair was frizzy, and her skin was pockmarked. She was wearing a very low-cut dress with pillow-like breasts spilling over the top.

"Well, if it isn't our old friend, Sherazade," Jaco said. "Are you still a saloon girl?"

"Not exactly," she replied. "Now I'm sort

of managin' the girls that work here at the Red Dog. What brings you here?"

"Nothin' in particular," Jaco said. "We just happen to be here."

"So the story wasn't true. You wasn't hung."

Jaco smirked. "You see us, don't you?"

"Yeah, I see you all right. Are you goin' back in business?"

"We might be. Why do you ask?"

"I know a man that's lookin' to partner up with somebody."

Jaco shook his head. "We ain't lookin' to take on no partners. But, if he would like to ride with us, I could see that, maybe. What's his name?"

"His name is Manny Dingo."

"What kind of name is that?"

Sherazade shrugged. "I don't know. It's his name."

"Good enough, I reckon. What do you know about 'im?"

"I know he shot a miner in California, then after that, he started sellin' his gun to the highest bidder. Don't know how many he kilt that way. He rode with Henry Plummer for a while. He's a good man. You won't go wrong by hirin' him on."

"Is he in town?"

Sherazade smiled, then pointed up. "He's

upstairs with one of my girls now. Do you want me to go up and get him?"

"No, I wouldn't want to interrupt a man while he's takin' care of business. When he comes back down, send him over to talk to me."

"All right."

It was no more than fifteen minutes later when Jaco saw Sherazade talking to some man who had just come down the stairs. She pointed toward Jaco and Putt, and the man came over to their table.

He stood there for a moment, running his fingers through his dark beard, his eyelids giving the illusion of being half-closed. He stared down at the two killers. "I'm Manny Dingo." He didn't offer his hand. "Sherazade said you wanted to talk to me."

"That depends," Jaco replied.

"Depends on what?"

"On whether or not you would be interested in what I have to offer."

"I don't know whether I am or not. She didn't say nothin' 'bout no offer. She just said that she thought I might want to talk to you. What is it that you have to offer? 'Cause I tell you right now, I ain't interested in buyin' nothin'."

"That's very good, because I have nothing

178

to sell . . . 'ceptin' mayhaps a way for you to make some money."

The expression on Dingo's face brightened. "You're offerin' a way to make money? How are you goin' to do that?"

"I'm puttin' together a gang. But not just any gang. I'm talkin' about a gang that will be strong enough to rob any coach, hold up any train, and take what we want from any bank."

"That's pretty bold talk, ain't it?" Dingo asked.

"Ain't bold if you can pull it off. And I can pull it off."

"Let's say that you do put together a gang that can do all that. Next thing you know, ever'one in the gang will have such a price on their heads that ever' bounty hunter in the whole West will come lookin' for us."

"I've got that all figured out, too. Once I get it all put together, we'll have us a place that no law and no bounty hunter will dare come lookin' for us."

"Where would that be?"

"I'll let you know when you need to know. What about it, Dingo? Are you with us?"

"Yeah," Dingo said. "I'm with you. How many is in the gang?"

"There's three of us," Jaco said. "Me, Putt, and you."

"Three? I thought you said this here gang was strong enough to do anythin' we wanted to do."

"It will be when I get it all put together."

"Who else you goin' to put in it?"

"I'm not sure yet. But they'll all be good men. You can count on that."

CHAPTER SIXTEEN

Sky Meadow Ranch

Ten cowboys were in the bunkhouse. Four of them were playing poker for matches, one was playing a guitar, accompanied by another with a Jew's harp. One cowboy was sleeping, and Dewey, Woodward, and Martin were gathered around Elmer next to one of the two potbellied stoves, which, in the winter, provided warmth for the building.

"You'll be gettin' paid extra for makin' this drive down to Cheyenne," Elmer said. "I'm the one that picked you out, so don't you embarrass me. You do a good job, you hear?"

"You know you can count on us, Elmer," Woodward said.

"Yeah, well, I hope I can. Duff, that is, Mr. MacCallister, needs this deal to go real smooth. I think it's kind of a special thing for him, bein' as this feller he's sellin' the beef to is an Englishman."

"Damn you! You palmed that ace!" The shout came from the other end of the bunkhouse where the poker game was in session.

Everyone in the bunkhouse looked toward the commotion to see what was going to happen next. Three of the cowboys who were playing were still seated. The one who was shouting in such anger was on his feet, pointing at one of the men.

"Sit down, Louie," one of the other players said. "You're makin' one hell of a row over nothin' "

"Over nothin' Hank? Over nothin'? Merlin dropped a palmed ace on us. He cheated! That's how he won the pot."

"Louie, how much did you lose?" Elmer asked, walking to the card game to intercede in the argument before it got out of hand.

"Well, I lost six . . . uh . . . matches." Louie said the word *matches* very quietly as if realizing the foolishness of his complaint.

"Was you cheatin', Merlin?" Elmer asked.

"I was practicin'," Merlin answered.

"You was practicin' cheatin'?"

"Yeah, I was practicin' cheatin'. Elmer, you know damn well them card sharks in the Wild Hog cheat all the time. I figure if I could get good enough at it, why I could turn the tables on 'em, so to speak. I've lost me a lot of money in the Wild Hog. If I can get this cheatin' down, I could get my money back."

"And if you don't get it down, you could get yourself kilt," Elmer said. "Hell, if Louie could catch you at it, how hard is it goin' to be for a professional gambler to see what you're doin'?"

"Yeah, I reckon you're right."

"You might say Louie just saved your life."

"Yeah, I reckon you could say that. Here's your matches, Louie." Merlin slid six matches across the bed toward him.

Louie chuckled. "That's all right. You keep 'em. And you keep on practicin'. I'd like to see someone take them card slicks down a notch or two my ownself."

Shaking his head, Elmer returned to where he had left Dewey, Woodward, and Martin. "You boys be ready tomorrow."

West Texas

The little town of Bibb lay twelve miles northwest of Comanche in northwestern Comanche County. By 1880 the community had a school, a church, two grocery stores, two saloons, a cotton gin, and a flour mill. It was a growing and industrious little town with a population of 360. It also had a mayor and a city council, and they'd hired

Wyatt Mattoon as a city marshal.

Mattoon came well recommended; he had been a deputy sheriff in Tarrant County, one of the most densely populated counties in Texas. In the beginning, Bibb thought they had chosen wisely. Mattoon managed to keep the peace when the customers got a little rowdy in one or the other saloons.

The problem was that Bibb wasn't able to pay very much, and Mattoon decided to augment his salary. Because of his position, he learned that the owner of the cotton gin had negotiated a loan from a bank in Waco. He was asked to meet the stage so as to escort the money safely into town. Instead, he met the stage, and relieved them of the money box, taking not only the thirty-five hundred dollars that had been borrowed by the cotton gin, but another two hundred and seventy dollars from the passengers.

Of course, Mattoon didn't return to Bibb. He headed for Brackettville, where he passed himself off as a cattle broker for buyers from the East, but in all the time he had been there, he had never bought a single cow.

At the moment, he was sitting in a saloon, nursing a beer. He had spent his ill-gotten gains lavishly, and was nearly out of money.

He was going to have to find something else soon.

Sky Meadow Ranch

Dawn broke on the morning the cowboys were to leave. The cattle had never been driven any distance before, and sensing something was about to happen, they milled about nervously, lifting a large cloud of dust that caught the morning sun and gleamed a bright gold.

Even though Elmer, Woodward, Martin, and Dewey were the only cowboys who would actually be making the drive, every cowboy on the ranch was mounted and helping to get the 600 cows herded together for the four-day push south. Finally the cattle gathered four abreast, and, under the urging of the cowboys, began the slow, shuffling walk that would take them to Cheyenne.

Duff slapped his legs against the side of his horse and urged Sky into a gallop, dashing alongside the slowly moving herd until he topped a small hill, then looked back down on the herd. Six hundred cattle were but a small percentage of his herd, but moving out at four abreast as they were, they made an impressive sight, the line stretching over a quarter of a mile long. The cattle

185

moved slowly but inexorably toward the Laramie Mountains.

From his position Duff could see the entire herd. The cowboys who would remain behind had already dropped off and returned to the ranch. Woodward was the flank rider on the left side, near the front, and Martin was riding flank on the right side, with Dewey riding drag, bringing up the rear. Duff had assigned Elmer to stay with Hanson, to "keep an eye on him" and the two men, with no fixed position, rode with the herd, moving from one side to the other, more as observers than participants.

Wang was driving the wagon, which was already a mile ahead of the herd. Duff wasn't riding in any specific position, but kept himself on the move, ready to react to any trouble that might present itself. Sometimes he galloped ahead to check in with Elmer and Hanson, sometimes he rode squarely in front of the herd.

The first day of the drive was uneventful. They stopped for the night, and Wang prepared a meal of fried pork rice with a hot mustard sauce he made himself. In addition, he had egg rolls.

Sitting next to Duff, Woodward said, "I tell you what, boss. I've been on a dozen or more trail drives, and most of the time I ain't never et nothin' more 'n beans 'n bacon 'n maybe some biscuits. This here is sure some good eatin'."

"What do you think, Mr. Wang? The boys like your cooking," Duff said.

Wang might have beamed in pride, but his face, as always, was inscrutable.

"Elmer," Duff said. "Why don't you tell us a sea story?"

"I got so many, I don't know what one to tell."

"Were you ever in a storm at sea, Elmer?" Hanson asked. "I mean one that had you thinking you would be transported to the Pearly Gates at any moment."

Elmer laughed. "Sonny, with the life I've lived, I ain't all that sure that it'll be the Pearly Gates for me. More 'n likely it'll be the fiery pits of Hell. But, I can sure spin you a yarn about a storm. 'Twas six days out of New Caledonia when up come the damndest storm I ever been in. It come up on us so sudden that the moon rakers warn't naught but strips of canvas, flapping from the arms, a-fore we could get 'em took down. We had to get other sails took in, 'n the bosun ordered men aloft, but nobody would go. The sails had to be took in or else we woulda foundered. More 'n likely all of us woulda drownded right then.

"Finally, me 'n two other men said we would climb the rigging, so up we went. Well, sir, I'm a-tellin' you, that ship was rollin' from side to side so much that I was hangin' out over the sea 'bout as much as I was over the deck."

Elmer stopped talking and took a swallow of his coffee, then bit into a sweet roll. "This is the best eatin' I ever done outdoors."

"Yes, well never mind all that. Just finish the story, will you, please," Dewey asked. He, Woodward, and Martin had been riveted to the tale.

"What do you mean finish the story? Seems to me like I purt nigh did finish it."

"No, you ain't finished it atall. Last you said was that you was hangin' on for dear life, sometimes over the deck 'n sometimes over the sea. So what happened?"

"Yeah," Woodward asked. "What happened?"

"Oh. Well, once we got the sails reefed, we just tightened up the hawsers that was holdin' the ship tied to the dock, 'n rode the storm out just as pretty as you please."

"Tied to the dock?" Martin said. "What dock?"

"Oh. Well, that would be the dock at Port Moresby."

"Port? You said you was in the middle of the ocean!"

"What are you talkin' about? I never said we was in the middle of the ocean."

"You damn sure did. You said you was six days from New Caledonia."

"That's right, we was. It took us six days to get from New Caledonia to Port Moresby."

Duff, and Hanson laughed out loud, but Dewey, Woodward, and Martin didn't appreciate it as much.

"Damn, Elmer, you're as full of it as a Christmas goose," Dewey said.

Duff put an end to the storytelling. "Elmer, it's time to get the night riders out."

"All right, I'll take it from now until ten. Dewey, you got it from ten till twelve, Martin, from twelve till two, and Woodward, from two till four. I'll relieve you at four."

"There's no need for you to do a double shift," Hanson said. "I would be glad to take the four o'clock watch."

Elmer glanced toward Duff.

"Why not?" Duff said with a smile. "They're his cows, after all. Who would have a greater interest in watchin' over the herd?"

"All right," Elmer said. "Mr. Hanson, I'll wake you at eight bells."

"Bells?" Woodward questioned. "What do

189

you mean, bells? Don't you go ringin' no bells in the middle of the night."

"There'll be no bells rung, you landlubber, you," Elmer said. "This is talk that only me 'n Mr. Hanson 'n Duff can understand."

"As long as there ain't no bells rung to wake me up."

"Don't you worry none 'bout gettin' woke up," Martin said to Woodward. "When it comes time for you to relieve me, if you don't wake up, I'll get you woke up with a bucket of water from the cook wagon."

"You no get water from my wagon," Wang said.

"Yeah, I will, too."

Wang picked up a knife. "How you carry water, if you no have hand?"

Woodward laughed. "Ha! The Chinaman got your butt, didn't he?"

"Yeah? Well, you just wake up when I come for you."

CHAPTER SEVENTEEN

Some nine hundred miles south of where Duff and company had spent the night, Val Cyr dismounted to relieve himself. He had seen a lot in his fifty-three years. He had ridden the outlaw trail even before the war, and when the war started he joined up with Bill Anderson where he continued doing what he had been doing all along — robbing, burning, and killing. But then robbing, burning, and killing became, according to Anderson, a patriotic duty.

Cyr remembered 1864 as a summer of violence, when the men riding with Anderson went on a campaign that killed hundreds.

Cyr was the bloodiest of all the raiders, surpassing even Bloody Bill Anderson in his killing. Then, on September 27, Anderson's gang captured a passenger train, the first time Confederate guerrillas had done so. Moving through the train, they robbed all the men onboard, taking almost ten thousand dollars. Twenty-four Union soldiers were among them, and they were taken off the train and shot. The civilian passengers were allowed to leave, but they had to do so on foot, because the train was set on fire.

With the train burning behind him, Anderson set out to pillage the town of Centralia, Missouri. When more than one hundred Union soldiers pursued them, the guerrillas were made aware that they were being trailed, and they turned from the pursued to the pursuers.

The Union soldiers had thought they were chasing no more than twenty or thirty men, but the number was much greater. They were surprised and ambushed.

"Bugler, blow retr—" That was as far as the captain got before he was cut down. Val Cyr personally shot the bugler when he lifted the instrument to his lips.

For the next several minutes, pistols, rifles, and carbines roared as gun smoke roiled up over the town in an acrid smelling, blue-gray cloud. Soon the saddle of every Union mount was empty, their riders either dead or dying on the ground. After the storm of battle was over, Cyr walked through the street shooting those who were wounded, and even the few who attempted to surrender.

"Ease up a bit there, Cyr," Anderson called out to him. "There ain't none of them boys goin' to be able to do us any harm."

"They're Yankees, ain't they?" Cyr asked.

"They're Yankees, all right."

"Then there ain't no need in leavin' any of 'em alive." Cyr saw one wounded soldier lying with his head on a young woman's lap. "Get away from 'im," he ordered.

The woman shook her head no. "This is my husband and I will not leave him."

"Have it your way," Cyr said. "But if you get a bullet in your leg when I shoot this damn Yankee, don't blame me." He pulled the hammer back on his pistol and aimed it at the head of the wounded soldier, but before he could pull the trigger, he heard the click of the hammer being pulled back on another pistol. Looking toward the sound, he saw Elmer Gleason pointing a Navy Colt at him.

Elmer shook his head no. "There ain't no need in killin' that feller, or any of the other ones that's already been shot. There can't none of 'em hurt us now."

"Like I told Anderson, he's a Yankee, and I'm goin' to kill him."

"If you kill him, I'll kill you," Elmer said calmly.

"What the hell's got into you, Elmer?" Cyr demanded. "Me 'n you is cousins. And now you're tellin' me you're goin' to kill me?"

"Yeah, I'm tellin' you that if you kill that man, I'm goin' to kill you," Gleason said. "Ambushin' these fellers while they was all armed, and comin' after us was one thing. But killin' 'em while they're lyin' there wounded 'n half dead, ain't right. I don't intend to do it 'n I don't intend to let you do it. Leastwise, not with any more of 'em."

"You're growin' soft, Elmer," Cyr said with a sneer. "You might want to think about gettin' into another line o' work." With that, he lowered the hammer on his pistol, then turned and walked away.

One month later, on October 26, 1864, the Yankees located Bloody Bill Anderson just outside Glasgow, Missouri. Though greatly outnumbered, Anderson and his men charged the Union forces, killing five or six of them, before encountering heavy fire. Only Anderson and Elmer Gleason continued the attack, Elmer riding side by side with his leader. The others retreated.

Anderson was hit by a bullet behind his ear and killed instantly. Not until then did Elmer turn and join the others in retreat. Four other guerrillas were also killed in the attack, but the rest of the men were able to escape.

After that battle, Cyr went out on his own, not to find another venue to fight the war, but to continue to rob and kill, though he was doing it for himself. By the time the war ended, he was too well-known to remain in Missouri, so he drifted into Kansas.

He knew all the saloons and gambling dens in all the wild towns such as Hays City, Dodge City, and Abilene. He spent his ill-gotten gains on the half-nude girls with pretty faces and heavily shadowed eyes who plied their avocation in such places, and lost money to the pale-skinned and thin-lipped gamblers with their broadcloth frock coats and wide-brimmed flat-crowned hats.

Cyr shook off twenty years of memories and buttoned up his trousers, remounted, and continued to ride through the deep, narrow, steep-walled canyons and flat mesas of the surrounding countryside. He was out of money, he was hungry, and he was thirsty for some whiskey. Then he saw something just ahead that would take care of that problem for him.

The small, ripsawed timber building had only one word on the sign out front. STORE. It was surviving in the middle of nowhere, precisely because it *was* in the middle of nowhere. The nearest town was twenty miles south, and across the line into Verde County.

Cyr dismounted in front of the store, blew his nose onto the ground, and pulled his pistol. Holding his gun down by his side close to his leg, he stepped in through the door. A small bell tinkled, announcing his presence.

The inside of the store was in deep shadows. Dust motes floated in the few bars of light that managed to make it through the dirty windows.

"I'll be right with you," a disembodied voice called from somewhere in the little building. "I've just been takin' me an inventory of what I'm a-goin' to be needin' to order when the wagon comes through next." A small, bald-headed man wearing a white apron and wire-rim glasses came out of the back room, rubbing his hands together. "Now, what can I do for you?"

Without so much as a word, Cyr raised his pistol and shot the man in the forehead. "You can die for me."

Stepping around behind the bar, he pulled out the cash drawer and smiled. "You was doin' all right for yourself, wasn't you? There must be over a hunnert dollars here." He gathered up all the money and stuffed it into his pocket. Then, taking three bottles of whiskey, a few cans of beans, and a couple cans of peaches, he left the store.

Chugwater

From the *Chugwater Defender:*

CATTLE ON THE MOVE

Though railroads have nearly put an end to the trail drives of old, it is still necessary for ranchers some distance removed from the nearest railhead to continue with the practice. That is the case with the cattle recently purchased by Mr. Cal Hanson, an Englishman who has come to America to go into the cattle business.

As reported in an article previous, Mr. Hanson chose to come to our own Laramie County where he has made the purchase of six hundred head of Black Angus cattle from local rancher Duff MacCallister. Mr. MacCallister is credited with introducing Black Angus into Wyoming, and indeed, is one of the earliest western proponents of the breed.

One can readily see the advantage of Black Angus cattle when it is realized that but one cow of this superior breed will bring, at the market, two times as much money as a Hereford, and four times as much as a longhorn. The current price of a Black Angus cow at the Kansas City Market is sixty dollars a head.

There were two saloons in Chugwater. One, of course, was Fiddlers' Green, owned and operated by Duff's friend Biff Johnson. The other was the Wild Hog. It made no pretensions toward gentility, nor even sanitation.

The Wild Hog existed for the sole purpose of providing inexpensive drinks to a clientele who didn't care if the wide plank floor was unpainted and stained with spilled liquor and expectorated tobacco juice. The saloon did offer food from a menu that was prepared in its own kitchen, primarily biscuits, bacon, eggs, beans, and fried potatoes. In addition to the plate lunches, a couple jars were always sitting on the bar, the vinegar in the jar discolored by unclean hands dipping into it to extract its contents, mostly boiled eggs and pickled pigs' feet.

One other major thing set it apart from Fiddlers' Green, and that distinction ensured a brisk business for the Wild Hog. The difference was in the women who were employed by the two saloons. Whereas the girls who worked the bar at Fiddlers' Green provided pleasant conversation and flirtatious company only, the women who worked at the Wild Hog were soiled doves, who, for a price, would extend their hospitality to the brothel maintained on the second floor of the saloon. Nippy Jones, who owned the Wild Hog, made it very clear to the girls he hired that they would be expected to offer that service.

Two of the Wild Hog customers, Vic Forney and Henry Crump, were nursing a beer at a table in the back of the saloon. Unable to afford any of the girls, though the opportunity to enjoy the services of the soiled doves had been presented to them, they had eaten a lunch, of sorts, from the free boiled eggs and pickled pigs' feet in the jars on the bar.

Crump had also picked up from the bar a free copy of the *Chugwater Defender* and was reading a story with great interest.

"Hey, Forney, you know what Black Angus cows is bringin' in in Kansas City?" Crump asked, tapping the newspaper with his finger. "They're bringin' sixty dollars a head."

"Well now, ain't that just real interestin'?" Forney replied. "But tell me, Crump, what the hell does that have to do with us?" He punctuated his question by taking a bite from the pig's foot he was eating.

"I tell you what it has to do with us. Money, that's what it means."

"You ain't talkin' about rustlin' them cows, are you? 'Cause oncet you rustle cows, the next thing you got to do is drive 'em somewhere. Then you got to sell 'em. You damn sure ain't goin' to be gettin' no sixty dollars a head for 'em when you sell 'em."

"You're right. That's how come we ain't goin' to be stealin' no cows."

Forney looked up from the pig's foot. "Then where at is the money comin' from?"

"The Englishman that bought the cows is the same one that put thirty thousand dollars in the bank here. Now you know damn well he didn't pay no thirty thousand dollars for the cattle, 'n that means he still has it on him. That's where we're goin' to get the money. We're goin' to take it from him."

"Where?"

"We'll find a place."

On the trail

The herd was three days out, and had stopped on the banks of Lodge Pole Creek. Water and good grass ensured that they would have no problem keeping the cattle together on what would be their last night out. Elmer had given Wang a night off, and cooked a breaded fried steak with biscuits and gravy for supper. Even Hanson had gotten in on it, making a bread pudding.

"Whoa, this is good," Martin said. "I ain't

200

never tasted nothin' like this before. Who woulda thought you could make old bread taste this good?"

"I do believe that this will be our last night on the trail. That is correct, is it not?" Hanson asked.

"Aye, 'tis correct. We'll be to Cheyenne by noon tomorrow, but the cattle train isn't scheduled to be there until day after tomorrow, so we'll put the cattle in holding pens and spend tomorrow night in Cheyenne. When we get there, I shall send a telegram to Jason Bowles, and I've nae doubt but that he'll meet you with some men to help get the cattle out to your ranch. Elmer, Wang, and I will be along as soon as we can get another train lined up."

"You're going on, are you, Wang?" Hanson asked.

"I wish to see Texas."

"Well, if you like Texas, and you want to stay there, I'd be happy to give you a job."

"I belong to Mr. MacCallister," Wang said.

"I understand, my friend. I truly understand."

"Who has first watch tonight?" Martin asked as he cleaned his mess kit and put it back into his saddlebag.

"I think you do," Dewey said. "I follow you."

"Good. Don't be late."

"Don't worry, I'll be there."

"If you ain't out there to relieve me on time, I'm just liable to dump a whole bucket of water on you," Martin said. "And it won't cost me my hand to do it, 'cause I won't have to get it from Wang's wagon this time. I can get it right out of the creek." He chuckled as he mounted his horse and rode out to keep watch on the herd.

"Hey, Martin," Dewey called. "How 'bout you sing to them cows a bit, get 'em all calmed down for me."

"Whoa, what are you talkin' about Dewey?" Woodward asked. "You ever heard that boy sing? He sounds like a coyote with his foot caught in a beaver trap."

The others laughed.

CHAPTER EIGHTEEN

After breakfast the next morning, they got the cattle moving for the last ten miles, and by noon they were in Cheyenne, on schedule, loading the cattle into the holding pens.

Woodward, Martin, and Dewey, after getting a bonus payment from Duff, started back home.

Cheyenne

Wang and Elmer stayed in town with Duff. They were going on to Texas to deliver half of the herd. The first train wasn't scheduled to arrive until the next day.

"Well, it would seem that we need accommodations for the night," Hanson said. "Have you a suggestion?"

"You can't beat the InterOcean Hotel," Duff said. "What do you say we go check in at the hotel, get cleaned up, then have us a good meal at the Cheyenne Club?"

"An excellent idea, even for a Scotsman," Hanson said with a little laugh. He looked around. "What happened to Elmer and Wang?"

"Cheyenne has a Little Chinatown. I expect they went there."

Two men were standing in front of the gate as Duff and Hanson started to leave the pen.

"Excuse us, gentlemen, we are going to have to open the gate," Duff said.

"Yeah, don't let us get in the way," one of the two men replied.

Henry Crump and Vic Forney had overheard all the discussion between Duff and Hanson.

"Well now, ain't that interestin'?" Crump said. "They're checkin' in to the InterOcean Hotel."

"What's so interestin' about that?" Forney asked. "There cain't neither one of us afford to stay there."

"We don't have to *stay* there. All we have to do is pay a little visit there."

"What for?"

"For money, that's what for. We're going to take it from the Englishman."

"How do you know he has any money?" Forney asked.

"I told you before. It was in the paper that

he put thirty thousand dollars in the bank back in Chugwater. He only bought six hundred head of cattle, so he didn't spend all that money, 'n you know damn well he didn't leave any of it back in Chugwater. That means he's got it on 'im. All we have to do is take it away from 'im."

"All we have to do," Forney said.

"Yeah. He's one o' them highfalutin' foreign dandies. Now you tell me, just how hard can it be? If he sees a gun, he'll more 'n likely pee in his pants."

"Yeah." Forney smiled. "I'll bet he ain't never even see a gun before."

In another part of town, Elmer and Wang were standing in front of a single-story, flat-roofed building. It was red, with gold trim, and the sign in front was in English and Chinese. AN LEE'S 李安

Wang was greeted in Chinese. *"Wei zhong guo ren. Gāi rén jiù shì Gweilo?"*

"The white man is my friend," Wang said in Chinese. "Do not call him a foreign devil, for in this country, *we* are the foreigners."

"Wèi biǎo shì wèn hòu," Elmer said, greeting the man who had greeted them.

"You speak our language?" the man asked in English, surprised at hearing Chinese spoken by this white man.

"A little."

"I am Han Sing," the man said with a slight bow. "You are welcome in this place."

"I am Wang Chow," Wang said, switching to English. "We would eat now."

Han Sing escorted them to a table. "We have cabbage and beef." He again spoke in English.

"That is good."

The meal was delivered, chopsticks provided for each of them. Elmer was able to use his quite adroitly.

Halfway through their meal three American men came in.

"An Lee!" they shouted. "An Lee, you slanty-eyed fishwife! Get yourself out here."

An older woman came from the kitchen. "Why are you here? Why do you disturb my guests?" the woman asked.

Besides Elmer and Wang Chow, eight others were eating in the restaurant. Three were Americans.

"You want to see your guests disturbed?" One of the men pulled his pistol and pointed it at a young Chinese woman who was sitting alone at one of the tables. "If you don't give me the money right now, I'm going to blow her head off. Is that disturbing enough for you?"

"What money is he speaking of?" Wang

asked in Chinese.

"Every week he comes into this place and demands that I give him money so that he will not do damage to my restaurant," An Lee answered in Chinese.

"You two quit babbling in that heathen tongue," the spokesman of the three said. "You got something to say, you say it in English."

"What is it, Wang?" Elmer asked as he stood up.

They walked over toward the three men who were causing the trouble. Elmer noticed that only one of the three had actually drawn his pistol.

"The three *Gweilos* are taking money from An Lee. If she does not pay them, they will do damage to her place." As he was speaking, Wang drew his knife and palmed it against his leg.

"Well now, ain't that somethin'." Elmer said. "You three polecats get on out of here and leave these nice people alone."

"I don't know who you are, mister, but this here ain't none of your business," the extortionist said.

"I just made it my business."

"Did you? Well, that was a mistake." The man smiled and turned his pistol toward Elmer. " 'Cause I intend to kill you and the

Chinaman."

"Now, Wang," Elmer said.

Wang whipped his hand up like the strike of a snake, and the knife crossed the distance between them before the extortionist could pull the trigger. The knife buried itself hilt deep into the man's chest, penetrating his heart. He fell, dead, before he hit the floor.

"What the hell!" shouted one of the other two men. He started to go for his gun, but stopped when he heard Elmer cock the pistol in his hand.

"You two boys want to shuck out of them holsters?" Elmer asked. "Wang, is there one o' them telephones in this place?"

Wang asked the question of An Lee in Chinese then shook his head "No."

"Well, tell 'em to drag that fella out to the alley so's he don't interfere with these folks that's eatin'. Me 'n you will take these other two polecats down to the jail."

Wang translated Elmer's words, and Han Sing answered him. Wang nodded. "Han Sing say that we did not finish our meal."

"Well, tell 'im we'll come back for it."

Half an hour later, Elmer and Wang had turned the two gunmen over to the sheriff and learned that the gunmen and Hobbs

Ketchum — the one Wang had killed — were wanted outlaws. They were in for a three-hundred-dollar reward.

"Sheriff, we ain't from here," Elmer said. "There ain't goin' to be no trial or nothin' 'bout this feller we kilt, is there? I mean they was a lot of witnesses that seen it, 'n they'll all tell you exactly what happened."

"Were all the witnesses Chinamen? I mean, I don't have anythin' against Celestials, you understand, but seems like the court pays more attention to white men."

"They was two white men and one white woman there," Elmer said.

The sheriff smiled. "If they verify your story, there won't be any need for a hearing. If you're still here tomorrow, come on back and I'll have the reward money for you."

He walked back to An Lee's Restaurant with Elmer and Wang, where all the Chinese and the three Americans gave eyewitness testimony that validated Elmer's story. Satisfied, he returned to his office.

Elmer turned to Wang. "Well, what do you say we finish our meal?"

They started toward their original table, but Han Sing waved his hand and shook his head. "You no go to that table. You come to this table." He escorted them to a table in the back corner of the room where red and yellow silk hung from the wall. The entire table was covered with food and wine, and it was being served, not on plain white plates, but decorative blue and white china. The table was being served by two young and exquisitely beautiful Chinese women.

One of them smiled at Elmer, put her hand on his cheek, and spoke to him in Chinese.

"Wang, I only know a little of your lingo," Elmer said. "I don't have any idee what she just said."

"She wanted to know if you are too old." Wang smiled, shocking Elmer, who had never seen him do that before.

Elmer frowned. "Too old for what?"

"Too old," Wang repeated inscrutably.

But it wasn't all that inscrutable. Elmer knew exactly what he was talking about. "No," he replied with a broad grin. "I ain't too old at all."

Wang nodded. "Let us enjoy our evening."

"Oh, I think I will."

CHAPTER NINETEEN

The bathing rooms of the InterOcean Hotel were at the end of the hallway. Well equipped, they had a tank in which the water could be heated by a kerosene flame. A pipe ran directly from the tank to the large, claw-foot tub, where it was controlled by a faucet handle. Another pipe allowed cold water into the tub to ameliorate the hot water.

Duff took his bath first, then rapped on the door to Hanson's room as he passed by. The Englishman opened the door.

"I'm out," Duff said. "Let me know when you're ready, and we'll go to the Cheyenne Club to eat."

Half an hour later, Hanson was out of the tub, dressed, and tying his shoes when he heard someone at the door. "I'll be out of here in just a moment, Duff."

The door opened and two men came in.

Both were carrying guns.

"You aren't Duff." Despite the fact that they were carrying guns, there was no hint of fear in Hanson's voice.

By coincidence, Duff had come out of his room at the precise moment the two men had gone into the bathing room. He pulled his pistol and moved quickly down the hallway. Through the door, he could hear the conversation taking place inside.

"You got the money on you?" one of the men asked roughly.

"What money would that be?"

"Don't play dumb with us, mister. We know that you put thirty thousand dollars in the bank in Chugwater, and you didn't spend all of it on them cows you put in the holding pen today."

"My word. You are the men we saw standing at the gate, aren't you?"

"Yeah, we was there. Now, where is the money?"

"You didn't expect me to bring the money into the bathing room, did you? It is in my room."

The man waved his gun. "Then let's go get it."

"Why should I?"

"What do you mean, why should you?

'Cause we'll kill you if you don't, that's why."

"Let me tell you how I view this situation, gentlemen. And, I must say, that I am using the term *gentlemen* in its widest application, for you two are certainly not gentlemen in any sense of the word. If I don't give you the money, you will kill me. But, if I do give you the money, you will kill me anyway. I would rather you kill me and not get the money, than kill me and get the money."

"What'll we do now, Crump?" Forney asked.

"Forney, you are damn dumb. What did you use my name for?"

"Oh, now you have put yourselves in quite a conundrum, haven't you?" Hanson said. "I know your names, which I will, of course, supply to the constabulary."

"What the hell is he talkin' about? Why don't he talk English?" Forney asked in frustration.

"Let me think, let me think!" Crump said.

"Yes, Mr. Forney. Let him think. You must know how difficult that is for him."

"Shut up! Just shut up!" Crump shouted.

Hanson kept talking. "May I offer a suggestion? Suppose I give each of you fifty dollars apiece. We can say it is for providing me with an exciting, Wild West experience.

There would be no need for me to inform the constabulary and no one will be hurt."

"Why the hell should we settle for fifty, when we can have all of it?" Crump asked.

At that moment, Duff jerked the door open. "Because you won't get any of it and you might find the alternative quite unsatisfactory."

Gasping, the two men whirled around to see a pistol pointed at them.

"Indeed you might," Hanson said, and hearing the hammer being drawn back on a pistol behind them, Crump and Forney turned to see that he, too, was holding a gun.

"Where did you get that gun?" Crump asked.

"Oh, do you like it? It is a Webley and Scott forty-five-caliber pistol that I picked up in the Gun Quarter in Birmingham, England. Duff, I believe you are familiar with that district."

"I am indeed," Duff replied, smiling broadly.

"Are you two men crazy? Or, are all foreigners like that?" Forney asked in frustration.

"I'm quite sane," Duff said. "But Mr. Hanson is an Englishman. And Englishmen are quite mad. All of them."

Hanson grinned slyly. "He's quite right, you know. Englishmen are mad."

"Cal, what I think they want to know is, where did you get the gun at this moment?"

"Oh, yes, of course, they would be curious about that, wouldn't they? It was right here under this towel." Hanson patted the towel he'd used after his bath. "Along with my money belt."

"Uh, that offer for fifty dollars apiece. Does it still stand?" Crump asked.

"Surely you jest," Hanson said.

"What is it I do?"

Hanson looked at the two men and sighed. "I will renew the offer, but with a codicil."

Forney looked at his partner in confusion and Crump asked, "With a what?"

"A condition," Hanson explained. "I will give each of you fifty dollars on the condition that you empty your guns and leave this hotel."

"And you ain't goin' to tell the sheriff nothin'?"

"I'll say nothing about our arrangement."

"All right. Yeah, we'll do it," Crump said.

Hanson gave each of them a fifty-dollar bill. "We plan to take our dinner at the . . . what was the name of that establishment, Duff?"

"The Cheyenne Club," Duff said.

"Yes, the Cheyenne Club. I would suggest you not go there to spend your money."

"Don't worry. There ain't no way we're goin' to go to a fancy place like that," Crump said.

Duff had one more condition. "Oh, Mr. Crump and Mr. Forney —"

"How did you know our names?" Crump interrupted.

"I heard you through the door. You called each other by name."

"That's right, Crump. We did," Forney said.

"Crump and Forney, disabuse yourselves of any idea that you might try this again. Next time, we will shoot you dead."

Crump looked at Hansen.

"You had better listen to him. He is a Scotsman, and they have been known to kill just for the pleasure of it."

"Don't worry, we ain't goin' to try this again," Crump said. "Come on, Forney. Let's go get drunk."

The two men took their money, then moved quickly through the hallway to the stairs. Their feet drummed loudly on the stairs as they hurried down.

Duff and Hanson looked at each other, then laughed.

216

Jaco had taken over a table in the Red Dog Saloon, and word went out that he was putting together a gang of men for what promised to be a very profitable operation for all concerned. Putt and Dingo were his top recruiters, and they had spread out over all of West Texas and East New Mexico to find men who were suitable for the operation.

Almost every day someone new would come into the saloon, then stand at the bar looking around nervously, trying to determine who it was that they were supposed to meet. It wasn't hard for Jaco to pick such a person out. He knew they were there to see him, but part of his testing was to see if they had enough confidence to come to him first.

As he sat at his table, someone came into the saloon who didn't have to be told who Jaco was. He knew Jaco, and Jaco knew him. He was Lou Miller, the trusty who had helped Jaco escape.

Miller quickly saw Jaco and he marched toward him. The expression on his face was one of anger. "You didn't meet me in Seven Rivers."

"I couldn't meet you there. I had to get out of New Mexico as fast as I could. I figured we'd meet up later, if not in Seven Rivers, then some'ers else." Jaco smiled. "And here we are, meetin' just like we planned."

"No, this here ain't at all the way we planned. The plan we had was that we would meet in Seven Rivers, 'n you would give me a thousand dollars. This ain't Seven Rivers, but if you give me the thousand dollars, I can forget that you wasn't there."

"I ain't got a thousand dollars," Jaco said.

"Get if from your stash."

"I ain't got no stash, neither."

"Then you lied to me, didn't you?"

"Would you have helped me escape if I hadn't told you that?"

"Hell no, I wouldn't have."

"Well, then, that's why I lied. But don't worry, I can make it up to you. I'm puttin' together a gang. You can join the gang, if you want to. Do that, 'n you'll have yourself a thousand dollars sooner 'n you think."

Miller smiled. "Oh, I'll have more 'n that, soon enough. You see, they's a twenty-five-hunnert-dollar reward for you 'n another twenty-five hunnert for Blue Putt. I done tole' the Shumla marshal about it. He didn't even know there was a reward out for you 'n Putt. But he knows now. He 'n his deputy is waitin' right outside. Soon as I give 'em the word, they're goin' come in here, arrest you, then inform the sheriff back in New Mexico that you two has been caught. That's when I'll get my money."

"You go ahead 'n tell 'em I'm here," Jaco said. "He ain't goin' to do nothin' to me."

"We'll see about that," Miller said.

Jaco waited until Miller turned to go back outside. As soon as his former fellow inmate presented his back, Jaco pulled his gun and shot him.

"Here! What's goin' on in here?" the city marshal shouted as he and his deputy dashed into the saloon with their guns drawn.

Jaco was waiting for them. He shot them down, killing both.

Two other men and four women, including Sherazade, were in the saloon.

"My, oh, my," she said. "You have had a busy day, haven't you?"

Jaco walked over to the two bodies, then reached down and removed their badges. He took the badges down to the two men standing at the other end of the bar. "Tell me, Puke, how would you like to be the new city marshal?"

The man's actual name was Poke Cage, though he had long ago picked up the sobriquet *Puke*.

"Yeah," Puke said. "I'd like that."

"You can be the deputy," Jaco said to the other man. "You two will answer to me."

"What about the mayor?" Puke asked.

"We don't have a mayor."

"Sure we do, it's —"

Jaco held up his hand to stop Puke in mid-sentence. "Wait here. I'll be back."

Ned Urban, the mayor of Shumla, was sitting at a workbench in his hat shop, blocking a hat. He was the only one in the store when Jaco stepped in.

"What can I do for you?" Urban asked, looking up with the practiced smile by which he greeted all his customers. When he saw that Jaco was pointing a pistol at him, the smile left his face. "What is this? A robbery? You must know that I don't keep very much money in my shop."

Jaco made no reply to the mayor's inquiry. He simply pulled the trigger, and the mayor died with a shocked expression on his face.

Jaco left the mayor's body lying on the floor, then walked back to the Red Dog Saloon. "It's like I said, Puke. We ain't got no mayor. You'll answer to me."

"Yes, sir!" Puke replied proudly.

"The first thing I want you to do is take care of the mayor's body, then round up every member of the town council and put them in jail."

"What are we puttin' 'em in jail for?" Puke asked.

"Someone killed the mayor," Jaco replied. "It's likely one of them done it, thinkin' maybe with the mayor dead, they could become the new mayor."

"Yeah," Puke said with a smile. "Yeah, more 'n likely it was one of them that kilt the mayor. And the sheriff 'n his deputy."

"No, the sheriff 'n his deputy, and Lou Miller, killed each other. We all seen it happen."

"That's right," Puke said. He glanced over to Owen Hayes, his deputy. "That's just how it happened, ain't it?"

"That's the way I seen it," Hayes said.

"Once you get the city council all rounded up and put in jail, then I want you to go to every business in town 'n tell 'em we're havin' a town meetin' here in the saloon at four o'clock this afternoon."

"How we goin' to do that?" Puke asked.

"It's simple. You tell them they will either attend the meeting or you will shoot them."

"No, I don't mean that. I mean that near 'bout ever'one that's on the city council also owns some kind of business in town."

Jaco stroked his chin for a moment, then nodded. "All right. I've changed my mind.

You don't have to put them in jail. Come to think of it, it wasn't none of them that killed the mayor, it was Lou Miller. Just bring 'em to the meetin', 'n I'll set everyone straight."

CHAPTER TWENTY

There were only twelve business establishments in town, and that included the mortuary and the feed and seed store. By four o'clock, everyone in town had heard of what happened to the town marshal, his deputy, and the mayor. All showed up for the meeting, including every member of the city council.

"The preacher ain't here," Puke said. "I tried to get him to come, too, only he said he wasn't goin' to go into no saloon, whether it was for business or not."

"That's all right," Jaco said easily. "I'm sure word will get back to him about what we're goin' to do here."

"What are we goin' to do, Jaco?" asked Rafferty, the owner of the grocery store.

"We're goin' to change this town. And the first thing I'm goin' to do as the new mayor is ask all of you that's on the city council to resign."

"What do you mean, as the new mayor? What happened to Ned Urban? I haven't heard anything about him resigning." The councilman was incensed.

"I'm sorry to say that Urban is dead. He was shot and killed by Lou Miller. When the city marshal found out about it, he and the deputy came to arrest Miller . . . right here in the saloon. Miller resisted arrest, and they had a shoot-out. They wound up killin' each other."

"Yeah? Well, that may be so, but how does that make you mayor? By rights, we as the city council would appoint a temporary mayor until a new mayor can be elected."

"All right. Go ahead and appoint me. That can be your last official act before all you resign. As mayor, I won't be needin' any council."

"Look here, I don't know what this is about, but I ain't goin' to vote to appoint you, and I ain't goin' to resign."

"Putt?" Jaco said.

Putt shot the protesting councilmen.

"As I said, gentlemen, your last official act, before you resign, will be to appoint me. Now, all who agree that I should be the new mayor, raise your hands."

The councilmen looked at each other nervously, then, with shaking hands, they raised them in a unanimous vote.

"Good," Jaco said. "Now, as your new mayor, I accept your resignations. As participating businessmen in this town, I'm sure you will all be interested in what I have to say.

"We're goin' to make it a place where the only law is our own law, 'n any outside law ain't welcome. It's goin' to be a place where someone with a price on their head can feel welcome."

"My word!" one of the businessmen said. "Are you talking about turning Shumla into an outlaw town? That is what you're talking about, isn't it?"

Jaco shrugged. "I suppose I am."

"Absolutely not! I'll have no part of this!"

"I'm sorry to hear that," Jaco said, and to the shock of everyone present, he pulled his gun and shot the businessman who had spoken out.

Two former members of the city council lay dead on the floor.

"Here's the thing about an outlaw town," Jaco said, continuing his talk as if nothing had happened. "The outlaws that do come here is goin' to need food, and liquor, and tobacco, and clothes, just like everyone else. The only difference is . . . they don't have no place else they can go to get such things, except right here."

"How's that any different from now?" Morris, the owner of the saloon asked. "Most of the folks that come into my saloon is from here. They ain't goin' to someplace like Van Horn to buy a beer."

"What do you think a beer costs in Van Horn?" Jaco asked him.

"Why, it costs a nickel, same as it does anyplace else," Morris said.

"You're right. It does cost a nickel in Van Horn. But that ain't the same it costs anyplace else. 'Cause here in Shumla, if anybody buys a beer from you, it's goin' to cost 'em a quarter."

"Look here, I like a beer ever' now 'n then, my ownself," said Silas Dunn, the owner of the meat market. "Are you tellin' me I'm goin' to have to pay five times as much for a beer as I do now?"

"Why not?" Jaco replied. "You'll be chargin' five times as much for your pork and beef, so you'll have more money. Ever'one will be chargin' five times as much."

"What about me 'n my girls?" Sherazade asked. "Right now, it don't cost but a dollar for a visit."

"Same thing," Jaco promised. "Anybody wants to visit one of your girls, it's goin' to cost 'em five dollars."

Sherazade smiled.

"We may have a problem you haven't considered," Rafferty dared to say.

"What problem is that?"

"If you turn this into an outlaw town, where are we going to get the goods to sell? I can tell you right now, there won't be any freight companies who are willing to come into a lawless town."

"You don't worry none about that," Jaco said. "You'll get your groceries all right. You'll have to pay more for them, but you'll get them."

"You keep sayin' ever'thing is goin' to cost a lot more," Morris said. "But what I want to I know is, where's all this money goin' to come from? We can't just all start chargin' more unless there's more money to begin with."

"Oh, there will be more money," Jaco said. "There will be a lot more money. You see, I have plans for the outfit I'm putting together. We'll find places to get more money, and, we're going to need someplace safe to come back to. Shumla will be that safe place, which means this is where we'll be spendin' the money."

"Yeah!" Morris said with a big smile on his face. "Yeah, I like that."

"In fact," Jaco said with a smile, "you'll all be making so much money that you won't even miss the twenty-percent taxes you'll have to pay."

"Twenty-percent taxes? What twenty-percent taxes?" Dunn asked.

"When you have people livin' here like the ones we're goin' to have livin' here, it's goin' to take a special kind of law to keep order in the town. And that law is goin' to be expensive."

"Are you talkin' about Puke Cage?" Morris asked.

"Puke will be wearin' the badge . . . but I'll be the law," Jaco said pointedly.

Eagle Pass, Texas

Sheriff Jason Bowles was at the train depot when Cal Hanson arrived with the three hundred head of cattle he had brought with him.

"So, you've arrived safely, I see," Jason said. "I got Duff's wire, and I've made arrangements for you to keep them in the holding pens until Duff arrives with the rest of your cattle. I've also hired some cowboys to drive your cattle out to your ranch when you're ready."

"That is very decent of you, Sheriff. Do you know if any of the men would be will-

228

ing to stay on with me? I shall require a number of men to help me operate the ranch."

"I'm sure you'll be able to find enough good men from this group. In the meantime, you are to be our guest tonight. Melissa insisted on it."

"That is most gracious of you," Hanson said.

As sheriff of Maverick County, Jason and his family lived in a house supplied by the county. It wasn't very large, but it was a nice house, and it was immaculately kept by Melissa.

Hanson was greeted by Megan when he arrived at the house.

"Miss Parker, how nice to see you again."

"I take it you had no trouble driving the cattle to Cheyenne," Megan said as Hanson stepped inside.

"None at all, and I must say, it was all very exciting. I hope I learned something from Duff and the others."

"They are good teachers and you are an intelligent man, so I'm sure you did."

"My, something smells very good," Hanson said.

"You have my sister to thank for that."

Melissa shared a trait with her sister, in that she was very talented. But while

Megan's talent was in designing and sewing dresses, Melissa's talent was in cooking. She was much more than just a "good" cook. She was a gourmet cook.

Dinner that evening started with a soup of chicken giblet consommé with egg. That was followed by leg of lamb with mushrooms and black olives, roasted potatoes, asparagus, and dinner rolls. Dessert was a peach pie.

"Oh, my," Hanson said, touching a napkin to his lips after the meal was concluded. "I haven't dined this elegantly since the officers' mess of the Royal Horse in Calcutta. I much appreciate the invitation."

"Ha, believe me, Mr. Hanson, Melissa appreciates you coming as much as you appreciate being here," Jason said. "She is always ready to show off her skills."

"As indeed she should be. And, if we are to be neighbors, shouldn't you call me by my Christian name? It is Cal."

"Very well. Cal it shall be," Jason replied. "Who is coming with Duff?"

"Elmer and the Chinaman will be traveling with Duff."

"Wang is coming with him?" Jason asked.

"Apparently Wang requested to go along so that he might see Texas."

Jason smiled. "I can understand that.

Texas is a wonderful place, and I feel sorry for anyone who doesn't live here."

"For heaven's sake, Jason, don't take on so about Texas. It isn't fitting," Melissa said.

"Say, I have a marvelous idea," Hanson said. "As soon as all the cattle have been moved out to my ranch, I should like to host all of you for a gala."

"For a what?" Timmy asked.

"A festive event."

"A party," Melissa said when she saw that Timmy still didn't understand.

Timmy smiled. "Oh, good! I like parties."

Shumla

As news of what Jaco was doing spread through the town and out into the surrounding area, the people who wanted no part of it began leaving the community. Some tried to sell their houses, but finding no buyers, simply loaded their belongings into a wagon and left, leaving the houses standing bleak and empty. Some burned the houses behind them, rather than let someone else move in and take over.

Jaco moved in quickly, establishing ownership of the abandoned properties by way of quitclaim deeds. Within a short time the only people left in Shumla were those who were complicit with Jaco or those who were unable to leave for one reason or another and had become victims of the new order Jaco had established.

But while many of the residents of the town were leaving, new ones were coming in. The news wasn't universally disseminated, but spread through the outlaw circuit by word of mouth. Word was, the town of Shumla had become an outlaw town, and anyone who was on the run was welcome there. Also, there was a moneymaking opportunity for anyone who would be willing to join a group being put together by a man named Jaco.

The Israel brothers, Lenny and Larry, having heard word of such an opportunity, decided to explore it. They thought they were on the right road, but they hadn't seen any signs indicating that Shumla was ahead.

"You think this is the right way?" Larry asked.

"I think so," Lenny answered.

A few minutes later, they encountered a wagon loaded with furniture coming toward them. A stern-faced man was driving the wagon, a sad-faced woman sitting beside him. Back in the wagon, sitting on some of the furniture, were a young boy and a young girl.

Lenny held up a hand to stop the wagon.

"Tell me, mister, we're lookin' for the town of Shumla. Is this the way?"

"Yes, it ain't no more 'n a couple miles on down this road," the man replied, pointing back.

"Movin' are you?"

"We aren't movin'. We're bein' run away from our own home," the woman spat out.

"What do you mean, you're bein' run off?"

"It has turned into an outlaw town," the woman said.

"Martha, you've said enough now." The man slapped the reins against the back of the team and the wagon started moving again.

"D'ya hear that, Larry? It must be true, what we heard," Lenny said as they continued toward the town.

"All she said was that this here was a outlaw town. She didn't say nothin' a-tall about some feller puttin' together a gang."

"Well, I reckon that won't be too hard to find out," Lenny said.

Fifteen minutes later, the two men dismounted in front of the saloon. They brushed some of the dust off their clothes.

"My mouth is as dry as this sand," Larry said. "I can damn near taste me that beer now."

"Yeah, well, let's quit talkin' about it, and

233

get us a beer." Going inside, they each put a nickel on the bar and ordered a beer.

"That ain't enough," Morris said. "It'll cost you each a quarter."

"A quarter? Why, there ain't nowhere in the whole state of Texas where a feller has to pay a quarter for a beer."

"There is now," Morris said. "If you want a beer in this saloon, you'll have to pay a quarter."

"Is there another saloon in town?"

"This is the only one."

"This ain't right," Lenny complained.

"If you don't like it, you can take it up with our mayor. That's him, sittin' back there with that real pale-lookin' feller. Mayor Jaco."

"Jaco?"

"Lenny, that's the feller we're lookin' for."

"Looks like we've found him. Give the man a quarter."

"A quarter?" Larry scrunched up his face.

"You want a beer, don't you?"

"Well, yeah but —"

"But nothin'. Give him a quarter." As Lenny spoke he put his own quarter on the bar. Then, with beer mugs in hand, the two approached the table where Jaco was sitting with the whitest looking man either Lenny or Larry had ever seen. They stared at him in curiosity for a moment.

"You two boys got business with me or did you just come over here to gawk at the albino?" Jaco asked.

"Oh. Uh, we got business with you. We hear you are putting together a gang."

"And you want to join the gang?" Jaco asked.

"Yeah."

"You ever used them guns?"

Lenny answered. "Yeah. Does it matter?"

"It matters. See that feller over there in the corner, sittin' all by hisself? I want you to walk over there and kill 'im."

"What? Why?"

"He's plannin' to start his own gang, and I don't need the competition. If you're goin' to be in my gang, you're goin' to do what I tell you to do. I want you go over and kill 'im."

"Want me to do it, Lenny?"

"Nah, I'm the oldest. I'll do it."

Lenny walked over to the table, raised his pistol, and shot the unsuspecting man in the forehead. Returning his pistol to its holster, he walked back to Jaco's table.

"You boys are hired," Jaco said.

Chapter Twenty-One

Eagle Pass

"I shall require a mount," Hanson said the next morning to Ernie Taylor, one of the four cowboys Jason had found for him.

"Clem Northington has some good horses for sale down at the stable. Me 'n Barnes will come with you 'n help you pick one out, if you'd like."

"Yes, thank you, that would be splendid."

Fifteen minutes later, the three men were standing outside the corral. Taylor pointed to a horse. "That looks like a good one there."

"Ain't that the horse that Coleman brung in?" Barnes asked.

"It's a good horse," Taylor repeated pointedly.

"Yeah, well, I didn't say it wasn't a good horse. I just said it was the one that Coleman brung in."

Clem Northington came toward the three

men then. He spit out a stream of tobacco before he spoke. "Kin I he'p ye?"

"Indeed you may." Hanson pointed to the horse that Taylor had indicated. "I am in the market for a horse, and my friends here have recommended that one."

"They did?" Northington asked, looking at Taylor and Barnes questioningly.

"Yes. Would you saddle him for me so that I might give him a trial ride?"

"All right." Northington turned to shout back toward the barn. "Moon! Put a saddle on Pepper!"

"You want a saddle on Pepper?" Moon called back.

"That's what I said," Northington answered.

"Is it all right if I get Mo to help me? I don't want to saddle that horse all by myself."

"Go ahead 'n get 'im if you want to. But just get the job done. I don't aim to keep this here gentleman standin' aroun' all day."

"We'll do it," Moon said.

"I take it by the discourse that Pepper is a spirited animal?" Hanson asked.

"Yeah, you might say he's got a lot of spirit. You a good rider, are you?"

"I consider myself a competent equestrian, yes."

"Mister, you got a funny way about talkin'. You must be that foreign feller that's started a ranch out in the county."

"Yes, that would be the Regency Ranch."

"Well, I'm glad you know how to talk English, even it is kind of funny soundin'. I'll go check on gettin' the horse saddled."

"Mr. Hanson," Taylor said. "Uh, maybe we should pick you out another horse."

"Oh? And why is that? Do you think Pepper might be lame?"

"No, sir, it ain't that. It's just that I was funnin' with you, only as I think about it, I'm a-feared you could actual get hurt 'n I sure wouldn't want to see that."

"Can the animal be ridden?"

"Oh, yes sir, he can be rode all right. It's just that, well, he ain't exactly what you call gentle."

At that moment, Northington and another man brought the horse to him. Walking on either side of the horse, each had a good grip of his halter.

"Here he is," Northington said, handing the reins to Hanson. "Maybe if you are real calm with him, I mean, don't try 'n make him do anythin' more than just walk, he'll be gentle enough with you."

"Thank you." Hanson swung into the saddle, slapped his legs against the horse's side, and gave a yell, a battle cry that was as old as England. "Ut! Ut! Ut! Ut!"

The horse burst forward as if shot from a cannon. He headed straight for a fence that separated the back end of the stable property from the rangeland beyond.

"Mr. Hanson, look out!" Taylor shouted.

"There ain't no way that horse is goin' to take that fence," Northington said. "He'll stop and throw his rider over, sure as a gun is iron."

To the surprise of all watching, Pepper sailed over the fence as easily as if he had wings.

"Ut, ut, ut, ut!" they could hear Hanson shout, and he rode about fifty yards beyond the fence before he stopped, turned the horse, and came galloping back toward the fence.

"That man is a damn fool!" Northington said. "He mighta got away with it the first time, but I know that horse. There ain't no way he's going to jump that fence a second time."

Barnes laughed. "Looks like that horse ain't goin' to listen to you," he said as, yet again, the horse literally flew over the fence.

Hanson rode back at a gallop, and just as everyone started to dash out of the way, he stopped the horse on a dime, Pepper lowering his back haunches and literally sliding to a halt.

Hanson hopped down, then patted the horse on its neck. Pepper lowered his head and brushed it against the Englishman's face.

"Oh, what a magnificent animal! This is a fine horse, a fine horse indeed," Hanson said. "Taylor, Barnes, I thank you very much for pointing him out to me. Mr. Northington, I should like to buy Pepper."

"Yes, sir," Northington said.

"How much are you asking for him?"

"Seven . . . that is . . . a hunnert dollars."

Barnes frowned. "Are you sure? I heard you was willin' to let 'im go for fifty dollars."

"Yes, but that was 'cause I didn't think he could be rode, and I was afraid I'd never be able to get the horse sold. But this here foreign feller wants him, so the price is goin' back up."

"If you raise the price on him, I'll see to it that there ain't a ranch in the whole county that'll do any business with you," Barnes said angrily.

"And we know lots of ranchers," Taylor added.

"All right, all right," Northington said, throwing up his hands in surrender. "He can have the horse for fifty dollars, 'n good riddance it is, too. I don't care if I don't never see that four-legged hellion again."

Hanson gave it some thought. "I tell you what, Mr. Northington. I intend to be a longtime resident here, and I expect you and I will be doing business together many times. I want our relationship to be most cordial, so to that end, I will pay you the one hundred dollars you are asking for."

"What? You are willing to pay me one hundred dollars when I said I would let it go for fifty?"

"As I said, I expect we will be doing a lot of business together over the next several years, and I do want us to be friends. So yes, I'm willing to pay you one hundred dollars."

"How about seventy-five dollars?" Northington said with a broad smile.

"See?" Hanson said, returning the smile. "We are already friends. Seventy-five it is."

He rode Pepper back to the holding pens, where the cattle, not used to being kept penned up so close, were bawling and moving around restlessly. Taylor and Barnes walked back.

"Gentlemen, I am grateful to the two of you for helping me find a horse and for speaking up for me when Mr. Northington tried to elevate the price. If either or both of you are looking for a job with some permanency, I would be glad to hire you on as hands out at Regency."

"You'd do that knowin' we was thinkin' the horse would throw you, but we steered you toward him anyway?" Barnes asked.

"Hold it, Barnes," Taylor said, sticking out his hand. "Mr. Hanson, Barnes is a good friend of mine, so he's just tryin' to take the blame along with me. But he didn't have nothin' to do with it. The whole thing was my idea 'cause I was wantin' to have some fun."

"As it turned out, I was the one having the fun. I most enjoyed jumping with Pepper," Hanson said. "You are both good men, and I would be proud to have you in my employ."

"Was you really goin' to give Northington a hunnert dollars even after you found out he was tryin' to cheat you?" Barnes asked.

"Oh, I don't think he was trying to cheat me," Hanson said. "Mr. Northington is a businessman, after all, and he was only trying to maximize his profit. There is nothing at all wrong with that, and Pepper is most definitely worth one hundred dollars. Were I to purchase him in London, I've no doubt

I would be paying twice that amount."

Taylor was impressed. "All I can say, Mr. Hanson, is that you are a good man. Maybe as good a man as I ever saw."

"That's very decent of you to say. Now, about my offer of employment?"

A broad smile spread across Taylor's face. "You got us, Mr. Hanson. You got both of us."

"Wonderful. Now, I have a proposal. To consecrate your agreement to a concomitant arrangement, suppose we have a very good meal, on me?"

Taylor laughed. " 'Bout the onliest thing I understood was you sayin' you was goin' to buy us dinner. That is what you said, ain't it?"

"It is indeed. Have you a suggestion as to where we might dine?"

"I'd say the Rustic Rock," Barnes said.

"They set a good table, do they?" Cal asked.

Barnes laughed. "Well, to tell you the truth, Mr. Hanson, I can't say, personal, that they have good food. I ain't never et there, bein' as it cost too much. But I've heard tell the food was just real good, and I've always wanted to try it."

"Then try it we shall," Hanson promised.

Val Cyr was the next man to show up in Jaco's town. "I'm lookin' for a man named Jaco," he told Morris.

"What do you want with him?"

"Mister, I don't see that that is any of your business."

"I'm tellin' you now, if you're law or a bounty hunter, you won't get out of Shumla alive," Morris said.

"Do I look like the law?"

"How am I supposed to know what the law looks like?"

"If this really is an outlaw town like I heard it was, then you ought to have some idea of what the law looks like." Cyr pulled his pistol and stuck it in Morris's face. "Now, either tell me how to find Jaco, or I'll blow your head off and find someone who will tell me."

"I'm Jaco," a voice said from behind Cyr.

"Jaco, I'm Val Cyr, and you just saved this man's life."

"What do you want with me?"

"I hear you're puttin' together a gang."

Jaco looked him over. "Ain't you a little old?"

"I can ride and I can shoot. What else do you need?"

Jaco chuckled. "Nothin' else, I reckon."

Although Duff had been told that the second of the two trains would arrive the day after the first, the wait to ship the remaining 300 heads of cattle still in the holding pens had stretched into an entire week.

Early in the morning of the seventh day, he was awakened by the sound of a train whistle. Finally! Getting up, he dressed, then moved along the upstairs hallway and stopped just outside Elmer's room. He knocked on the door. "Train's here, Elmer."

From the other side of the door, he heard a grunt that might have been a reply.

He continued on into the dining room. The clock showed that it was ten minutes until six. Whether the train was the one he had ordered or it was one of the regularly scheduled trains, Duff didn't know, but whichever it was, he knew he had time for breakfast.

Only two other customers were eating at the early hour. They were drummers waiting for the morning stage, and their sample cases sat on the floor beside them. They nodded a greeting toward Duff.

The waitress set a cup of steaming coffee in front of him and he ordered a stack of pancakes, two eggs, a large piece of ham, biscuits, and redeye gravy.

Elmer joined him and ordered his own breakfast, which was every bit as large as that ordered by Duff.

"Have you heard from Wang?" Duff asked.

"I saw him where he's staying in Little Chinatown yesterday. Told him you thought the train would be here today," Elmer said. "I asked him to join us for breakfast."

"There he is, now." Duff nodded toward the door of the dining room where Wang was standing, his bag by his side.

"Hey, Chinaman, are you sure you are in the right place?" one of the drummers called to him. "There ain't no slant-eyes allowed here. Just whites."

Elmer stood up abruptly.

Duff grabbed his arm. "Elmer, *dinnae* be for making a scene. We'll be checking out shortly."

Elmer nodded. "I will be very quiet." He walked over to the table where the drummers were sitting.

"May I help you?" asked the same man who had called out to Wang.

Elmer pulled out a chair and sat down as if to have a friendly chat. "Do you know who owns the InterOcean Hotel?"

The drummer shook his head. "No, I don't."

"His name is Barney Ford, 'n he is a black man, not a white man. The Chinaman you just insulted is Mr. Wang. He is a Shaolin priest."

"I don't care what church he goes to. He doesn't have any business being in here."

"I'm afraid you don't understand. When I say he is a priest, I ain't talkin' 'bout someone all dressed in black 'n wearing a white collar, who prays for your soul. Mr. Wang doesn't give a damn about your soul. A Shaolin priest is a special kind of fella, who has a special way of fightin'. He could come over here, jerk your tongue out of your mouth, and hand it to you before you would even know what happened. I've seen men like him kill a bull in full charge, just by hitting the beast between his eyes with the edge of their hand. And you have just insulted him."

"I . . . just called out to him. I didn't mean anything by it," the drummer said nervously.

"Yes, but the Chinese set quite a store by what they call honor. I seen the expression in his eyes when you insulted him. Does your friend know how to get in touch with your next of kin?"

"What? No, please . . . I . . . I didn't mean anything."

"Then sit here quietly and don't say

another word. Mr. Wang is my friend, and I believe I can convince him not to come after you."

"Yes, do! Please do!"

Elmer put his hand on the drummer's shoulder. "I'll do what I can," he promised.

Wang had joined the table by the time Elmer returned.

He sat down, put his napkin on his lap, and picked up his fork. "I told you I wouldn't make a scene."

Duff chuckled. "You handled it quite well."

CHAPTER TWENTY-TWO

After breakfast, Duff, Elmer, and Wang walked down to the depot. The locomotive that would take them and their cattle to Texas sat hissing and popping while a thin column of smoke rose from the smokestack. Behind the train were ten cattle cars, each one capable of carrying thirty head of cattle. Two additional cars were attached to the train, a Pullman car, providing accommodations for Duff, Elmer, and Wang, and a caboose for the train crew.

Duff went to the station master to make arrangements for the train to be loaded and dispatched. "How long will it take to reach our destination?"

"Five days and four nights," the dispatcher replied.

"Isn't that an unusually long time?"

"Not at all. I'm sure you understand that because this train is carrying cattle instead of people, it will not get priority. There will be many times during your trip when the train will be shunted off the main line and onto a side track to allow the passenger trains to pass through."

"All right," Duff said. "I can understand that. Even if it takes five days, that is much quicker than it would be if we had to drive the herd south."

The dispatcher chuckled. "To be sure, sir.

"We're going to be on the train for five days," Duff said when he returned to the others.

"That's all right," Elmer said. "I've got a deck of cards. Do you play poker, Wang?"

"I do not know the game."

Elmer smiled. "I'll teach you."

Shumla

When Wyatt Mattoon rode into town, he studied both sides of the street and appraised everyone he saw. It was a matter of habit from having been a lawman for fourteen years. He had been a deputy for Red Angus in Johnson County, for Isaac Parker, the Hanging Judge in Arkansas, and for Wyatt Earp.

He had also served as a city sheriff in some of the smaller towns in Arizona and New Mexico. Those small towns couldn't pay enough . . . sometimes they couldn't even pay what they had promised. And so, his law career had ended a year ago when he killed the driver and guard and took the money from a money shipment he was supposed to escort.

Having to live on the run, the money hadn't lasted all that long, so he'd pulled a couple smaller jobs since then. Recently he'd heard of the outlaw town being run by a man named A. M. Jaco.

As deputy for Wyatt Earp in Dodge City, Mattoon had once arrested Jaco. He knew he was taking a chance coming to see him, but it was a chance he was willing to take.

Dismounting in front of the saloon, he went inside and up to the bar. "Whiskey."

"That'll be half a dollar."

"I thought it might be something like that." Mattoon paid for the drink. Lifting it to his lips, he looked in the mirror and saw Jaco sitting with a woman in the back of the saloon. He tossed down the drink, wiped his mouth with the back of his hand, then turned and walked back to the table.

Surprised, Jaco looked up.

"Do you recognize me, Jaco?"

"No," he grunted.

"You should. The name is Mattoon, and I arrested you five years ago." Aware that nearly every man in the saloon drew their pistols, he held up both hands. "Hold it, boys. I ain't in the law business any more. Fact is, I'm on the other side. I'm a wanted man, same as I expect most of you are."

"What are you doin' here, Mattoon?" Jaco asked.

"Hidin' out from the law is one reason. The other reason is, I hear you're lookin' for some good men to put together a gang. I want to ride with you."

"How do we know this ain't all a phony, so as to get in with us, 'n arrest us?" Putt said.

"Yeah," Jaco said. "Like Putt said, how do we know you ain't just tryin' to work your way in with us?"

"I am tryin' to work my way in with you, but not to arrest you. I told you. I want to ride with you."

Jaco shook his head. "I ain't willin' to take that chance."

"You would be missing a good opportunity," Mattoon said. "Because I was the law once, I know how they think."

"He's right about that, Jaco," Cyr said. "Having a lawman on our side would give us an edge."

"But how do we know to trust him?"

"There is a jail in this town, isn't there?" Mattoon asked.

"Yeah, there's a jail."

"Put me in jail until you check me out. If you find out that I'm still with the law, you won't have to come looking for me to kill me. I'll be right there."

"All right," Jaco replied, stroking his chin. "Puke?"

"Yeah?"

"Take Mattoon down to the jail and lock him up until we get this all figured out."

Puke stood up. "Come along, you."

Mattoon didn't move. "Don't you think you should relieve me of my arms?"

"What?"

"The first thing you do when you arrest someone is take their guns from them."

"Oh." Puke started toward Mattoon, and a pistol suddenly appeared in his hand so fast that nobody even saw him draw. Puke gasped and stepped back.

Mattoon smiled, then turned the pistol around and handed it to Puke, handle first. "What time will you feed me?"

"I don't know," Puke replied. "I ain't never had no one in jail before."

"Yeah, well you got someone now, and you damn well better feed me well. If you don't, soon as Jaco finds out I'm for real, and I join his gang, I'll be visitin' you."

"Don't worry, Mattoon, we'll feed you.

'Cause if you don't check out, I'm goin' to hang you. And I want you fattened up, just like a hog for the slaughter." Jaco laughed at his own joke.

Later that same day, after Jaco was satisfied that Mattoon was all right, he gathered his newly organized gang in Sherazade's room upstairs at the Red Dog Saloon. He wanted to make plans for their first job, and he didn't want anyone to overhear.

"We are going to be different from any other gang operating out there," Jaco told them. "We are going to kill as many people as we can."

"Why?" Mattoon asked. "Not that I have anything against killin' when it needs to be done. But what do you mean, we're goin' to kill as many as we can?"

"It's a matter of tactics. If we make a name for ourselves as men who come in shootin' 'n killin', then folks are goin' to be a-scared of us. And when folks is a-scared of us, they're goin' to be a lot less likely to get in our way. It'll make it a lot easier to take what we want."

"Yeah," Putt said. "I think that's a good idea."

The others, even Mattoon, nodded in agreement.

"Our first job will be in Bitter Creek," Jaco said. "They got a bank there that's just waitin' for us."

Bitter Creek, Texas

Just after nine o'clock the next morning, Jaco halted his men near the small town located thirty-five miles northwest of Eagle Pass and divided them into four groups of two.

He and Val Cyr approached the town from the north. Blue Putt and Johnny Dane came in from the south, Manny Dingo and Wyatt Mattoon rode in from the west, while Larry and Lenny Israel entered town from the east.

Riding in pairs slowly, and deliberately, they aroused no suspicion. Not until all eight converged in front of the Bitter Creek Bank and Trust did anyone notice, and even then, the only thought was that the bank was getting busy. After all, the men hadn't arrived together. However, they did go into the bank together, at least four of them did.

Neither the Israel brothers, nor Dane and Mattoon went into the bank. They remained mounted out front, each holding the reins to a horse belonging to one of the men who'd gone inside. They also kept a sharp eye out for anything that might interfere with the job at hand.

Inside the bank, Jaco stepped up to the woman standing at the teller's cage. Grabbing her, he pushed her roughly to one side. She let out a little cry of alarm.

The well-dressed man with white hair and a white beard stood up quickly from the desk at one side of the room. "See here! What is this?" he shouted angrily.

"This is a bank robbery," Jaco said. "That's what this is." He added a malevolent chuckle.

"What? How dare you?"

"Are you the head of this here bank?"

"I am."

"Then give us all the money." Jaco waved his gun around.

"I will not."

Jaco turned the pistol toward the teller, who was looking on in shock and fear. Jaco shot him.

"My God! What did you do?" the bank president shouted.

"What's it look like I done? I shot your bank teller. Now, give us all your money like I told you to."

"No, I will not."

Jaco shot the woman.

"You! You are insane!"

■ ■ ■ ■

From their position outside, Mattoon and the others could hear the shooting coming from inside, and they drew their pistols, but did nothing.

A man walking up the boardwalk also heard the shooting. Startled, he headed toward the front door of the bank.

"Mattoon?" Lenny asked.

"Let 'im go in," Mattoon replied. "No sense gettin' the whole town stirred up yet. Jaco will take care of 'im."

"What's all the shootin'?" the man asked, stepping into the bank.

Dingo shot him.

"Now," Jaco said, pointing the gun at the banker. "Give us all the money, or I'll shoot you, too."

"You . . . you can't shoot me. If you do, there will be nobody left to give you the money."

"That's no problem. We'll kill you, then go find us another bank to rob." Jaco pulled the hammer back on his pistol.

"No! No! Wait!" The bank president held his hands stretched out in front of him. "Don't shoot me! Please, don't shoot me! I'll give you the money!"

"Jaco, this is startin' to take too long," Putt said. "What if some others come into the bank?"

"Cyr, you and Dingo get on back outside," Jaco ordered. "Tell the others I want you to kill anyone you see on the street."

As the two men stepped outside, the bank president hurried around behind the counter, then opened the safe. Several stacks of bound bills were in the vault.

"Whoowee, look at that, will you, Putt? You ever seen anythin' so purty as that? How much is there, banker?"

"Twenty-two thousand dollars."

"Well, get the money put into this bag, pronto."

From outside came the sound of shooting, as well as some loud shouts of men and a few screams from women.

Working as quickly as he could with shaking hands, the banker put all the money in a cloth bag, then handed it to Jaco.

Jaco took the bag with his left hand, then lifted the gun with his right hand and pulled the trigger. The banker went down with a bullet hole in his forehead.

"All right. Let's go!" Jaco said.

With the money in hand, he and Putt ran out of the bank, then mounted. The other six men were already mounted, busy shooting up the town.

"As we ride out, kill ever'one you see!" Jaco shouted.

Slapping their legs against the sides of their horses, the eight men rode out of town, shooting through the windows of the buildings. Not one person stepped out onto the street to challenge them as they left.

Riding back into Shumla, they made their presence known by whooping and shouting and shooting into the air. Jaco reached down into the sack and withdrew handfuls of one-dollar bills, which he promptly tossed aside, allowing them to flutter down into the street behind them.

"Lord almighty!" one of the citizens of the town shouted. "That there is real money he's tossin' around!"

Most of the town had been standing by, watching the riders gallop into town with a mixture of fear and curiosity. But upon seeing real money being tossed aside, they dashed out into the street to recover it.

Jaco and his gang pulled up in front of the saloon, where they were met by Sherazade and half a dozen of her girls. Puke Cage was there, as well, the marshal's badge on his shirt clearly visible.

As the men and girls rushed together, Jaco stepped up to his city marshal. "Puke, go round up all the town's leading citizens, and bring 'em down here to the saloon. Tell 'em that the drinkin' will be free."

"Yes, sir!" Puke replied with a big smile on his face.

As Puke started out on his errand, Jaco went into the saloon, where he gave the bartender one hundred dollars. "Give anyone who comes in here a free drink. And you can keep the drinks goin' until you run out of liquor or run out of money, whichever is first."

The bartender laughed. "As long as I've got water, I won't be runnin' out of drinks."

Chapter Twenty-Three

The bank robbery and wanton killing at Bitter Creek made the front page in newspapers all over the state. The article in the *San Antonio Daily Express* was typical of the articles carried in other newspapers.

Terrible Crime in Bitter Creek, Texas

Nine Killed by Outlaws

Among Them Women and Children

A gang of eight outlaws robbed the bank in Bitter Creek, Texas. As both the bank teller and the bank president were killed, it is not known how much money the robbers got. The vault was standing open, however, and there was no money, except for change, remaining.

The robbers not only killed the above

mentioned victims, but also a woman customer who was in the bank at the time.

As the robbers rode out of town, they continued their murderous spree by firing indiscriminately onto the sidewalks, and into the stores and business establishments of the town. Two additional women and two children were among the victims of this murderous gang of outlaws.

The identities of this nefarious group of outlaws are not known.

Eagle Pass

The first half of the herd had been on Regency Ranch for just over a week when Hanson sent Ernie Taylor into town to check on when the train was due to arrive with the second half of the herd.

"It'll be here sometime tomorrow morning," dispatcher Sterling Bobe said. "But I'll have a clearer read on the exact arrival sometime in the morning."

Taylor smiled. "Well, I reckon I'd better spend the night here in town."

"You want to sleep in the waiting room, Ernie? If you do, it's all right." Sterling chuckled. "I know that when you were brakeman for the T and P, you more 'n likely spent quite a few nights in depots."

"Yeah, too many. Thanks, Sterling, but

there's no need. I'm ridin' for Mr. Cal Hanson now, 'n he's already paid me enough money to get me a room in the hotel."

"I'm not surprised by that," Sterling agreed. "Mr. Hanson hasn't been here very long, but everyone knows that he is a gentleman of means."

Leaving the depot, Taylor walked down to the livery to board his horse.

"I hope you're not comin' here to tell me that Mr. Hanson has broke his neck on Pepper," Northington said.

"Listen, you don't understand. Mr. Hanson is the best rider I done ever seen," Tyler replied. "Why, he purdee much rides that horse like it's a part of 'im." Tyler laughed. "He wanted me to tell you again, how much he appreciated the deal you give 'im."

"He's a good man," the liveryman said.

"Especially since you was trying to cheat 'im, Northington. And, it wouldn'ta been right for me to stand by 'n watch my boss man get cheated now, would it? Besides, I've got a idee that he's goin' to wind up bein' the biggest rancher in the whole county. You will be wantin' to do business with him, won't you?"

Northington smiled. "Yeah, I guess that's right, ain't it? Me 'n him made up. You seen it yourself."

"How much do I owe you for leavin' my horse here?"

"I ain't a-goin' to charge you nothin' at all on this first night, on account of you 'n Barnes was the ones that brung Hanson to me to do business with in the first place."

"Well, that's just real decent of you, Mr. Northington."

With his horse taken care of, Taylor walked back out onto the board sidewalk in front of the livery stable where he stood for a moment, rubbing his hands together in eager anticipation of doing a night on the town.

The boardwalk ran the length of the town on both sides of the street. At the end of each block, planks had been laid across the road to allow pedestrians to cross the road without having to walk in the dirt or mud. Taylor waited patiently at one of them while he watched a lady cross, daintily holding her skirt up above her ankles to keep the hem from soiling.

"Good afternoon, miss," he greeted, touching the brim of his hat with two fingers.

The woman returned his greeting with a nod.

Once she passed, Taylor stepped onto the plank himself. Walking around town for a bit more, he stopped and stared in the window of a leather goods shop. His attention had been caught by a pair of good-looking boots he would love to have. The boots he owned were so worn there were holes in the leather. He had held off buying new ones because he could still wear them, and other things had held a greater priority. But, with a job now, he was beginning to think that the boots might just be in his near future.

He strolled all the way up one side of the street and down the other, finally winding up at the High Pockets Saloon. Pushing his way through the batwing doors, he stepped up to the bar.

The bartender approached carrying a damp rag with him, which he used to make a swipe just in front the cowboy. The rag reeked with a sour stench. "Hello, Taylor. What you doin' in town? I heard tell that you and Barnes was workin' for that foreign feller."

"His name is Mr. Hanson," Taylor said. "And yes, we're workin' for him. He ain't no foreign fella. He's a good man, is what he is."

"Didn't mean nothin' by it," the bartender said. "What'll you have?"

"Whiskey."

The glass was set before Taylor and he

took it, then turned with his back to the bar to survey the room. The evening customers were just beginning to gather, and the soiled doves were moving about the room like bees working in a field of wildflowers, going from table to table to ply their vocation. Soon the tables were filled with drinking, laughing customers, and at one of the tables, a card game was in progress. One of the players left the game, and Taylor walked over to the table.

"Mind if I join you?"

"You got money now, Taylor?" asked a tall man with a handlebar mustache.

Taylor smiled. "I got a little. I also got me a job."

"Then sit in." The man with the mustache pushed a chair out with his foot.

An hour after Taylor joined the game, he was fifty dollars richer and decided that, instead of getting a room at the hotel, he would spend the night right there with Peggy. He didn't choose her by chance. For the last three months, anytime he could afford one of the working girls, she was always the dove of his choice. But it was the first time he had ever been able to spend the entire night with her.

Later, as they lay together in bed, Peggy

raised up on one elbow and turned toward Taylor. Her naked breast swung forward as, with her other hand, she reached up to brush back a fall of Taylor's hair. "I'm glad you could stay with me tonight, honey, 'cause I'll be leaving soon."

"What? Where? Where are you goin'?"

"You ever heard of a town called Shumla?"

"Yeah, I've heard of it."

"Well, that's where I'm goin'."

"Why? I thought you liked it here in Eagle Pass. I know Sheriff Bowles don't give none of you no trouble, 'n far as I know, he ain't takin' no money from any of you, is he?"

"No, Sheriff Bowles is a good man. That ain't got nothin' to do with why I'm leavin'."

"Is it Gibson?" Taylor asked, referring to the owner of the High Pockets Saloon. "Is he cheatin' you? Is he beatin' you? 'Cause if he is, I'll take care of that."

Peggy laughed softly, then bent down to kiss him on his forehead. "My brave cowboy. I really think you would. No, I have a friend in Shumla, and she told me that if I came there, I could make five times as much money as I can here."

"What? How? That's impossible!"

"She said it's what they call an outlaw town. It's a place where people wanted by the law can go and be safe. But they have to

267

pay a lot more to live there."

"Don't go, Peggy," Taylor said. "It don't sound to me like that's the kind of place you need to be."

"But if I went and stayed for just one year, why, I'd make enough money I'd never have to be on the line again."

"Then what would you do?"

"I don't know. Maybe I'd go back East and get married." A smile spread across her face. "I could marry you. You'd like to marry me, wouldn't you? I know you like me."

"I do like you, but I don't want to go back East. 'N I don't want you goin' to no outlaw town."

"Why? Would you be worrying about me?"

"Yeah, I would."

"Then I've got an idea. Why don't you come with me?"

"Peggy, I ain't proud of ever'thing I've ever done before, but I ain't never rode the owlhoot trail, 'n I got no plans to start now."

"You wouldn't have to be an outlaw to live there," Peggy said. "Sherazade said that ever'body that lives there is makin' a lot of money. You could find somethin' to do there. I know you could."

"I got me a job now, Peggy. A good job with a good man. Why, you don't have to go to no outlaw town. If you want to get married, me 'n you could get married right now, 'n you could move out to the ranch with me. More 'n likely, you could get on with Mr. Hanson, too."

"And what would I be paid? Twenty dollars a month and found? Why would I do that, when I can make much more money in Shumla?"

"There's more to life than money," Taylor said.

"There may be, honey, but it takes money to find it."

"I tell you what. Why don't I just go down to the hotel for the night? That way, you'll be free to make even more money."

"Now, honey, don't get all upset. You don't have any hold on me, and I don't on you. I'm flattered that you will be worried about me, but I can take care of myself."

"I'm sure you can," Taylor said as he swung his legs over the edge of the bed and reached for his trousers.

Shumla

Silas Dunn, owner of the meat market and one of the businessmen who'd stayed in town when so many others left sat in the saloon, wasting his morning.

Jaco walked up and gave the butcher one

hundred dollars. "Dunn, I want you to set up a spit right in the middle of town and roast half a steer. Think you can do that?"

"Well, yeah, I can do that," Dunn replied. "But that's going to be a hell of a lot more meat that you 'n your men can eat."

"Oh, it isn't just for us. It's for the whole town." Jaco turned to the bartender. "And Morris?"

"Yes, Mr. Jaco?"

"Maybe you'd better hold back a barrel of beer. This town is goin' to have a party!"

"Yes, sir!" Morris said.

Dunn left the bar at a clip, set up the spit, and started cooking the meat. For the rest of the day, an enticing aroma swept through the town. News that there was to be party with free food and beer spread through the community.

By sundown the party was in full swing. The meat was cooked and Sherazade and her provocatively dressed girls moved around, teasing the men.

Jaco climbed up onto a buckboard, and pulling his pistol, fired two shots into the air. That got everyone's attention, and all looked toward him.

"Ladies and gentlemen, this is just an example of what this town is going to be like. We have declared our independence from the state and from the country. We are a free town with our own laws, and we will not allow any U.S. Marshal, Texas Ranger, or county sheriff inside the city limits. If they do come here, they'll stay here." He pointed to the cemetery. "We'll make a special lawman's section over there in the graveyard."

The others laughed.

"We can have a fine place here as long as ever'one understands that the only laws in this town are the laws that I declare."

"Wait a minute," one of others said. "If we really are goin' to be a free town, seems to me like we ought to all have some say-so in whatever laws we're a-goin' to have."

Jaco raised his pistol and shot the protester. Gasps and cries of alarm came from several of the others.

"Is there anyone else who wants to have a word about who will be makin' the laws in this town?"

The others looked at each other with expressions of shock and fear, but nobody spoke.

Smiling, Jaco returned his pistol to his shoulder. "I didn't think there would be. Now, what do you say that we get back to the celebration?"

CHAPTER TWENTY-FOUR

Onboard the train

"Damn." Elmer hung his head. "I shoulda know'd better 'n to gamble with a Chinaman. I've been to China, I know how good they are."

"I thought Wang *dinnae* know the game," Duff said.

"It don't make no never mind that he don't know the game. He's a Chinaman."

"How much did he win from you?"

"He won the whole hunnert 'n fifty dollars that was my share of the reward money we got back in Cheyenne."

Duff chuckled. "Aren't ye glad then, that you own half the gold mine that's on Sky Meadow?"

"Yeah." A broad and satisfied smile spread across Elmer's face. "Yeah, I reckon when you think about it like that, it don't really matter all that much that Wang won all my money."

272

Duff was referring to an old abandoned mine in which Elmer had discovered a new vein. He had been working the mine before Duff bought the land, but had never filed a claim.

Duff recalled how he and his cousin, Falcon, had first encountered this man who was not only his foreman, but his best friend.

A creature had appeared on the first day Duff and Falcon had been working the mine, but then not again until the third day. For three days, they worked and though they had not made a significant find, they had found enough color in the tailings to make their efforts worthwhile.

Examining the nuggets they had recovered, Falcon estimated that they had at least one hundred dollars' worth of gold. "If we keep getting these results, you will get enough money to build your herd," he said.

"Aye, and that is my intention," Duff replied.

They were ready when something hit the tripwire, causing the empty tin cans to rattle.

"Did you hear?" Falcon asked.

"Aye."

"Get ready."

Duff picked up the lantern and moved it about fifty feet back toward the entrance, leaving them in the dark, but that was part of their plan. When the creature passed them, Falcon stepped out behind it and threw a loop of rope down over the creature. Falcon jerked the rope back, tightening the loop, which secured the creature's arms by his side.

The creature let out a bloodcurdling scream as Duff leaped out behind it to knock him down. The creature struggled, but Duff and Falcon were too strong, and within a moment Falcon had looped the rope around it enough times to have both his arms and legs restricted. The creature continued to scream.

"Get the lantern, Duff. Let's see what we have here," Falcon said.

Duff hurried back to get the lantern then returned and held it up.

Falcon rolled the creature over. "I'll be. It's a man."

The man's hair hung down to his waist and he had a full beard. He was wearing clothes made of wolf skin and his fingernails were long and curled.

"Of course I'm a man! What did you think I would be?" the man replied in a gravelly voice. "Turn me loose!"

"So you can try to kill us again?" Falcon asked.

"I wasn't tryin' to kill you. I was tryin' to scare you away."

"Like the three men you killed?"

"I only kilt two."

"There were three — Elmer Gleason, Ethan Post, and Sam Hodges."

"Is that what their names was? They never told me."

"Why did you kill them?"

"I kilt 'em 'cause they tried to kill me. They wanted me to show 'em where the gold was, and when I wouldn't do it, they pointed a gun at me and said they was goin' to shoot me. I got away from 'em, and when they come after me, I kilt 'em. Then I dragged their bodies outside as a warnin' to anyone else as might come around."

"Those were Post and Hodges. What about Elmer Gleason? Did he try to kill you, too?"

The man laughed a high-pitched, insane cackling laugh. Then he stopped laughing and stared at Duff and Falcon, his eyes gleaming in the light of the lantern. "What are you doin' here? You got no right in here. This is my home."

"Sure 'n you aren't for sayin' you live here in this mine, are you?" Duff asked.

"Yes, I am a-sayin' that. Now, I want you to turn me a-loose and get out of here."

"How do you live? What do you eat? What do you drink?" Falcon asked.

"Bugs, rabbits when I can catch 'em, such

wild plants as can be et. And they's a pool of water back a-ways."

"What is your name?" Duff asked.

The man laughed again, the same, high-pitched insane laugh as before. "You already know my name. You done said it."

"What do you mean we've already said it?"

"I'm the feller I didn't kill."

"Mister, you've been in this mine too long," Falcon said. "You aren't making any sense at all. What do you mean, you are the man you didn't kill?"

"Wait a minute," Duff said. "I think I know what he means. Are you trying to tell us that you are Elmer Gleason?"

"I ain't tryin' to tell you nothin, sonny." He laughed again. "I'm a-doin' it. I am Elmer Gleason."[1]

Duff shook his head to clear it. By rights, he knew the entire mine would have belonged to him, but he'd filed the claim in both his and Elmer's names. They kept the mine secret, accessing it only rarely when there was a need for funds. None of the cowboys on the ranch were even aware of it, and as far as they knew, Elmer was no more than a ranch foreman.

1. From *MacCallister: The Eagles Legacy*

"What?" Duff had been lost in his memories and hadn't paid a bit of attention to Elmer.

"Yeah," Elmer repeat. "Having part of that mine does make it easier for me to be a good loser." He glanced toward Wang. He'd already put the money away and was preparing their lunch in the small kitchen that was part of the private railroad car.

Eagle Pass

Taylor could have eaten his breakfast in the hotel, but he chose to go to the saloon for bacon and biscuits. The real reason was because he wanted to see Peggy one more time. He went right up the stairs and knocked on the door to her room, taking a chance that she didn't have anyone with her.

To his surprise, she opened the door immediately. She was dressed, not in the provocative attire of her profession, but in the more modest clothes any woman might wear. On the bed behind her, he saw her luggage.

He frowned. "You are really leaving town?"

"Yes."

"Well, before you go, can you at least come down and have breakfast with me?"

Peggy smiled. "I can do that."

■ ■ ■ ■

Half an hour later, Taylor pushed his empty plate away and lifted his cup of coffee. Peggy was still eating, and he studied her over the rim of his cup. "I wish I could talk you out of leaving. Especially out of going to that place."

"And I wish I could talk you into coming with me. My friend, Sherazade, said that everyone who is there can make a lot of money, not just the working girls. Ernie, you could get a real good paying job. We would stay there no longer than a year, save our money, and we could go someplace where nobody would ever know I had been a soiled dove. We could buy a ranch and have a good life."

"I think we could have a good life working for Mr. Hanson. And we could get married right now."

Peggy shook her head. "No, Ernie. I'm sorry. I'm going to Shumla, and I wish you would come with me."

Taylor stood up. "Good-bye, Peggy. I hope it all works out for you." He turned and walked away.

He had been assured that the train bringing the rest of the cattle would arrive this morning, so he headed to the depot to meet it.

One of the most important events in any town in the West was the arrival of the train. Many people would come to watch the trains even if they had no personal stake in the arrival or departure. As the townspeople began to gather, the crowd would take on a carnival atmosphere, the environment often accented with salesmen, and sometimes, entertainment.

Outside the Eagle Pass depot, a fiddler was playing for the crowd, an upturned hat on the ground in front of him inviting people to express their gratitude for the music by making donations. The high, skirling sound of the fiddle could be heard all over the depot, even above the laughing and joking of those waiting for the train.

Taylor found a place away from the jostling crowd and leaned against the depot wall. He rolled a cigarette, lit it, and smoked quietly as he waited. He had asked Peggy to marry him last night, and she had turned him down. As he thought about it in the light of day, he realized it was probably a pretty good thing that she had turned him down. She was a soiled dove, after all. Someone was bound to make a comment about it, and he'd wind up killing him. Or getting killed.

Besides, he didn't even know her last name. For that matter, he wasn't even sure that her name really was Peggy.

He had left her on a sour note but had to admit that he was worried about her going to an outlaw town. He wasn't all that sure exactly what an outlaw town was, but it didn't seem like a place a normal person would want to be.

"Here comes the train!" someone shouted.

Immediately upon the heels of the shout came the sound of the train whistle, announcing its arrival.

"It's right on time," another said.

It wasn't the train that Taylor was waiting for, but he wasn't surprised. He had worked as a brakeman for the railroad once, and he knew that "the varnish" as passenger trains were called, always had "the high iron." That meant they always had the right of way, Freight trains would be pushed onto a side track to allow the passenger trains uninhibited passage.

The laughing and joking ceased as everyone grew quiet to await the train's arrival.

Taylor didn't join the crowd of people as they pushed closer to the track to stare in the direction from which the train would come. It could be heard quite clearly, not only the whistle but the hollow sounds of the puffing steam coming from the engine, then rolling back as an echo from the surrounding hillsides. As the train drew even closer, the crowd could see clouds of black smoke billowing from the diamond stack.

The train pounded into the station with sparks flying from the drive wheels and glowing hot embers dripping from its firebox. Following the engine and tender were the rapidly passing windows of the passenger cars. The train squealed to a halt. Inside, people who would be getting off there stood and moved down the aisles toward the exits at the end of the cars.

Several who weren't getting off the train remained in their seats, some reading a paper, some engaged in conversation, and many of them just looking out at the town they were passing through.

Taylor watched the arriving passengers, then he watched the departing passengers board the train. Not until the train had left the station, and the crowd dispersed, did he go speak with Sterling Bobe, the station master.

"What's the latest?" he asked. "Any news on the train I'm here to meet?"

"I just got a telegram from Spofford," the

dispatcher told him. "The stock was shunted aside while the varnish came through. The stock train left about ten minutes later. There's nothin' else in front of it, so I expect it'll be here in another ten or fifteen minutes."

"Thanks, Sterling." Taylor went back outside, and finding an empty baggage cart, sat on it as he waited.

A few minutes later, Sheriff Bowles, his family, and another lady came walking up.

As they approached, Taylor hopped down from the four-wheeled baggage cart. "Hello, Sheriff."

"Hello, Taylor. Hanson send you in to meet the train?"

"Yes, sir. Sterling said the train would be here in another few minutes."

"Yes, he called my office to tell me."

"You brung your whole family to meet the train?"

Jason nodded then turned to Megan. "This is my wife's sister, and we have a friend on the train."

"You don't say."

"What about Hanson? Does he know the train is arriving this morning?"

"Mr. Hanson don't have no telyphone out at the ranch, so I sent someone to tell him the train would be here this mornin'. I expect he'll be along soon with enough hands to take the cows on out to the ranch."

Onboard the train

Even though the special car Elmer, Duff, and Wang were riding in had four beds, privacy provided by curtains, as well as a small kitchen, dining, and seating area, it hadn't all been plush and comfort during the journey. It had been necessary that they stop several times during the trip in order to make certain that the cattle were well watered and fed.

"I reckon this must be Eagle Pass," Elmer said as the train began slowing. "You think we'll be takin' the beeves right out to Mr. Hanson's ranch or will we be puttin' 'em in a holdin' pen?"

"I expect that Cal will meet us or make arrangements for us to be met," Duff replied.

Even as the train was coming into the station, it was shunted onto a side track to keep it out of the way from regularly scheduled trains passing through.

Elmer looked out the window. "The whole Bowles family is here and I see Megan, but I don't see Mr. Hanson."

"I expect he'll be along shortly," Duff said.

CHAPTER TWENTY-FIVE

Runnels, Texas

Initially, Jaco and his gang, which had grown to twelve men, called themselves Jaco's Raiders. One newspaper had dubbed them the "Kingdom Come Gang" because they slaughtered every man, woman, and child in sight during their raids. That name stuck and became a sobriquet that the men wore as a badge of pride.

As a single column, their leader A. M. Jaco at the head, they had ridden through the star-filled, moonless night, arriving just as the sun was coming up, a red disc on the horizon behind them. The town had been built in the hope that it would become a railroad stop, but the tracks had bypassed it, and it was already struggling for survival.

Jaco held up his hand, bringing the column to a halt.

For a moment, the riders were quiet, staring down at the just awakening town.

A rooster crowed.

A dog barked.

A baby cried.

Blue Putt, his milky white skin nearly luminescent in the dawn's early light, rode up alongside his leader, spit out a wad of tobacco, then wiped his mouth with the back of his hand.

"Look down there," Jaco said. "If ever there was a town just waitin' to be picked, like pullin' an apple from a tree, this here is the one. They don't have one idea that we are here."

"What if they heard about us, 'n they're just waitin' for us?" one of the gang's newer men asked.

The door opened at the rear of one of the homes and a man started across the back yard toward the outhouse. He hadn't put on a belt or galluses, and was holding up his pants as he walked.

"Does that feller look to you like he's waiting on us?" Jaco asked as the man stepped into the outhouse and closed the door behind him.

"Well, it ain't like they'd be likely to let us know they're expectin' us, is it?" the new rider asked.

"Why don't we find out?" Jaco pulled his pistol and looked at the others. "Let's ride in, makin' a lot of noise 'n shootin' up the town. Anyone you see out in the street, kill 'im."

The others pulled their pistols and looked over at their leader, waiting for orders.

"Let's go!" Jaco shouted, firing the pistol toward the town.

The twelve men of the Kingdom Come Gang started forward at a gallop.

Just as they entered town, they saw a woman heading to the barn with a milking stool in one hand and the milk bucket in the other. Frightened by the sound of gunfire and thundering hoofbeats, she dropped stool and bucket and started running back toward the house.

"Kill her!" Jaco shouted, following his own order by shooting toward the woman.

Several of the riders fired at the same time and the woman fell, bleeding from a dozen bullet wounds.

A small group of workers had gathered outside the freight wagon warehouse, waiting for it to open. None of them were armed. They were more curious than alarmed by the unusual activity of the riders coming into town.

"Kill them!" Jaco shouted, and he began firing at the workers. The other riders of the Kingdom Come Gang followed suit, and the young, inexperienced workers were cut down like sheep in a slaughtering pen.

A few of the townspeople came out into the street, many still in their nightgowns and nightshirts. Seeing what was happening, they retreated quickly back into their houses.

While the early risers were now lying in the street dead or gravely wounded, Jaco turned his attention to the townspeople. "People of Runnels!" he shouted. "I want you out of your houses! All of you! Turn out into the street, now!"

No one came.

Jaco looked over at Dingo, who was holding a flaming torch. Jaco pointed to the roof of the general store. "Burn it down," he ordered.

Dingo tossed the flaming brand onto the shake roof. It caught fire and, within a few moments, the entire building was ablaze.

Jaco fired a few shots into the air. "Now, if you people don't come out into the street right now like I ordered you to, I'm goin' to burn down ever' buildin' in this town. Do you understand me? Ever buildin' in the town is goin' to be burnt down, if you don't come into the street."

Hesitantly, fearfully, the people of the town started going outside.

"Well now, you're finally beginnin' to get smart," Jaco noticed that they had stopped in front of a restaurant. "Who owns this restaurant?"

"I own it," a man said, stepping down from the porch. Unlike most of the others, he was dressed and wearing an apron.

"I want you to fix breakfast for us."

"Yes, sir, I'd be glad to. Breakfast is a quarter apiece. How many of you are there?"

"It don't matter how many of us there are, this mornin' breakfast is free."

"Why, sir, I can't give you a free meal. I'm a businessman," the restaurant owner protested.

Jaco looked out over all the people he had called outside. He saw one old man with wrinkled skin, white hair, and a long, white beard. He shot him, and the man died with a look of shock on his face.

Screams and shouts of alarm came from several of those gathered on the street.

"Let me tell you what I'm goin' to do, Mr. Restaurant Owner," Jaco said. "I'm goin' to start killin' people, 'n I'm goin' to keep on a-killin' people until you get back inside 'n start cookin' our breakfast. How many I kill depends on how long it takes you to get back inside."

"No! No!" the restaurant owner shouted, holding both his hands out. "Don't kill nobody else! I'm a-goin' back inside now 'n I'm a-goin' to start in a-cookin' your breakfast."

"And you ain't goin' to charge nothin' for it," Jaco repeated.

"No, sir. I ain't goin' to charge you nothin' a-tall."

"You're a good man." Jaco turned to the others. "This man just saved your lives . . . all of you. So I think you need to give him a lot of business after we leave."

"Ha!" Putt said. "He owes us a free breakfast on account of you drummin' up business for 'im."

Over breakfast of bacon, eggs, and fried potatoes, Jaco addressed all his men. "Blue, after we get through here, you, Larry, and Lenny go to the bank. Have the banker open his vault and clean it out. Clean out the cash drawers, too. Then, kill whoever is left in the bank."

"All right," Putt said.

"Dingo, I got somethin' special I want you to do. I want you to take three, maybe four more men with you and kill fifteen or twenty people."

"Anyone in particular?"

289

"No, it don't make no never mind who it is . . . as long as we kill a bunch of 'em. The more we kill, the more people will be afraid of us. And the more people are afraid of us, the less chance anyone is goin' to try and go agin' us. You all right with that?"

Dingo grinned. "Yeah. That'll be fun."

Jaco nodded. "I thought you might like that." He picked out the former law man. "Mattoon, I want you and Cyr to visit every store and select the best merchandise the store has to offer. I also want you to visit every house and take all the jewels and money you can find. If anyone protests, kill them."

"Where you goin' to be, Jaco?" Putt asked.

"I'm goin' to be right out front, drinkin' coffee 'n enjoyin' the show."

When the Kingdom Come Gang rode out of town early that afternoon, they had sacks filled with money and anything else they could find of value. Behind them, more than thirty people lay dead and a dozen buildings were burning.

Johnny Dane was feeling particularly satisfied. One of the dead lying on the street behind them was a sixteen-year-old girl. He had kept her alive until he was finished with her, so he could enjoy the terror in her eyes.

It had been good. So good.

Eagle Pass
Totally unaware of the terrible drama taking place some fifty miles north of them, Jason, Melissa, and Megan greeted Duff and the others warmly.

"I thought Cal would be here to meet us," Duff said. "I expect I had better make arrangements to get cattle into the holding pens until he gets here."

"Are you Mr. MacCallister?" a man asked, approaching him.

"Aye. And you would be?"

"My name is Taylor. I work for Mr. Hanson. I've done sent word that his cows is here. He'll be along directly, I reckon."

"We're here now, Mr. Taylor," an English-accented voice said as Hanson approached them. "Hello, Duff, Miss Parker. Good morning Sheriff and Mrs. Bowles." Hanson shook hands with Duff and the sheriff. Then, seeing Elmer and Wang, he shook hands with them as well.

After the greeting, he turned to Taylor. "Mr. Taylor, if you would like to join Mr. Barnes and the others, I think we can eschew the holding pens, and start straight away to get the beasts relocated to the ranch."

"Bless you," Taylor said.

Hanson looked at the cowboy with a confused expression on his face. "Was the thought of putting the cattle in the pens so daunting that you feel you must bless me?"

"What? No, I was just blessin' you 'cause you sneezed."

"I beg your pardon. When did I sneeze?"

Duff laughed. "I think it was the word *eschew*."

Taylor nodded. "Yeah. You mean that wasn't a sneeze?"

It was Hanson's turn to laugh. "No, dear boy, that wasn't a sneeze. But I thank you for your response, anyway."

"Well, if it warn't no sneeze, what was it?"

"*Eschew* is a perfectly good word. It means that we will avoid using the holding pens."

"Yes, sir. Well, that deserves a bless you, as well. I expect I'd better get over there 'n start helpin' Barnes get all them cows offen the train."

Hanson shook his head as Taylor left. "How can two nations approach the same language with such vast differences?"

As the cattle were off-loaded from the cars, Elmer and Taylor, who was the ranch foreman, kept a head count by tying a knot in a strip of rawhide for every tenth cow.

When a strip had ten knots, they started another strip. The final tally was 306, the additional cows added as an extra measure in case any were lost along the way.

None were lost, and Duff threw them in as a bonus.

Three hours later, Hanson's cowboys had all the cattle off-loaded from the train. Since the depot was on the east end of town and Regency Ranch was seven miles from the west end of town, it was necessary to drive the herd down Main Street right through the middle of town.

Because Black Angus was a new breed, many of the people of the town who had not seen the first half of the herd watched with keen interest as the black, hornless creatures passed by.

"What kind of cows did you say them was?" someone asked.

"They're what you call Black Angus, 'n there ain't no better tastin' beef anywhere in the world," Elmer replied.

"You don't say. Well, I'd love to eat me somethin' other 'n pork 'n stringy beef all the time," another man added.

Near Shumla
On Bullhead Trail, approximately ten miles east of Shumla, Matt Garrison was driving

a single wagon down a rutted road. His wife Jennie sat on the seat beside him while their ten-year-old-boy Ethan was riding in the back, wedged in between boxes of clothing, a few items of furniture, household goods, a plow, and several more farming implements.

"Do you think we'll have any trouble farming out here?" Jennie asked.

"Trouble? Why should we have trouble? Look around you. Things are growing everywhere. I think we'll make a good crop the very first year. I plan to grow cotton."

"I'm not talking about whether or not we can make a crop. You're a good farmer, Matt. I've seen that. But Uncle Jake says this is cattle country. I'm worried that ranchers won't be welcoming us."

Matt chuckled. "Don't worry about that. I've got that all planned out. I bought fifteen hundred acres from Philbin, 'n I don't plan on usin' more 'n eighty acres. Leastwise, not for some time. I figure to let the cattlemen use the rest of the acreage for grazin'. That'll do two things. One is, it'll get us in good with the ranchers, so's there won't be no trouble. Another thing is, it'll keep the weeds from overtakin' the land so that when I'm ready to farm more, it'll all be there for us."

"I wish you had waited until there were

two or three more wagons wantin' to go in the same direction," Jennie said. "I would feel a lot safer."

"We couldn't wait for another wagon," Matt said. "You heard what Philbin said. If we don't take possession of it within a month, the land will revert to the county."

"So, what if it does?" Jennie replied.

Matt looked at his wife as if she had lost her mind. "This is good land, Jennie. It can set us up for life. Most people go a lifetime and don't get a chance like this."

"I'm just worried about what Mr. Philbin said about why he left. He said the town had turned into an outlaw town."

"Why would that bother us? We won't be livin' in town. We'll be livin' out in the country."

"But we'll need to be goin' into town from time to time for supplies 'n such," Jennie said.

"There ain't nothin' says we got to go into Shumla. I've looked on the maps. They's a town named White's Mine that ain't but about twelve miles farther away, 'n it's in the opposite direction so we wouldn't never even have to go through Shumla."

"I wonder what the house is like?"

"Philbin said the house was in good shape when he left it. There's even some furniture in it that comes with it. Why, I'll just bet we can move into it in no more 'n a couple hours."

Jennie reached over to take Matt's hand. "You're right. It will be nice to have a place all our own."

CHAPTER TWENTY-SIX

Eagle Pass

Hanson invited his new friends from Chugwater and Eagle Pass to his ranch for dinner that evening, and to prepare the meal, he'd hired the sous-chef from the Rustic Rock. The meal was a great success, and afterward they gathered in the parlor where the Englishman surprised them by playing several classical pieces on the piano.

"You play beautifully," Melissa said. "I had no idea you had such talent."

"It was my intention, at one time, to be a concert pianist," Hanson said. "But, alas, that was not to be."

"Why not?"

"I am the . . . or I was, the Heir Presumptive to the Earl of Warwick. Members of the peerage do not engage in such pedestrian pursuits as concert pianists."

"You said you were. You mean you aren't the heir anymore?" Megan asked.

Hanson smiled and shook his head. "I'm afraid not. One is not allowed to keep a title in the United States."

"Oh. Are you sorry you came here?" Melissa asked.

"Not at all, my dear lady. I gladly gave up my title and commission to live here in this marvelous country. How could anyone not want to live in a place as vibrant and alive as America? Duff, you having come from Scotland, you must feel the same way."

"Aye." Duff chuckled. "It pains me to find myself in agreement with an Englishman, but agree I must. 'Tis no country on earth like the United States, and while I wasn't born here, 'tis here that I call home, now. But we aren't the only ones who have left our native land to come to America." He glanced toward Wang.

"Yes," Wang said. "I too, am glad to be in America."

"Wang, why don't you show some o' them magic tricks I've seen you do?" Elmer said. "I expect these people would enjoy seein' them."

"You are a magician?" Timmy asked, excited by the prospect.

"They are called illusionists," Hanson said. "There is no such thing as magic. But a good illusionist can make you think it's

298

magic. Please, Mr. Wang, do give us a demonstration."

"Yes," Timmy said. "Please do."

"Jin ze de Shaolin moshu," Wang said, looking at Elmer.

"They will never know," Elmer replied. "Go ahead, there is no danger."

"Yes, no danger," Wang said. "I will do."

"Good!" Hanson said.

"Blindfold me please," Wang said. Jason applied a blindfold, then satisfied himself that Wang couldn't see.

"I ask all of you to find something in this house, something small enough that you can hold it. Cover it so that no one can see it and only you know what it is. Then come back. Madam Bowles, I ask that you stay here and keep an eye on me, so that others will know I have not seen."

Melissa agreed, and the others left to find an object, then returned. Everyone had their object covered, Duff, Elmer, and Jason had whatever they were holding, covered by a hat. Hanson and Timmy covered their objects with a table napkin, Megan had her object covered by a stole from her dress.

"They are all back," Melissa said.

Wang turned his back to them. "Point to someone. Do not tell me who you have pointed to," Wang said.

Melissa pointed to Jason.

"You have pointed to your husband. He is holding the picture of a man. It is Mr. Cal Hanson. He is sitting on a white horse, and he is wearing the uniform of a British officer."

Jason pulled the picture from his hat, and the others gasped in surprise.

Wang did that successfully with everyone else. Then, to the applause of all, he turned back around and removed his blindfold.

"You did not choose anything," Wang said. "Please tell your husband what you would have chosen."

Melissa whispered something to Jason, speaking so quietly that no one else could hear her.

"You would choose a silver spoon from the dining table," Wang said.

"How the hell can you do that?" Jason asked with a gasp. "That's exactly what she said!"

"I learned many things in the temple," Wang said without further elaboration.

Shumla

True to her word, the woman Ernie Taylor knew as Peggy left Eagle Pass for Shumla. Two miles outside town, she stopped and changed out of the jeans and shirt she had worn for the ride, into a very low-cut and formfitting dress. She applied makeup with the artistry of a master.

"Dancer," she said to the horse she was riding. "Say good-bye to Peggy. We're going to leave her here. Say hello to . . . hmm . . . who shall I be? What about Belle? Yes, I shall be Belle."

She mounted the horse. "All right, Dancer, let's get Belle to town."

The sight of a woman riding into town alone was unusual enough to draw a great deal of interest. The fact that she was a very pretty woman caused even more attention, and when the people of the town saw that the dress she was wearing was an obvious advertisement for her profession, being that of a lady of the evening, the interest grew even more intense. Men began pouring out of the buildings that fronted the main street, hurrying down the street on each side, looking on in curiosity and unrestrained lust.

Belle stopped in front of the Red Dog Saloon and smiled when she saw that a least a dozen or more men had followed her. She leaned forward to pat her horse on the neck. That action, by design, showed the tops of her breasts almost all the way to the nipples. Looking out at the crowd of men, she put on her prettiest smile. "Tell me, gentlemen, do any of you know where I might find a lady named Sherazade? She is a friend of mine."

"Sherazade a lady?" one of the men called from the crowd, and several of the others laughed.

"Is that a nice thing for you to say?" Belle asked, rolling her lips out in a pout. "I've been thinking about moving here, but if that is the way you treat ladies, then I may have to change my mind."

"Cooper didn't mean nothin' by it," one of the other men said. "Did you, Cooper?"

Several of the others glared at Cooper.

"No, I didn't mean nothin' by it. If you ask me, Miss Sherazade is a lady. Same as all the ones that works for her."

"What are you lookin' for Sherazade for?" asked the man who had chastised Cooper.

"Oh, I thought I might join her in providing" — she paused for a moment, then leaning ever farther forward, finished the sentence is a husky, breathy tone — "a pleasurable experience for any gentleman who is willing to pay for it."

Upon hearing that, the men cheered, whistled, and applauded.

"Unless, of course, this town has an ordnance against pleasure," Belle said.

"Miss, we ain't got a ordnance against

anything," Cooper said, and everyone laughed.

"Of course, I only intend to entertain real gentlemen. Do you think you could be gentlemen?"

"I can be the dandiest, most sissified gentleman you done ever seen." Holding one hand out, Cooper curled his finger.

"Oh, I want a gentleman, not a girly-man," Belle said, and again the others laughed.

"What's your name?" one of the men in the crowd asked.

"My name is Belle."

"Well, Miss Belle, once you meet up with Sherazade, how soon do you think it will be before you start . . . uh . . . doin' business?"

"Oh, I plan to start working right away," Belle replied enthusiastically. "I see no reason to delay, do you?"

"No, none a-tall." The one who'd asked her was already rubbing himself in anticipation.

The Garrison farm
It took Matt, Jennie, and Ethan the rest of the day to get the wagon unloaded and the house ready to move in to.

"I'm glad he left the stove here," Jennie said.

303

"I checked the pump. It's pumpin' water just fine," Matt said.

Jennie crossed her arms across her chest and looked around. "Oh, Matt, I'm sorry I was ever against this. Why, it's really nice. All it will take are some curtains and maybe a little paint here and there."

"And fixin' those two boards that's missin' on the front porch," Matt said. "I can get them put back in no time."

"Our own house," Jennie said, her eyes blazing in excitement.

"More 'n our own house. This here is our own *land*. Why, by this time next year, we'll have made a fine crop of cotton —"

"And don't forget the garden," Jennie said. "You can't eat cotton."

Ethan laughed. "Mama, I don't think Papa meant we was goin' to eat cotton."

Jennie ran her hand through her son's hair and laughed. "I know that. That's why we're going to put in a garden. The finest garden you've ever seen. We'll have potatoes and corn, beans and peas, carrots, lettuce, celery, beets, tomatoes and cucumbers, bell peppers."

"And maybe some watermelon?" Ethan asked.

"You want watermelon?"

"Yes, ma'am!"

"Then we'll have watermelon."

"First thing we're goin' to have to do is get us a milk cow and some chickens," Matt suggested.

"Oh, Matt, you mean we'll have to go into that awful town?"

"No, I told you about White's Mine, remember? It's a mite farther away than Shumla, but I think I'd just as soon stay away from Shumla as much as is possible."

"Yes," Jennie said. "I agree."

Eagle Pass

Jason, Melissa, and Timmy had come to the depot to see Duff, Megan, and Elmer off for their return trip to Wyoming.

Elmer and Timmy were on the opposite side of the waiting room. Timmy was playing with the intricate ball in a hoop toy Elmer had carved for him.

"Elmer and Timmy seem to have hit it off quite well," Jason said.

"Aye, so it would appear," Duff said.

"You wouldn't think so, would you? I mean, a man like Elmer, you wouldn't think he would have much interest in spending any time with a young boy."

Duff looked at him. "Why would you say that?"

"I don't know. It's just that Elmer seems a

rather odd sort."

"He seems sad," Melissa said. "As if he has some great tragedy in his past."

"I've no doubt but that he has," Duff said. "I'll say this, he has the most storied past of anyone I know or have ever known."

A whistle announced the approach of the northbound train.

"Well, this is it," Duff said. "I thank you for being such gracious hosts."

Duff and Jason shook hands as Megan and Melissa embraced. Then Melissa and Duff embraced as did Megan and Jason. Wang, who had been silent for the entire length of time, stood off to one side, the expression on his face as inscrutable as always.

As they started to board the train, the conductor stopped them. "This is a first-class car. No Chinamen allowed on this car. He'll have to ride in the immigrant car."

"I have paid for a first-class ticket for him," Duff said.

"You can write to the railroad, and I'm sure they will refund you the price of your ticket. But that Chinaman will not be allowed in a first-class car."

"Look here, I'm Sheriff Bowles, and these people are friends of mine," Jason said in protest. "All of them are, including Mr. Wang."

"Sheriff, I don't care if you are the governor," the conductor said. "This is the rule of the Texas and Pacific Railroad, and there's nothing I can do about it."

Duff turned to his friend. "Jason, would you be for doing me a favor, lad? Would you send a telegram ahead to San Antonio and arrange for a private car? I'll not be for having my friend treated so."

"I'll be glad to."

"Until then, I'll be riding in the immigrant car."

"So will I," Elmer said.

"Megan, there's no need for you to give up your first-class ticket,"

Megan smiled. "Duff MacCallister, you just try and keep me from that car."

"But I don't understand," the conductor said as the four of them started toward the back of the train.

"I don't expect you would understand," Melissa said, beaming. "But I've never been more proud of my sister."

Chapter Twenty-Seven

Unlike the cushioned seats of the regular cars and the even more plush seating in the first-class cars, the immigrant car had benches made of wooden slats. The seats were crowded close together so that there was very little legroom.

More than two languages were spoken, and the car smelled of unwashed bodies and exotic, odiferous foods.

"Mr. MacCallister, you should not ride here," Wang said. "I am all right here, but you are a *zhòngyìyuán,* a gentleman, and Miss Parker is *guìfùrén,* a gentlewoman. This is no place for you."

Elmer nodded. "Wang is right, Duff. You and Miss Parker go on back up to the first-class car. I'll stay back here with Wang."

"We'll all stay here," Duff said pointedly.

Wang put his hands together, prayer-like, and dipped his head. "You are not only my boss, you are my honored friend."

The four took their seats, though they were unable to get them all together. Elmer had to sit a few rows separated from the others. Looking out the windows, they saw that Jason, Melissa, and Timmy had moved down on the platform to better able to wave good-bye to them.

The waves between Elmer and Timmy were particularly enthusiastic.

Elmer was napping, his head bobbing with the movement of the train.

Megan chuckled as she pointed to him. "How can he possibly sleep on seats like this? Do you think Timmy wore him out?"

"He may have. Timmy is a young man who is brimming with energy, and Elmer is a man who is, as they say, coming into the ripeness of his years."

Megan laughed. "What a quaint way to say that he is getting old. But you had better not let him hear you say such a thing."

Even as they were talking about him, Elmer Gleason was lost in a dream.

He was walking behind a mule, watching the dirt fold away from the plowshare as it opened a deep, new furrow. His nine-year-old brother was walking a few yards in front of him, picking up rocks that might be hit by the plow and tossing them aside. Half the field had already been tilled, and the coal-black dirt glistened with the nutrients that made the soil so fertile.

Elmer looked toward the two-story white house where they all lived and at the barn, granary, and machine shed that made up the Gleason farm in Jackson County, Missouri. The windows in the house were shining brightly in the sunlight; first silver, then gold, then red. The color spread from the windows to the side of the house, then to the roof, and then to the other buildings. But as the color intensified, Elmer realized that he wasn't seeing reflected sunlight . . . what he was seeing was flames. The house, barn, and all the outbuildings were engulfed in a blazing inferno!

Elmer looked away from the burning buildings and saw his brother lying in a pool of blood. The Kansas Redlegs, firing pistols and rifles into the air, were shouting and laughing. On the ground were the bloody bodies of his brother, mother, and father.

"No!" Elmer shouted.

"Elmer, are you all right?" Duff's calm voice asked.

Elmer awakened with a start and saw that Duff had come to his seat and was looking down at him. Outside sounds were intruding . . . the rattle and squeak of a train in motion, the rhythmic clicking of wheels over track joints, the conversations of other passengers. Time and place returned and he realized that it wasn't pre-war Missouri . . . it was post-war Texas.

"Are you all right?" Duff asked again.

Elmer ran his hand across his face as if wiping the sleep away. "Yeah." He sat up straight in the seat. "Yeah, I'm all right."

Duff chuckled. "I think you might have been dreaming."

"Yeah," Elmer agreed. He thought, but didn't say aloud, that it was the boy who had brought on the dreams. Timmy was about the same age as his brother Wes had been when the Jayhawkers killed him and his parents and burned the farm.

"You want to come back and join Megan and me? I'm sure we can convince the gentleman across the aisle from us to change seats with you, if I make it worth his while."

"Nah. I don't want to be intrudin' on the talk between young folks." Elmer smiled. "Especially, you two. Why, you might be talkin' 'bout gettin' married 'n all, 'n I sure wouldn't want to get in the way of that."

Duff laughed again and put his hand on Elmer's shoulder. "Well, if your dreams get too bad, you can always come visit with us."

Elmer nodded as Duff returned to his seat.

"Is everything all right with Elmer?" Megan asked.

"Aye. 'Twas a bad dream, I think, and nothing more."

"A bad dream? I wonder what it was about."

"I'm not sure you would want to know," Duff said. "I'm not sure I would want to know. There is no telling what devils one might find in his past. For them to still torment a man like Elmer, they must be bad indeed.

After Duff walked away, Elmer looked out the window and remembered.

He was with Bloody Bill Anderson, and they were pillaging a small town in Missouri. Pistols, rifles, and carbines roared as gun smoke roiled up over the town in an acrid smelling, blue-gray cloud.

By noon the small town resembled a smoking funeral pyre with a large portion of the town's business and residential districts burned or still burning.

They had been pursued into the town by one hundred Union soldiers, but once the Yankees realized the tide had turned, many of them tried to run. For the most part, running did nothing to save them, but merely provided additional entertainment for Anderson's Raiders. His men on horseback chased them down, then killed them without compunction.

Elmer had been shooting as well, but he killed only two and he justified the shootings by the fact that they were armed and were shooting at him. Unable to watch the unmitigated carnage going on around him, he rode between two houses in order to get off the main street.

In the back of one of the houses, he saw a woman with her skirt spread out backed up against the house by a man that he presumed to be her husband. He looked directly at her, and the woman stared defiantly back at him.

"Anything back there, Gleason?" one of the Bushwhackers called out, shouting from the street.

Elmer stared at the woman's face for a moment longer, admiring her courage and appreciating her beauty. Neither of them said a word.

"Gleason?" the Bushwhacker called again.

"Nothing back here, Cyr," Elmer replied. "Not a thing." To the woman he said, "Just stay back here. And keep quiet."

"Thank you. God bless you," the woman said, crossing herself.

■ ■ ■ ■

Even as Elmer was remembering that woman in Missouri, he saw a woman on the train crossing herself. It startled him. He could almost believe that the woman sitting in the back of the train car was the same woman he was just thinking about. He knew that couldn't be. He'd seen her over twenty years ago. The woman he had seen then would be much older than the woman he was looking at now.

He turned his attention to Duff, Megan, and Wang. Duff and Megan were talking and, upon occasion, laughing. Wang was sitting silently, the expression on his face unreadable. They were good people. He didn't deserve to have such good people as his friends.

When they reached San Antonio, Duff saw a private car sitting off on a side track and smiled in the realization that Jason had managed to make the arrangements for him. As he and the others left the immigrant car, he saw a rather self-important-looking man, wearing the jacket and cap of a railroad official, standing by the Wagner Palace car, studying all who detrained. He was holding a piece of paper in his hand, which Duff took to be a lease agreement for the car.

He counted out one thousand dollars. "Wang, if you would, go make the arrangements for the private car," he said, handing Wang the money and pointing to the uniformed railroad official.

Wang nodded, took the money, and approached the official.

"Whatever you want, you're just going to hold it for a moment," the official said. "I have some business to attend to."

"Why do you watch that car?" Wang asked.

"I told you, Chinaman, don't bother me now. If you got business, go into the depot and take care of it. But stay on the immigrant side."

"Thank you," Wang said with a nod. He left the official standing by the first-class car and went into the depot, being careful to stay in the immigrant section. He stepped up to the counter.

"Yes, can I help you?" a well-dressed man asked.

"Yes, please."

"What can I do for you?"

"I wish to pay for the private car."

"What?" the man asked, a surprised look on his face. "Look here, are you talking about the car on the side track?"

"I believe it is one thousand dollars?"

"That's what it is, all right. Do you have one thousand dollars?"

"I do."

The official behind the counter frowned. "I don't understand. Why didn't Arnie come in here with you?"

"I do not know Arnie."

"He's standing out there on the platform." Walking over to the window, the official pointed to the man Wang had approached earlier. "There he is. You should have gone to him."

"He would not speak with me. I think he is waiting for someone in the first-class car."

The man laughed. "Yes, he would be. Look at the dumb idiot still standing there. Come along with me. I'll get you all fixed up. Are you to be the only passenger?"

"No, there are three others."

"Where are they?"

"They are waiting. They rode on the immigrant car, as I did."

The man laughed again. "This is funnier 'n hell."

Once they stepped out onto the platform, Arnie came toward them. "Mr. Scott, you may as well tell the engineer to go on. Whoever was supposed to pick up the private car didn't show." Seeing Wang, he glared at him. "What are you hanging around for, Chinaman? Didn't I tell you to take care of your business inside?"

"He did take care of it inside," Scott said.

"Oh, Mr. Scott, I'm sorry. When I sent him inside, I had no idea he would bother you."

"Get the private car attached, would you, Arnie?"

"What for? I told you nobody showed."

"The car is for this gentleman," Scott said, indicating Wang.

Duff had seen Wang dismissed, and he had followed what was going on. He laughed at the expression on the face of the man who had been watching for the first-class passenger to disembark.

Shumla

Jaco was sitting at a table in the back of the saloon, playing a game of solitaire, when Sherazade came over to talk to him.

"Jaco, we've got a problem."

"What kind of problem?"

"It's Peg . . . uh, Belle, the new girl.

"What about her?"

"She's not like my other girls. She's a little more refined. She's not used to being treated the way your men are treatin' her."

Jaco laughed. "A refined soiled dove.

317

That's something new."

"Yes, well, she wasn't always such. I guess because of that, some of you men are findin' her ways a little strange and they've hit her a few times. I wish you'd tell your men not to do that."

"If my men are hitting her, she probably brought it on herself. I don't need to be talking to my men. You need to be talking to her. Tell her not to try and come across as somethin' so high 'n fancy, 'n more 'n likely my men will quit hitting her."

"I just wish you would help," Sherazade said.

"When you women take it in mind to be soiled doves, you know what you're lettin' yourself in for, same as we do when we start ridin' the outlaw trail. Now, don't bother me with any more foolishness." Jaco made a dismissive wave with his hand, and though Sherazade looked as if she might say something else, she held her tongue, then turned and walked away.

Jaco returned to his game of solitaire.

"I need to talk to you," someone else said, approaching Jaco's table. It was Rafferty, owner of the grocery store.

"Hell's bells," Jaco said, slapping one of the cards down on the table. "Can't a man get a little peace around here?"

"Well, you are the mayor."

"All right. What is it? What do you want?"

"I just thought I'd let you know that I'm goin' to be runnin' out of groceries soon, and you'd better do somethin'. 'Cause if this town runs out of groceries, things is goin' to get pretty ugly."

"How do you get your groceries?"

"Normally, they come by train to Eagle Pass, then Tucker Freight brings them to us by wagon. But there don't nobody want to come into Shumla, now. I mean, not with us bein' a outlaw town 'n all."

"I'll take care of it," Jaco said.

"When?"

"How many days of groceries do you think you've got left?"

"I don't know. A week, I reckon. Could be maybe a week and a half."

"Then it ain't a big deal yet, is it?"

"Not yet. But it's goin' to be."

"Like I told you, I'll take care of it."

Chapter Twenty-Eight

As Rafferty left, Val Cyr approached the table. "Hey, Jaco, you know the Philbin ranch?"

Jaco found himself needing a black eight, and he looked through the facedown cards until he found one. Slipping it out from the pile, he put it on the red nine. "Ha," he said as he connected an entire string of cards to it, opening another space. "Yeah, I know it. Only it ain't the Philbin place no more. It's my place. I got me a quitclaim deed on it."

"Yeah, well, there's somebody livin' there now."

Jaco looked up, irritated by the information. "What do you mean somebody is livin' there? There ain't nobody goin' to live there without I tell 'em they can live there."

"Yeah, that's what I thought, too. But someone's livin' there."

Jaco needed a red queen, and again, he had no compunction about mining the facedown cards until he found it.

"You shoulda burnt that house down the moment Philbin moved away," Cyr said. "That way there wouldn't o' been nobody that come to live in it."

"It ain't too late to burn the house down. It's too early."

"Too early? What do you mean, too early?"

"We'll wait until it's dark tonight." Jaco made the last connection of the cards. "Ha! I won again."

The Garrison farm, 11:30 P.M.
Ten-year-old Ethan opened his eyes, puzzled by what he was seeing. The wall in his bedroom was glowing orange. Turning in his bed, he saw a brighter glow through the window.

He got up and moved quickly to the window, and saw that the barn was on fire. "Pa!" he yelled. "Pa! The barn! The barn is on fire!"

Ethan ran out of his room and saw that his father was already responding to the alarm. Though he was still dressed in his long johns, he ran to the front door. "How in the world could the barn catch on fire?"

His question was answered as soon as he opened the door. At least four riders were illuminated by the light of the burning barn.

321

He stepped out onto the front porch. "Here! What do you men think you are doing?" he shouted angrily.

"Mister, you're trespassin' on land that ain't your'n," one of the riders called back.

"This here is too my land, 'n I got the deed to prove it!" Matt held out his arm and pointed. "Now you men get off my land!"

Watching through a window, Ethan saw a muzzle flash, then heard a gunshot. Matt tumbled back into the house in the glow of the burning barn, which had cast a golden bubble of light through the whole front of the house.

"Pa!"

"Matt!" Jennie screamed.

"Get out of here, now," Matt said in a strained voice. "Go out through the back door."

They could hear the screams of the terrified horses.

"Pa, the horses. They're still in the barn. If we don't get them out, they'll get all burnt up."

"Leave the horses," Matt said. "Jennie, bring me my rifle, then take the boy and go, like I told you."

"I can't leave you here. Besides, we're not dressed."

"I'm done for anyway," Matt said. "There can't no doctor do anythin' for me, even if I could live long enough to get to a doctor. Now, please, Jennie, if you care anythin' at all for me, do what I say. Bring me my gun, then you 'n Ethan skedaddle on out the back!"

"Ethan, get dressed as fast as you can," Jennie said. "I'll get your pa's rifle and my own clothes."

As soon as the rifle was put in Matt's hand, he began firing through the front door. As he was shooting, Ethan and Jennie were getting dressed. By now the screaming of the horses had stopped.

"You 'n your family better come on out of there now," a voice called. "On account of, if you don't come out right now, we aim to burn you out."

Matt fired again. "Go, please go," he said, his voice much weaker. "I can't hold on much longer."

"You heard what they said, Matt," Jennie said. "They're goin' to burn the house down. I'm not goin' to leave you alone in a burning house."

Matt didn't answer.

"Didn't you hear what I said? I'm not going to leave you in a burning house!"

Matt still didn't answer, and Jennie moved

closer to him. She saw that his eyes, though still open, were fixed in a blank stare.

He was dead.

"Matt!" she screamed.

"Pa?"

A blazing torch was tossed onto the front porch, and as soon as it landed, the flames leaped up.

Somewhere, Jennie found the courage she needed, and she reached for Ethan's hand. "Your father is dead. Come, Ethan, let's leave through the back like he said."

"No, Ma, they'll be back there, too."

"We can't stay in this house! It's on fire!"

"I know another way out. It's in here." Ethan raced into his room.

Jennie followed and watched as he lay on his stomach and reached under his bed. "What are you doing?"

"There's a trapdoor here," Ethan said.

"How do you know about this?"

"I found it first night after we moved in. I didn't tell nobody about it, 'cause I've gone through it sometimes when you 'n Pa thought I was in bed. You ain't mad it me for that, are you, Ma?"

"No, Darlin', I'm not mad at you. I'm proud of you."

Ethan and his mother dropped down through the trapdoor then crawled under the house and he pointed to a natural crevice. "This here draw will take us behind the machine shed, and they won't never even see us. You have to stay real low."

"All right. You lead the way," Jennie said.

"You folks must be gettin' awful hot in there!" a voice called. His shout was followed by high-pitched laughter.

"What are you goin' to do? Just stay in there and burn up?"

The voice was ameliorated by distance. Ethan and his mother were at least a hundred and fifty feet away from the burning house and from those who had the house surrounded.

The fire cooked off the rounds that remained in Matt's rifle.

"Damn! They shot themselves!" someone whined.

Nobody had seen them. When they reached the back of the machine shed, they dropped down into a ravine and followed it for more than a mile before they stopped.

Not until then did Jennie allow herself to cry over her dead husband.

Fredericksburg, Texas
Since Crump and Forney were wanted men in Wyoming, they had made the decision to go to Texas. Neither had ever been there, so

they were sure they wouldn't be known. After several days of travel, which they financed with the money the Englishman had given them when they'd tried to rob him, they were sitting in a saloon in Fredericksburg.

Conversation floated around them and they learned about the town of Shumla.

"Ain't no law there," they were told. "Ain't no law there at all."

"What if someone was a wanted man?" Crump asked the man standing next to him at the bar. "Not me or Jones. We ain't neither one of us wanted. But say someone was wanted up in Wyoming or someplace like that?"

"Or Alabama or, say, Ohio?" Forney added. "Me 'n Jones ain't wanted in none of them places, neither."

"I thought he was Jones." The man pointed to Crump.

"We both are," Crump said quickly. "Only we ain't no kin."

"Well it don't matter where you're wanted, not even Texas. They don't allow no law to come into Shumla. It's called a outlaw town, 'n from what I've heard, there's a fella down there puttin' himself together a gang."

"A gang of what?" Crump asked.

"It's an outlaw town, ain't it? He's puttin'

together a gang of outlaws. I s'pose a man could make hisself quite a bit of money ridin' with an outlaw gang like that. They was a bank holdup a while ago, 'n it's said that the bank robbers got twenty thousand dollars."

Forney whistled. "Twenty thousand dollars? Was it this gang you're a-talkin' about?"

"They don't nobody know for sure, but if you was to ask me, I'd say it was them."

"I say we go to Shumla," Crump said.

"You think whoever it is puttin' together that gang will let us in?" Forney asked.

"Why wouldn't he?"

"Well, we ain't ever actual done anythin' real big."

Crump smiled. "He don't have to know that."

On the road to White's Mine

"Mama, I'm hungry," Ethan said. He and his mother were afoot on the road, having walked several miles since escaping from the men who had attacked their farm.

"I know you are, darlin', but we're just going to have to keep going until we can find food somewhere."

"You think Pa is in heaven?"

"I know he is. And I know he is very proud

327

of you for finding a way for us to escape."

"What are we goin' to do now? We ain't got no farm, we ain't even got us a place to live."

"As soon as we can find a town, I'll get a job somewhere."

"What kind of job will you get?"

"I don't know. Maybe I can get one at a hotel, cleaning rooms, or with a restaurant, cooking or even washing dishes. You don't worry about that, Ethan. That'll be my worry."

"Someone's comin', Ma!"

"I see them. But they are in a wagon. I don't think the men who killed your father and burned our farm would be coming after us in a wagon."

Despite himself, Ethan chuckled. "No ma'am, I don't reckon they would, either."

The driver of the wagon, seeing woman and a young boy afoot, called out to his team. "Whoa!" he said, pulling back on the reins. He set the brakes on the wagon. "Ma'am, what are you and the boy doin' out here on the road, afoot and all by yourselves?"

"Could you help us, please?" Jennie asked. "Some evil men attacked our farm. They killed my husband, and they burned our home."

"Oh, I'm mighty sorry to hear that. Yes, ma'am, I'll be glad to help you. Come on up into the wagon."

CHAPTER TWENTY-NINE

Eagle Pass

Sheriff Jason Bowles had just poured himself a cup of coffee from the blue steel pot that sat on a grate just outside his office. In the winter, he kept the coffee going on the stove inside, but in the summer the stove put out too much heat. He'd gotten around that by making a concrete fire pit just behind the jail.

"Billy, you want any coffee?" he called through the back cell window to his only prisoner.

A red face with white hair appeared in the window. "You don't reckon I could talk you into puttin' a little whiskey in that, do you?"

"Billy, that's what got you in trouble in the first place."

"What can it hurt, Sheriff? You already got me in jail. And I got the cravin' somethin' awful, right now."

Jason chuckled. "I'll see what I can do."

Taking two cups of coffee back inside, he poured a little whiskey into Billy's cup, then walked over to pass it through the bars.

"Thanks, Sheriff."

At that moment, the front door opened, and Boyd James came in. He drove a freight wagon for Tucker Freight company.

"Hello, Boyd, what brings you here?" Jason asked.

"I picked up a couple people out on the road when I was comin' back from White's Mine. I think maybe you better talk to 'em."

"All right," Jason said, curious as to what Boyd was talking about.

He stepped out front. A woman and a young boy about the age of his own son were sitting on the seat of the wagon. It was obvious that both of them had been crying.

"Ma'am, I'm Sheriff Bowles."

"They killed my husband, Sheriff. They killed my husband, and they burned our house down."

"Why don't you 'n the boy climb down and come inside so you can tell me all about it. I just made some coffee, if you would like some."

She nodded. "Yes, thank you. That would be wonderful."

"You got anything to eat?" the boy asked. "We didn't have no breakfast."

"Ethan, that isn't polite," she scolded.

"You come on in. I'll get something for you to eat."

The two followed Jason into his office, and he pointed out a couple chairs where they could sit. Then he walked over and unlocked the cell.

"Billy, you've got three days left. I'm goin' to let you out early because I want you to go down to Kirby's and get breakfast for these people." He turned to the boy. "I've got a boy about your age, and he loves pancakes. Is that all right for you?"

"I love pancakes, too," Ethan said with a big smile on his face.

"We, uh, weren't able to bring any money with us," the woman said. "I'm afraid we won't be able to pay for the breakfast."

"Don't worry about that. The county will pay for it." Opening the drawer, he took out a dollar bill and handed it to Billy. "Don't you stop for a drink on the way there or back. If you do, I'll keep you in here another month."

"I'll be right back, I promise," Billy said, taking the dollar bill.

"Sheriff, if you've no need for me, I got to report in to Mr. Tucker," Boyd said.

"No need for you to hang around," Jason replied.

As the wagon driver turned to leave, the woman said, "Mr. James. I can't thank you enough for your kindness to my son and me."

"I was glad I could do it, ma'am," Boyd said, touching the brim of his hat.

With Boyd and Billy both gone, Jason was alone with the woman and her son.

"Now, Mrs. —" Jason paused, waiting for the woman to supply the name.

"My name is Jennie, that is, Virginia Garrison. This is my son, Ethan."

"They killed my pa."

Jason turned to Ethan. "Who killed your pa?"

"Those men who came in the middle of the night. They set fire to the barn and when Pa went out onto the porch, they shot him."

"And then they set fire to the house," Jennie said. "With us in it."

"How did you get away?"

Jennie smiled at Ethan, then she reached out to put her hand on his head. "Ethan saved us."

The Garrison farm

Jaco dismounted as soon as he and five of the gang members arrived at the burned-out place. He started poking around through the charred wood of the burned house. "You're sure you didn't see anyone leave?"

"Nobody left," Cyr said. "We were watchin' the front and the back doors. If anyone had left, we woulda seen 'em."

"They wouldn't have just stayed here and burned up in the fire."

"They didn't. We heard shootin' after the fire got to goin' good. We figure the farmer shot the rest of his family, then shot his ownself."

"I suppose." Using a long stick, Jaco moved some of the charred wood to one side and looked under it. "You'd think we woulda found more 'n just one body, though."

"Not back there." Cyr pointed to the back of the house. "The fire got real hot back there. Any bodies that was back there woulda more 'n likely burned up to nothin' more 'n cinders. I doubt you could tell the difference between a burnt body and just a part of the house."

"I suppose you're right. Too bad we had to burn the house, though. I prob'ly coulda got rent for it."

"You wouldn'ta got no rent from this here fella. He claimed that he owned the house, 'n he said he had a deed to prove it."

"He had a deed, huh?" Jaco asked.

"That's what he claimed."

"Ha. Where's his deed now?" Jaco laughed, and the others laughed with him.

Wyatt Mattoon came riding up then with a big smile on his face.

"It's just like you said, Jaco. They's three wagons carryin' groceries from Eagle Pass to White's Mine."

Jaco nodded. "Good job of scoutin'. What do you boys say we take those groceries to Shumla?"

"What will we do with the wagons after we sell the groceries?" Dingo asked.

"We'll sell 'em," Putt said.

Jaco shook his head. "No, we'll burn 'em."

"Why would we burn perfectly good wagons?" Dane asked. "We could prob'ly get pretty good money for 'em."

"We can make good money without worryin' about the wagons. We're goin' to burn 'em," Jaco insisted.

On the road to White's Mine

The three wagons moved slowly but steadily down the road, the clopping sound of hoofbeats providing a rhythmic background to the crunching music of rolling wheels and the creak and rattle of the wagons.

Only the drivers were with the wagons. Sometimes, if the wagons carried a special cargo, like guns or industrial dynamite, an armed guard would accompany the driver, but these wagons were carrying flour, sugar, and canned goods — nothing that would present an attractive target to road agents. The three drivers had no reason to be feeling apprehensive.

As the wagons crested a small rise in the road, they were surprised to see half-a-dozen mounted men in front of them. Seeing that many mounted men wasn't, by itself, that disturbing. What made it disquieting was the fact that all six men were holding guns, and all six guns were pointed toward the wagon drivers.

Gib Crabtree, the lead driver, hauled back on the reins to stop his team. "What do you men want? Why are you pointin' guns at us?" He was a man with a swarthy complexion.

"We want what you have in those wagons," the leader of the group of armed men responded.

"Are you crazy? We ain't got nothin' but groceries in here," Crabtree said.

"You men, climb down offen them wagons, like I said."

"What for? I told you, we ain't carryin' nothin' that would be of any interest to you folks."

"Get down offen them wagons or we'll shoot you and drag you down," the armed man repeated.

Pete, in the second wagon, had had enough. "Damn, Gib, I think them men mean just what they say."

"All right," Gib said. "Climb down, boys. I don't know what they think they're gettin', but ain't no sense in gettin' ourselves kilt over it."

The three drivers climbed down from the wagons, then, by motion of the guns, were directed to the side of the road.

Gib tried once more to get an identity. "Who are you men?"

"You may as well know. My name is Jaco, and we are what the papers are callin' the Kingdom Come Gang."

"Hey, Gib, I've heard of them people!" exclaimed Harry, the third driver.

"Have you now?" Jaco asked, an evil smile spreading across his face. Without another word or provocation, he and the other five armed men began shooting, and the three drivers went down.

"All right. Let's get these wagons back to town."

Crabtree had been hit only once, in the hip. He lay quietly on the ground, not moving a muscle until he heard the wagons pull away. He remained motionless until he could no longer hear them, then he opened his eyes and looked down the road as the last wagon went around a curve and out of sight. "Pete? Harry?" he called. "They're gone." Crabtree stood up then. "Pete? Harry?"

As he looked at them, he realized they weren't going to answer him. Both men were dead.

Shumla

The three wagons rolled to a stop in front of Rafferty's store. Rafferty came out onto the front porch. "Well, I see you managed to get some groceries here. Who do I give the one hundred dollars to?"

"It will be five hundred dollars, and you'll give it to me," Jaco said.

"Five hundred? Are you crazy?"

"We discussed this, remember? You said you were unable to get groceries delivered to you, and I said I would take care of it." Jaco pointed to the three loaded wagons. "I did take care of it, and here are your groceries. Now, pay me the five hundred dollars or I'll use these groceries to start my own store."

"All right, all right. I'll pay you. Like you said, I'll be chargin' more anyway. I'm interested, though. How much did you have to pay for them?"

"What we paid for 'em?" Manny Dingo said from the seat of one of the wagons. "What we paid for 'em was —"

"None of your business," Jaco said sharply, cutting off Dingo in mid-sentence.

Eagle Pass

Joe Lingle was standing on the loading dock at Tucker Freight when he saw someone walking into town. It got his attention right away, because the man wasn't riding. He wasn't walking with an upright stride. He was slightly bent over and holding one of his hands over his hip.

As the walker came closer, Lingle's mere curiosity turned to shocked surprise. The hand over his hip was covered with blood, as were his pants, and the man coming up the road was no mere stranger. It was his friend, Gib Crabtree.

"Mr. Tucker! Mr. Tucker! Come quick!" Lingle shouted as he jumped down from the loading dock and ran toward the wounded Crabtree. "Gib! What happened? Where's your wagon? Where are the others?"

"Dead," Crabtree said with a strained voice. "It was the Kingdom Come Gang.

339

They shot us, and stole the wagons."

"Were you in Maverick County?" Sheriff Bowles asked, having been summoned down to the warehouse.

"No, we was already in Uvalde County." Crabtree winced as the doctor poked around in his wound.

"I'm goin' to have to get the bullet out of there, Mr. Crabtree," the doctor said.

"Yeah, go ahead, Doc," Crabtree said.

"I'm going to send a telegram to the sheriff of Uvalde county and let him know that the Kingdom Come Gang is operating in his county. I wouldn't be surprised if they were the ones that burned out the Garrison farm."

CHAPTER THIRTY

Sheriff Bowles returned to his office. He wasn't surprised to see Cal Hanson because he had sent for him.

"Sheriff, you wanted to see me?"

"How are the men I sent you working out?" Jason asked.

"You chose the men quite wisely," Hanson said. "They are all doing very well. I couldn't ask for better hands."

"How about your house?"

"I beg your pardon?"

"Do you need someone to cook and clean for you?"

"Yes, as a matter of fact, I do need such a person. How did you know that?"

"Mr. Hanson, you are a man living alone. It doesn't take a genius to figure out that you could use a good woman to keep house for you."

"Do you know such a woman?"

"I might. Wait here for a few minutes, and

I'll get her for you." Jason went to his house, where, for the last two days, Jennie Garrison and her son Ethan, had been their guests.

Melissa heard him come inside. "Jason, doesn't the house smell good? Jennie is preparing a pot roast for supper."

"It smells wonderful. Do you enjoy cooking, Mrs. Garrison?"

"You show me a Missouri farm wife who doesn't enjoy cooking, and I'll show you a woman who has no business living on a farm," Jennie replied.

"Would you like a job cooking and cleaning house?"

"Jason, what are you saying?" Melissa asked, with a look of confusion on her face. "You know we can't afford to hire anyone to do anything like that. We certainly couldn't afford to pay what someone like Jennie should be paid."

"I'm not speaking about us," Jason replied. "I'm speaking about Cal Hanson."

The look of confusion was replaced by a wide smile. "Yes," Melissa said, enthusiastically. "Oh, yes. Jennie, this would be a wonderful opportunity for you."

"That is, if you are looking for employment," Jason added.

"Oh, Sheriff Bowles, I am most definitely looking for employment. I've greatly appreciated being your guest these last two days, but I do need to find a way to earn an income for my son and me."

"You and your husband owned your own farm. You wouldn't feel that being a cook and a housekeeper is beneath you?"

"Sheriff, no one is above honest employment," Jennie said resolutely.

Jason chuckled and nodded. "That is exactly what I expected you to say. Come with me. I'll introduce you to His Lordship, Cal Hanson. He will be your employer."

"Wait a minute," Jennie said, holding up her hand. "His Lordship? What are you talking about? What do you mean, His Lordship?"

"Cal Hanson is . . . who did he say he was now?" Jason frowned a moment. "Oh yes, he is the Heir Presumptive to the Earl of Warwick."

"No he isn't, Jason. Not anymore," Melissa said. "He told us that he plans to become a citizen of America, and here, he can't use his title."

"I don't know about working for a lord," Jennie said nervously. "Why, I wouldn't even know how to act around such a person."

"You would just be yourself," Melissa said. "He might be the presumptive heir to

343

a title, but there is nothing presumptuous about him, I guarantee. He is as nice a man as you will ever want to meet."

Jennie met Hanson then returned to the house to check on her pot roast, leaving Hanson and Jason alone.

"I don't know," Hanson said to Jason a few minutes later.

"What is it that you don't know?" Jason asked. "I know she can cook. She's preparing a pot roast right now, and the smell in my house is so good that it'll make you want to eat the leather chair."

Hanson chuckled. "It isn't that, dear boy. I have no doubt as to her culinary qualifications. It's just that I expected someone . . . different."

"Someone different? Different how?"

"By different, I mean someone much older . . . and someone much less attractive."

Jason laughed out loud. "For heaven's sake, you aren't going to complain because she is too pretty, are you?"

Hanson smiled, as well. "No, I suppose not. Now that would really be foolish, wouldn't it?"

"Before she comes to work for you, I think I should tell you a little about her. She and her husband recently arrived here from Missouri. Have you heard of Missouri?"

"I know about Missouri. St. Louis is in Missouri. I passed through it when I came west from New York."

"She and her husband recently arrived from Missouri, and they started farming up in Uvalde County. A few days ago, a gang of outlaws attacked and burned their farm. They also killed her husband, so you need to understand that she is still going through a period of grief."

"Oh, the poor lady, of course she would be," Hanson said. "I will keep that in mind. Do you have any idea who did it?"

"I suspect it was the Kingdom Come Gang."

"Oh, yes, I have read about them in the newspaper. Will you be going after them? It sounds like quite a formidable job for one man."

"This happened in Uvalde County, and I have no jurisdiction there. But if they come into Maverick County, I certainly will raise a posse and go after them."

Chugwater

"How was your trip to Texas?" Biff asked when Duff went into Fiddlers' Green for the first time after returning home.

"It went well," Duff said. "We got all the cows delivered to Mr. Hanson without losing any."

"Well, you can't ask any more than that. The first one is on me. Sort of a welcome home, so to speak." Biff poured the scotch, then corked the bottle.

Duff picked up the drink, held it out toward Biff, then tossed it down. "Ah, Biff m' lad, 'tis truly the nectar of the gods, distilled from the mist on the moors, and aged in hickory kegs in fields of heather."

Biff laughed out loud. "Duff, have you ever kissed that Blarney Stone people talk about?"

"*Och, mon,* has your own dear sweet Scottish wife not told you that the Blarney Stone is for Irish? Not Scots?"

"Irish, English, French, Scot, it makes no difference who it is when you are telling a big one."

Duff chuckled. "Sure 'n you've got me dead to rights there, lad. But 'twas paying you a compliment, I was, for having the intelligence to stock, in your establishment, a drink that is so fine."

After the drink, and exchanging a few pleasantries with some of the other customers in the saloon, Duff bade his friend goodbye, then walked down to Megan's Dress

Emporium. She was with a customer when he went in.

"Oh. I *dinnae* know you were busy. Shall I come back later, then?"

"Don't you dare run away, Mr. MacCallister," Mrs. Matthews said. "I need only to buy a new scarf to go with the new dress Megan is making for me, and she's already selected the one that will do best. I'll just be a minute. I'll not be the reason for you not being able to visit with your lady friend."

"That is very nice of you, Mrs. Matthews. But please, take your time. I'll sit over in the corner 'n read today's newspaper."

"Oh, I'd hate for you to have to do that."

Megan smiled at her customer. "Take my word for it, Edna, you'll not be putting him out. Scotsman that he is, and so unaccustomed to spending money, he doesn't bother to subscribe to the newspaper. He just reads mine."

Duff chuckled. "Aye, I'm afraid the lass knows me too well."

KINGDOM COME GANG
STRIKES AGAIN

Texas Suffering Under
Criminal Activity

Three days ago, while engaged in the peaceful pursuit of business, three freight wagons were set upon by the gang of ruffians known as the Kingdom Come Gang.

Two of the drivers were killed. The third was left for dead, but surely would have been finished off if the outlaws had realized they had not killed him.

The strangest thing about the attack on the wagons was that they were carrying nothing that would normally be of interest to such men. The cargo was foodstuffs, consigned to grocery stores in the town of White's Mine, Texas.

Regency Ranch

Jennie brought Hanson's dinner in and put it on the table before him.

"Oh, Mrs. Garrison, that looks and smells perfectly marvelous," Hanson said. "I believe you said this is called chicken and dumplings?"

"Yes."

"Well, I've never before seen chicken and

dumplings. Chicken, of course, roasted, stewed, even fried. But never anything quite like this." He took a bite of one of the dumplings, then lifting his hand to the side of his mouth, he rubbed his thumb and forefinger together. *"Très délicieux."*

"I beg your pardon?"

"That is French for *very delicious.* I used French because the English language, wonderful though it might be, doesn't have the words to do justice to this extraordinary fare. Only the French language can give it its proper due."

Jennie laughed. "Mr. Hanson, you have the most marvelous way with words of anyone I have ever met."

Hanson stood and gestured toward the table. "Won't you please join me?"

"Oh, no, I . . . I don't think it would be quite proper," Jennie said. "After all, I'm working for you."

"But surely, if you sat at the far end of the table — it is quite long, as you can see — there could be nothing untoward in that."

"Mr. Hanson, I don't know how to thank you for hiring me and giving me a way to make a living and allowing me to live here in such a beautiful house. I just don't want to do anything that would cause any problems for you."

"Nonsense, how could having you dine at my table cause any problems?"

"Mrs. Bowles said you are an English nobleman. I'm just a country girl from Missouri. I'm a commoner."

Hanson laughed. "Believe me, Mrs. Garrison, in the few weeks I have known you, I have been able to observe that there is absolutely nothing common about you. However, if dining with me would make you uncomfortable, please, forget that I ask."

"Thank you."

"No, Mrs. Garrison. I thank you for coming to work for me. As you can see, you are most needed here. And I thank Sheriff Bowles for introducing us."

"I'll leave you to your dinner," Jennie said.

"Give my regards to your son," Hanson said as Jennie withdrew from the room.

Returning to the kitchen, Jennie took her place at the kitchen table with Ethan. He was eating his dinner with gusto. "You know what, Ma?"

"No, but I imagine you are going to tell me."

"Chicken 'n dumplin's is my most favorite thing to eat in the whole world."

"It was your father's favorite, too."

"Did you learn to make it because it was his favorite food?"

"Yes. His mother, your grandmother, taught me how to make it." Tears began sliding down Jennie's cheeks.

"Why are you crying, Ma?"

She shook her head, forcing a smile through her tears. "I'm sorry. I'm just a crybaby I guess."

"That's all right. I know why you're cryin'. You're cryin' because you miss Pa, aren't you?"

"Yes."

"It's all right if you cry, Ma. Sometimes when I get to thinkin' about him, I cry, too. But don't worry. I'm goin' to look out for you. Someday, I'll be a man, and I'll look out for you, I promise."

Jennie got up from her chair, walked over to him and put her arms around his head, pulling him into her side. "Ethan, you are already a man. You are as much a man as just about any adult I know."

He looked up at her. "Oh, Ma. Timmy invited me to go ridin' with him tomorrow. Is it all right if I do?"

"What are you going to ride?"

"Mr. Taylor said he would find me a horse to ride."

"In other words, you would be riding one of Mr. Hanson's horses. Is that what you are saying?"

"Yes ma'am, but Mr. Taylor says there aren't hardly any cowboys who own their own horse. They 'most all ride horses that belong to the ranch where they're workin'."

"Well, there it is, then. You aren't working here. You are just living here."

"But you're workin' here, Ma. And that's near 'bout the same thing."

"You could be working here, too, if you would like," Hanson said, the sudden intrusion of his voice startling them.

"I'm sorry if I startled you or butted into a private conversation, but I've finished with my meal — it was exceptionally good, by the way — and I thought I would bring my plate and utensils back to the kitchen so you wouldn't have to."

"There was no need for you to have to do that, but I thank you," Jennie took the dishes and silverware from him.

"What, do you mean I could be really working? For actual money?" Ethan asked.

Hanson chuckled. "Yes, for actual money. You can be my hostler."

"Your what?"

"You can be the person in charge of taking care of the horses. That is, with your mother's permission, of course."

"Ma, can I? Please?"

"Yes. And Mr. Hanson, I don't know how

to thank you."

The rancher smiled. "And, as my hostler, you are certainly entitled to a horse."

"Then I can go riding with Timmy tomorrow, can't I?"

Jennie smiled and ran her hand through her son's hair. "Yes, Ethan. You can go."

CHAPTER THIRTY-ONE

New Fountain, Texas

Henry Crump and Vic Forney were making their first foray with the Kingdom Come Gang. For two men who had spent a lifetime participating in petty crime, it was a totally new experience. They were riding with a gang that now numbered a little over twenty riders.

"You know what this means, Forney?" Crump asked. "This means there can't nobody, nowhere, do nothin' to us, 'cause we're too strong. There ain't no sheriff in all of Texas with enough deputies to take us on."

"No, no posse neither," Forney said. "Leastwise, I ain't never seen a posse this large."

Jaco held up his hand, and the sound of hoofbeats grew silent as the group of horsemen stopped. "There it is, boys. New Fountain."

Slightly below and spread out on plains before them was a small town consisting of approximately thirty buildings. The road they had been following widened somewhat and turned into the main street of the town.

"The bank is at the far end of the street, on the left-hand side," Jaco said. "What do you say we ride in and help ourselves?"

"Jaco, I know this is me 'n Forney's first time out with you, but do you think it's wise for us to all ride in together like this? I mean, bein' as there is this many of us, we're sure as hell goin' to get ever'body's attention."

Jaco laughed. "Oh yeah, we're goin' to get their attention all right. That's what we want to do."

"I don't understand. Why would we want everyone's attention?"

"Just pay attention and do what we do." Jaco pulled his pistol, and all the other riders followed suit. "Now!" he shouted.

The sound of twenty-three galloping horses caused a thunder that swept over the little town.

The first two citizens of the town to go down under the fusillade emanating from the Kingdom Come Gang were a young mother and her small daughter.

Bullets crashed through windows. Anyone

caught out on the street was shot. Those who attempted to escape were chased down by mounted gang members and shot down in cold blood.

One of the gang turned his horse toward the front of a dressmaking shop and horse and rider crashed through the window. Laughing demonically, he shot down the seamstress and her customer, her ability to flee limited by the pinned-up dress she was wearing.

When the outlaws reached the bank, at least six of them rushed in, but found the bank empty, employees and customers having run away at the sound of the guns. The vault door was standing open, whether by invitation or the fact that everyone had run away too quickly to close it.

The outlaws scooped up all the money, then went back outside and to a restaurant. Three dead diners were the only persons still inside the restaurant, having been killed by random gunfire as the gang had ridden into town. The men moved back to the kitchen and began serving themselves.

Three miles outside Eagle Pass
"When you jump over somethin', what you do is kind of stand in the stirrups, 'n keep your ass off the saddle," Timmy explained.

He chuckled. "Don't tell Ma I said *ass*, else she'll give me a whuppin'."

"Don't worry," Ethan said. "I won't say nothin'."

"Good. Now watch me and I'll show you —" Timmy stopped in mid-sentence as he saw several riders coming toward them. "That's funny."

"What's funny?"

"Seein' that many riders all bunched up like that. I wonder what they want?"

As the riders rode up to them, Timmy noticed that several had their pistols drawn. "Run, Ethan, run!" he shouted, jerking the head of his horse around and slapping his legs against the side.

Guns were fired, and both horses went down, spilling the boys from their saddles.

The riders came to them just as they were getting up.

"You're goin' to be sorry you kilt that horse!" Ethan said. "That was Mr. Cal Hanson's horse, 'n he's an important man."

"And my pa is the sheriff!" Timmy said.

Dingo aimed at the two boys.

"Wait a minute," Mattoon said. "Don't kill 'em."

"Why not?"

"They may be worth more to us alive. I've read about this Hanson fella. He's an

357

Englishman that's startin' him a ranch somewhere close. He may be willin' to pay a lot of money to get the boy back."

"What about the sheriff's brat?" Dingo said. "No need to be keepin' him alive, is there?"

"Don't shoot either one of 'em, yet," Jaco said. "I've read about the Englishman, too, and Mattoon might be right. The boy could be worth some money to us. And hangin' on to the sheriff's kid might give us an edge."

"What are we goin' to do with 'em?"

"We'll take 'em back to Shumla with us."

Eagle Pass
Sheriff Jason Bowles was pinning WANTED posters to his bulletin board when Larry Yeargan stuck his head in. "Sheriff?"

"Hi, Larry, what can I do for you?"

"There's somethin' a couple miles out of town you ought to see. Two horses that's been shot dead."

"Two of them, you say? Well, that is a little unusual."

"Here's what's more unusual. Both of 'em is still saddled."

"You're right. It probably is something I need to see. Let me get my horse saddled, and you can take me out there."

■ ■ ■ ■

"Oh Lord, no," Jason cried as they approached the two horses. "God in heaven, no!" he shouted, urging his horse into a gallop.

"Sheriff! What is it?" Yeargan called after him, putting his own horse into a gallop to catch up.

Jason looked around frantically. "Where are the boys? Did you see the boys anywhere?"

"What boys?" Yeargan asked. "Sheriff, I don't have any idea what you are talking about."

"I'm talking about the two boys who were riding these horses." Jason took a deep breath. "One of them was my son. The other one is staying out at the Regency Ranch with Cal Hanson."

"Oh, Lord. I didn't know nothin' about that, I didn't see no boys," Yeargan said. "I'm sorry, Sheriff. I'm just real sorry."

Going back through New Fountain, Jaco saw that all the bodies had been gathered in front of the church — fourteen total — as many women and children as men. Seeing the riders coming through again, the

359

townspeople assembled for an impromptu funeral service started to scatter.

"Hold on there, hold on!" Jaco shouted, stretching his arm out toward them. "We ain't here to do no more shootin'. No need for you to be runnin'."

"What are you here for?" one brave soul asked.

"We're here to get a couple horses," Jaco said. "Round up a couple saddled horses, and we'll be gettin' on our way. You won't be seein' no more of us."

Shumla

Late that afternoon, Jaco and his gang returned to town with Timmy and Ethan bound and riding on horses that were being led. They stopped in front of the Red Dog, then poured into the saloon, laughing and talking loudly.

"How much do you think we got from the bank?" one of the riders asked.

"What do you care? Your share will come to more 'n you would get from a whole year of punchin' cows."

"You got that right."

"What are you bringin' them two kids in here for?" Belle asked, when she saw Timmy and Ethan. "They're too young to be comin' into a place like this."

"Well now, Belle, me 'n some of the others was thinkin' that maybe you could break these two boys in. You think you could handle that for us?"

"I don't believe in robbing the cradle," Belle said. "Oh my goodness. You . . . You've got those two boys tied up! Why are they tied up?"

"Well, hell. It's obvious, ain't it? We've got 'em tied up 'cause we don't want 'em runnin' away."

"Wait a minute. One of those boys is the sheriff's son. I've seen him before."

Jaco nodded. "That's right."

Sky Meadow Ranch

Duff was filing the blade of a hay mower when he saw a boy, no older than fifteen, riding toward him. On the boy's head was a Western Union cap.

Dismounting, and clutching a yellow envelope in his hand, the messenger started toward the house.

"Lad, I'm over here," Duff called, wiping the back of his hand across his forehead.

The boy turned and came toward him. "You've got a telegram, Mr. MacCallister."

"Aye, I assumed as much." He reached for the message. "Please wait. I'll likely be wanting to send a return message."

361

"Yes, sir," the boy said.

Duff opened the envelope.

TIMMY AND YOUNG WARD OF HANSON
TAKEN BY OUTLAWS STOP MELISSA
VERY UPSET STOP NEED HELP STOP
CAN YOU COME STOP JBOWLES.

"Wang!" Duff shouted.

The door opened, and Wang stepped out onto the porch.

"Bring a pencil and three dollars!"

Without responding, Wang went back inside.

"Dewey?" Duff called out to the cowboy repairing a broken board in the corral fence.

"Yes, sir, Mr. MacCallister?"

"Would you be for telling Elmer that I should like to see him?"

"Yes, sir." Dewey hurried away on his errand.

Wang returned with a pencil and three dollars.

"Do you have any spare paper with you?" Duff asked the Western Union messenger.

"Yes sir." He produced a sheet of paper.

Taking the pencil, Duff wrote on the message sheet. *Will be there soon as possible.*

Turning over the telegram he had just received, he wrote on the back.

Megan, as you can see by this message, your sister needs you. Make arrangements for your store. We will leave tomorrow morning in time to catch the noon train from Cheyenne.

He gave the messages and the money to the telegram messenger. "See to it that this gets sent by return telegram, and that this message gets to Miss Parker. Do you know her?"

"Yes, sir. She's that pretty lady who runs the dress store."

"Aye."

"But Mr. MacCallister, that's too much money."

"See that the messages are both taken care of and keep the rest.

"Yes, sir!" the boy said with a wide smile.

To Elmer and Wang, Duff explained what had happened in Texas. "We'll spend tonight in town," Duff told Elmer. "We'll leave at daybreak tomorrow."

"Do you want me to go?" Wang asked.

"I appreciate the offer, but it won't be necessary."

"Duff, I've seen Wang . . . and his kind in action," Elmer said. "I think havin' him along could come in real handy."

"I've no doubt but that he would be an asset," Duff replied. "But, you saw how it was on the train. I think we need to get there right away. We won't —"

"Mr. MacCallister. You have been at sea. Mr. Gleason has been at sea. You have seen how it is for people in steerage. For the Chinese coming to America to work on the railroads, it was even worse. Please, do not be concerned that I will ride in the immigrant car. It will not bother me."

"I'll ride in the immigrant car with him," Elmer said.

"In that case, we'll all —"

Elmer held up his hand. "Don't you expect Miss Parker will be going?"

"Aye, 'tis my expectation that she will be."

"Then you two ride first class, as you should. Me 'n Wang will get along just fine in the immigrant car."

"All right. If you say so."

At six o'clock the next morning, Duff, Megan, Elmer, and Wang rode south out of town, the hollow clopping sound of the hoofbeats echoing back from the buildings fronting First Street. Already, the smell of coffee and frying bacon scented the cool morning air. If Vi Winslow had not provided an early morning breakfast for them, the aromas would have been difficult to take.

They passed by the Matthews Building, where a couple wagons were already taking on freight for the day's run, and the Chinese laundryman was building his fire under a tub of water. As they passed the laundry, Chang Ly and Wang Chow exchanged waves, but did not speak.

As the town fell behind them, they continued south on Chugwater Road.

They reached Cheyenne in time to make arrangement to secure passage and have their horses shipped on the same train.

"You are a good customer, Mr. MacCallister. I see no reason why your Chinese man can't ride in the first-class car with you."

"Can you guarantee that when we change trains in Denver?" Duff asked.

"Uh, no sir. Once you leave the Union Pacific, I won't be able to vouch for your accommodations."

"I think it would be better for Wang if he knows what to expect for the entire journey."

"Yes, sir, I understand."

CHAPTER THIRTY-TWO

Shumla

"Jaco, you are going to have to do something about those two boys," Sherazade said.

"What do you propose that I do about them?"

"I don't know, but they can't stay here, tied up in the corner of the saloon. This is no place for them. This whole town is no place for them. It's not safe."

"It's not safe for who? If you're talking about them, I don't care whether it is safe or not. But consider this. One of them is the son of the sheriff of Maverick County. The other belongs to the richest man in Maverick County. As long as we have them, nobody is going to come in here with guns blazing. They won't dare take a chance for fear of one of the boys getting hurt. In fact, I guarantee that they *will* be hurt, because if we are attacked here in this town, I will kill them. I will kill both of them."

"It's not just their safety I'm worried about. Having them in the saloon all the time isn't good for business — not for my girls' business, not even for the drinkin' business."

"Then what do you suggest?"

"I don't know. I don't have any suggestions. I just don't want them down here, tied up in the corner of the saloon, in front of everyone."

"Yeah? Well for the time bein', that's where they're goin' to stay. Unless you think you can come up with a better idea."

Sitting at a table away from Jaco, Forney and Crump were nursing a beer. They had put the beer on their tab, which Morris allowed since they had participated in the bank robbery and would be getting money when Jaco divided up the proceeds of the robbery.

"Did you hear them say where one of them kids is from?" Forney asked.

"Yeah, I heard. One of 'em is the sheriff's kid," Crump replied.

"Yeah, but that's not the one I'm talking about."

"What about the other kid? He ain't nothin' is he?" Crump asked. "Belongs to some cattleman, they said."

"Yeah, but not just any cattleman. Don't you know who he is?" Forney asked. "He's the one we tried to rob."

"You sure?"

"Yeah, I'm sure. Crump, this ain't no place for us."

"You mean because of the kid?"

"Not just because of the kid. I mean because of all that killing that went on in that town where we robbed the bank. Whoever heard of doin' somethin' like that? We rode in 'n everyone began shootin'. Dane told me it was always like that with Jaco. Hell, Dane was even laughin' about it. He enjoyed it. But, I didn't shoot nobody, and I don't think you did, either."

"No, I couldn't hold with all the killing for no reason at all."

"So like I said, we need to get out of here."

"Even before we get our money?"

"I'm not sure Jaco will even give us our cut. I say we leave tonight."

"Do you think he will let us go?"

"I don't plan on even askin'. I say we just leave when nobody's payin' any attention to us."

Jaco had told the others that he would divide up the bank money that night, so the entire gang was gathered in the saloon in anticipation of their share of the loot. "I tell you what, boys. Before I divide up the money, let's have a good time. Morris, drinks are free. You keep a count, then let me know how much the bill is.

"Sherazade, your girls are going to get a workout tonight," Jaco added, and the others laughed. They shouted in eager anticipation of the activities of the night.

"This ain't right," Sherazade said to the other girls.

"You mean we aren't goin' to get paid?" one of the girls asked.

"No, we'll get paid. What ain't right is to keep these two kids here in the saloon while all this is goin' on."

"I'll take them," Belle said.

"Take them where?" Sherazade asked.

"I'll take them to my room and keep them with me up there."

"Ha!" Sherazade replied with a laugh. "That would be worse than leaving them down here. If those two boys stay in your room, they are going to get an eyeful. They will grow up real fast."

"No, they won't. They won't see anything. As long as I have them with me, I won't be with any of the men."

"If you don't plan to be with any of the men, how do you plan to make any money?"

"I've thought about that," Belle said. "Maybe everyone can pitch in just a little bit and pay me to keep an eye on the boys. That way it won't cause any of them any trouble."

"Yeah," Sherazade said. "Yeah, that might work. All right. I'll put out the word. You'll get fifty cents for every man any of the girls have tonight. And all you'll have to do is keep your eye on the two boys. I'll have to clear it with Jaco, though."

"Yeah, go ahead," Jaco said in response to Sherazade's request. "I'm gettin' a little tired of lookin' at 'em myself."

"Thanks. It'll be much better this way." Sherazade looked over at the two boys. "You boys have been tied up down here for three days now. I'll bet you'd like to have a bed to sleep in, wouldn't you?"

"Yes, ma'am!" Timmy replied.

"Ha!" Jaco laughed. "Saying yes ma'am to a soiled dove. Now there's a boy that's got hisself some manners."

"Something you obviously never had," Sherazade said. "Come along, boys."

"You keep them tied up, you hear me, Sherazade?" Jaco called. "You keep 'em tied up."

She took the two boys up the stairs, then

down a hallway flanked on both sides by doors.

"Is this a hotel?" Ethan asked. "I've never been in a hotel before."

Sherazade chuckled. "I suppose you could call it a kind of hotel." She knocked on the door and Belle opened it. "Here they are. They're all yours."

"Jaco agreed to it?"

"Yes. But he said you have to keep them tied up."

"All right. I will. Come on in, boys. My name is Belle, and you're going to be my guests for a while."

Downstairs the party was getting louder and drunker.

"I wonder when Jaco plans to divide up the money?" Crump asked.

"In due time," Mattoon said. "In due time."

"Yeah. Don't get in such a hurry. What would we spend it on but liquor and ladies of the night, anyway? Right now, the liquor is free, and you have to stand in line to get a woman, so just keep your britches on." Cyr laughed. "That is, keep your britches on until you do get one of them women." He laughed again. "Did you get that joke, Mattoon? I said he can keep his britches on till he gets with one of them soiled doves."

"I got it," Mattoon said. "Speakin' of which, they's two of 'em comin' downstairs now. You want to stand here jawbonin' with these two or get your turn?"

"I'll take my turn," Cyr said, hitching up his trousers as he and Mattoon started toward the foot of the stairs to meet the two women.

"Let's go now, while nobody's payin' any attention to us," Crump said to Forney after the two men left.

"You mean don't wait for any of the money?"

"We don't want any of the money. If we take it, we'll be as guilty as anyone else."

"We already are. We was there, remember?"

"Yes, but what we do now is goin' to be the thing that says whether or not we're really guilty. I say let's go now, without the money."

"Damn! You're cheatin'!" a loud voice shouted.

The exclamation was followed by a gunshot.

Looking toward the table where the charge of cheating had been made, Forney and Crump saw one of the townspeople grabbing the bullet hole in his stomach, shocked at the sudden turn of events.

The shooter, still holding the smoking gun, was Manny Dingo. "Nobody calls me a cheat." He returned the gun to its holster.

"Let's get out of here, now," Forney said.

"How we goin' to do it? If they see us both walkin' out, they might get a little suspicious."

"We'll go out the back door," Forney said. "People been goin' out back to take a leak all night long. Nobody will even notice."

"Yeah, good idea."

The two men left through the back door, then slipped away from the saloon. Saddling their horses, they rode off into the night. True to Forney's prediction, nobody noticed their absence.

"Miss Belle, what are they going to do to us?" Ethan asked. "Are they going to kill us?"

"No, honey, they aren't going to kill you. I wouldn't let anything like that happen to you."

"I don't think they want to hurt us because if they do, they know that Pa will come after them," Timmy said.

"And I think your pa would," Belle agreed. "Your pa is a good man."

Timmy's eyes grew large. "You know my pa?"

"No, honey, I don't really know him. I just know who he is, him being the sheriff and all."

Timmy smiled. "Almost ever'body knows my pa. He's kind of famous, isn't he?"

"You might say that."

"I think we should try to escape," Ethan said.

"I wish you wouldn't try that," Belle said. "I think it would be too dangerous for you."

Eagle Pass

Forney and Crump rode into town the next morning. Locating the sheriff's office, they dismounted and stepped inside.

The man at the desk looked up. "Can I help you?"

"Are you the sheriff?" Forney asked.

"I'm Deputy Smith."

"We need to talk to the sheriff."

"He's not here right now, and anyway, this isn't a good time to be talking to him."

"Because of his kid?"

Deputy Smith's eyes narrowed. "What do you know about Timmy?"

"If you'll get the sheriff, we'll tell him what we know."

Deputy Smith drew his pistol and pointed

at them. "Take off them gun belts."

"What for?"

"Just take 'em off."

Forney and Crump looked at each other for a moment, then Forney shrugged. "We may as well take 'em off," he said as he began unbuttoning his gun belt.

Once their pistols were on the floor, Smith made a motion toward the jail cell. "Get in there."

"What? Look here, what's goin' on here?" Forney demanded.

"You came here bringing news about the sheriff's son. The only way you could have information about him is if you are involved. Now, both of you get in the cell. I'll bring the sheriff to you."

"This ain't right," Crump said. "This ain't no way right at all."

"Just do it," Smith ordered with a wave of his pistol.

Grumbling, but compliant, the two men allowed Smith to put them into the cell, then close and lock the door behind them.

"Wait here," Smith said.

"Yeah? Well, where else would we wait, Deputy?" Forney asked, his voice dripping anger.

"This ain't right," Crump complained after Smith left. "This ain't no way right a-tall. We shoulda just kept on a-goin'."

A moment later, Deputy Smith returned with another man with him. "This is them, Sheriff."

"Is it true, what my deputy said? Do you have news about my son?"

"Is your son named Timmy?"

"Yes," Jason said. "What has happened to him? Where is he? Is he all right?"

"A feller by the name of Jaco has him," Forney said. "And yeah, he's all right. Leastwise, he was all right when we left him last night. But I don't know just how long he will be all right. Jaco is about the evilest damn man I done ever run into."

"We ain't like that, which is why we left," Crump added.

"And also to tell you about your son, and Mr. Hanson about his."

"Cal Hanson doesn't have a son," Jason said.

Forney frowned. "Is that true? We thought . . . that is, I thought the other kid was his."

"No, he belongs to Mr. Hanson's cook."

"Maybe so, but knowin' Mr. Hanson, I don't doubt but that he'll be a-worryin' about that kid 'bout as much as he would if it was his."

Jason paid close attention. " 'Knowing

Hanson'? Are you telling me that you two actually know Cal Hanson?"

Both outlaws nodded. Crump spoke. "Yeah we know 'im. We . . . uh, done some business with him a while back. And we sure don't want to be a party to somethin' that might hurt him."

"I'll see that he gets the word," Jason said. "You haven't told me yet where the boys are."

"We'd like to tell you 'n Hanson at the same time, if you don't mind," Forney said.

"All right. You two just wait right here, and I'll ride out to get Mr. Hanson," Deputy Smith said.

"We'd rather you take us out to see 'im," Forney said. "We don't want to be talkin' to him from a jail cell. Besides which, neither of us actual done nothin' to make you want to put us in jail in the first place."

"Let 'em out, Smitty," Jason said.

"But, Sheriff, don't you think —"

"Let 'em out," Jason repeated.

CHAPTER THIRTY-THREE

Regency Ranch

"Yes, I do indeed remember you two," Hanson said when Forney and Crump confronted him.

"They know where the boys are," Jason said.

"Are they all right?"

"Yes, sir, they are for now. Jaco is holdin' them back in Shumla."

Hanson frowned and looked to Jason. "Shumla?"

"It's a small town in Uvalde County," Jason explained.

Hanson looked back at Forney and Crump. "Who is this man, Jaco? And what do you mean he is holding them?"

"Have you read anythin' in the newspapers about an outfit that's called the Kingdom Come Gang?" Forney asked.

"Yes, I believe I have."

"Well this man, Jaco, he's the head man

of the gang."

"Is he demanding ransom for the two boys? Because if he is, I will gladly pay it to see to their safe release."

"No, sir, I ain't heard him say nothin' like that. I think he's just holdin' them to keep anyone from comin' after 'im."

Hanson looked at Jason again. "What about the sheriff in Uvalde County? Can we expect any help from him?"

"You don't understand, Mr. Hanson," Forney said. "Jaco ain't just holdin' them two boys in the town. He's holdin' the whole town."

Surprised, Hanson asked, "What do you mean?"

"Shumla is what you call an outlaw town. There ain't no law there a-tall 'ceptin' whatever law Jaco says there is."

"That is totally unacceptable," Hanson said sharply. "We must do something."

Jason had listened carefully to the conversation, keeping his thoughts to himself. Finally, he stepped in. "I agree, but there's no sense in going off half-cocked. I have sent a telegram to Duff MacCallister. I expect him to be here soon. Once he arrives, we'll come up with a plan."

When Duff and the others reached Eagle Pass, they were met by Jason, who asked them to go with him out to Regency Ranch. "There are a couple men out there I would like you to meet. Actually, Mr. Hanson says you've met them before. They have some information that might be helpful."

"Where is Melissa?" Megan asked immediately. "I want to go to her. Bless her heart, I know she has to be having a very difficult time with this."

"She is. We both are," Jason said. "She is already out at the ranch. She and Mrs. Garrison are sort of comforting each other."

"Mrs. Garrison?"

"Jennie Garrison. Her son Ethan is Timmy's age, and the two boys were out horseback riding when the Kingdom Come Gang came upon them."

The name rang a bell with Duff. "The Kingdom Come Gang? I believe I read something in the paper about them. A gang of outlaws?"

"Much more than just a gang of outlaws," Jason said. "They are cold-blooded killers . . . and there are at least twenty of them. Well, two less now, since the defection."

"What defection?"

"The two men you'll be meeting defected

from the gang."

A half hour had passed by the time they got their horses off-loaded and rode out to Hanson's ranch. Everyone had gathered in the large keeping room. Melissa and another woman had obviously been crying, and Megan hurried over to embrace her sister.

Melissa wiped her eyes. "Megan, this is Jennie Garrison. Her son Ethan was with Timmy when they were taken by those evil men."

Megan embraced Jennie. "Have you heard anything else about them? Do you know where they are?"

"Yes, they are in Shumla," Melissa said.

"Duff, it was good of you to come," Hanson said. "I've two men I would like you to meet. They are out in the bunkhouse with Mr. Taylor."

"They would be the defectors Jason spoke of?"

"Yes. You have met them before."

"I have?"

"Yes. Ah, here they are. I told them to come up to the house when they saw you arrive."

Duff looked toward the two who were arriving, and remembered, at once, where he

381

had seen them before. "*Och,* you would be the two men who attempted to rob Mr. Hanson now, would you?"

"Yeah, we're awful sorry 'bout that," one of the men said. "He's Crump, I'm Forney."

"You are a long way from your territory, aren't ye now? 'Twas thinkin', I was, that you were in Wyoming."

"Yes sir, well, that's where we mostly was, but we decided it would be better for us if we left Wyomin' an' come to Texas," Crump said.

"Which is how we come to join up with Jaco. Only, we seen our mistake soon as we joined up," Forney explained.

"Jaco? What is Jaco?" Duff asked.

"Jaco is a who, not a what," Jason said. "His name is A. M. Jaco. He and an albino by the name of Blue Putt were about to be hung over in New Mexico, but they managed to escape the night before they were to hang. I've got paper on both of them. According to Crump and Forney here, Jaco and Putt are heading up the Kingdom Come Gang."

"And they're the ones who have the two boys?" Duff asked, to clarify.

"Yes."

"Tell me about this other boy, the one who was with Timmy when they were taken.

There's *nae* chance he's mixed up in it, is there?"

"No chance at all," Hanson said. "His mother works for me, and they live here on the ranch." He explained that Ethan's father had been killed, most likely by the Kingdom Come Gang. "I needed help and Mrs. Garrison needed a job," he concluded. "That's how they wound up here."

"And you two" — Duff wagged a finger at Forney and Crump — "how did you two wind up here?"

"Look, Mr. MacCallister, me 'n Forney ain't goin' to lie to you. We ain't exactly led what you would call decent, law a-fearin' lives. Only we ain't never done nothin' like what Jaco 'n his men are doin'. We ain't neither one of us ever actual kilt anyone, 'n soon as we seen what this here gang was like, we know'd we'd made us a big mistake."

Forney told about the bank robbery in New Fountain. "Only, it warn't like no bank robbery I ever heard o' before. You'd think that all you would want to do is take the money 'n git, 'n if you can do it without no shootin', the better it be. But not these men. When we first rode into New Fountain, well Jaco, he told us to commence a-shootin'. It was real crazy."

383

"Not so crazy. I can see that. By discharging your weapons into the air, it would generate a degree of shock, enough to divert people's attention," Duff said.

"No, it warn't nothin' like that a-tall," Crump said. "What Jaco told us to do was to start shootin' *people*. Men, women, even little children. If they was out on the street, we was s'posed to shoot 'em. 'Cept me 'n Forney, we didn't do none of that."

"How did you avoid it?" Jason asked.

"We just commenced to shootin', but we wasn't shootin' at nobody in particular," Forney said.

"Then, what we done," Crump continued, "is we made up our mind that soon as we got our share of the money, we was goin' to quit the gang 'n ride back up to Wyomin'. I mean, me 'n Forney, we'd done a little robbin', but we ain't never kilt no one a-fore."

"When we brung in them two kids, we didn't want no part of that, so we decided we wasn't goin' to even wait around for our cut," Forney said. "We was goin' to go right back to Wyomin'."

"Only you came to my office," Jason said.

"Yeah, we come there."

"Why?

"We come there when we larn't that one o' them two kids belonged to Mr. Hanson,"

384

Crump said.

"He was real good to us, if you remember," Forney said. "I mean, here, we tried to rob 'im, 'n what does he do? He gave us money."

"So we decided to tell the sheriff what we knew," Crump said.

"You did the right thing," Duff said.

"Yeah, well, truth is, even if it hadn't been for the kid belongin' to Mr. Hanson 'n all, we woulda prob'ly done the same thing, anyway. There wouldn't nobody in their right mind want to be around Jaco," Forney said.

"That's how it is. I mean, nobody around him is in their right mind. 'Cause Jaco 'n near 'bout ever'one with 'im is crazy," Crump added.

"Who are some of the people with him, do you know?" Duff asked.

"Well, sir, there's Jaco and Putt. They're the two leaders of the gang," Crump said. "Jaco, he's some kind of a breed, half Mex or half Injun, I don't know which. And Putt, he's one of them people that ain't got no color. All white, you know."

"An albino," Duff suggested.

"And Manny Dingo. You ever a-heered o' him?" Forney asked.

"He's a young gunslinger," Jason said,

interrupting the conversation. "He's fast with a gun. I mean he is really fast, and he likes to use it."

"Then there's a feller by the name of Johnny Dane. He's kinda funny," Crump said.

"Funny? How is he funny?" Hanson asked.

"I don't mean funny so's he does things to make you laugh. I mean he's funny 'cause he's odd. He likes little girls."

"And when Crump says little girls, that means real little girls, like maybe thirteen or fourteen years old," Forney added.

"What you are saying is, he is a pedophile," Hanson suggested.

Crump frowned. "I don't know what that word means. I just know that he likes real young girls."

"Then there's a couple men that I think are brothers. Can't recall their names though. Do you, Crump?"

"I think one of 'em is Larry or Lenny. Somethin' like that. Oh, and there's Mattoon. He's sort of an odd duck, too."

"Mattoon? Wyatt Mattoon?" Jason asked.

"You've heard of him?" Duff asked.

"Yeah, he was a peace officer once. People like him give anyone who has ever worn a badge a bad name."

"The only other name I recall is the one called Cyr. He's the oldest of the lot, and damn well may be the meanest."

"Cyr?" Elmer asked, speaking up for the first time. "Would that be Val Cyr?"

"I don't know. I never heard his first name spoke," Forney said.

"Well, let me ask you this. What about his right ear? Is there a piece of it missing?"

Forney nodded. "Yeah. Now that you mention it, he is missin' 'bout half his right ear."

"Elmer, how is it that you knew that?" Duff asked.

"I know it, 'cause I'm the one that bit it off."

"My word, you bit off half his ear?" Hanson exclaimed.

"Yeah, I done it when we was kids."

"You and Cyr knew each other when you were children?" Duff asked.

"Val Cyr is my first cousin. We joined up with Quantrill together, 'n some later, when I first come back from the sea, we rode the outlaw trail together for a while."

"You heard the way Forney and Crump have been describing this gang of brigands as thieves and murderers. And you say this fellow is your kinsman. Do you think he is capable of such a thing?" Duff had a lot of faith in his foreman.

"Yeah," Elmer said with a single nod of his head. "Yeah, I do."

"What about the townsmen?" Duff asked. "Does Jaco enjoy their support?"

"I'm not sure I know what you mean by that," Forney admitted. "He enjoys the soiled doves that work in the saloon."

"I mean, do the townspeople support Jaco? If it came down to a battle between Jaco and someone from outside, would everyone in the town fight for Jaco?"

Forney shook his head. "No, I don't think they would. Most of the folks that was in town left when Jaco took over. The ones that stayed thought they'd be makin' a lot of money, and I s'pose they are. Folks that's come to town since then done it just 'cause it is a outlaw town. Onliest thing is, it's costin' them a lot just to live there. Plus, Jaco is collectin' what he calls a tax."

"Forney's right. I 'spect more 'n half of the ones that stayed would just as soon Jaco move on."

"That's good to know," Duff said.

"But that don't mean he don't have a lot who would fight for him."

"How many?" Duff asked immediately.

"At least twenty. Maybe a few more," Crump said.

"But that ain't all of it," Forney said. "I know that he plans to use them two kids as a way to keep anyone from comin' after 'em."

"We can't just let those boys stay there," Jason said. "We've got to get them out, one way or another."

Wang spoke for the first time. "You know this town," he said to Forney and Crump. "Are there any Chinese people there?"

"Any Chinamen? No, I don't think so," Crump said.

"Yeah, there are," Forney said. "The laundry is run by some Chinamen, don't you remember?"

"Oh, yeah. I forgot about them."

"That is good," Wang said.

Duff turned to his cook. "Wang, you have an idea?"

"Yes. I will go into town and get the two young Americans out."

Frustrated, Jason asked, "How are you going to do that?"

"No one will see me."

"Ha!" Forney said. "Believe me, Jaco will be keeping an eye on those two boys."

"I will be invisible," Wang said.

"What do you mean, you'll be invisible?" Forney asked. "Somethin' else I don't understand."

"I do," Duff said. "Remember, Mr. Crump didn't even know there were Chinese in the town."

"Yes, I, too, am aware of the phenomenon," Hanson said. "The ubiquitous servant is often invisible because of his lack of standing in the perceived social order of the elite."

Forney and Crump looked at each other and shrugged. Hanson's explanation offered no help in understanding.

"All right, Wang. So you can get into Shumla without being seen. Then what?" Jason asked.

"I will find a way to save Timmy and his friend."

"You can't do this all by yourself," Jason said.

"I have seen Wang in action," Duff said. "I believe he can do it."

"How long will you need?" Jason asked.

"Two days."

Jason nodded.

CHAPTER THIRTY-FOUR

"Tell me, Forney, how'd you two boys get joined up with Jaco and the rest of 'em?" Elmer asked.

"It was easy. We just rode into town 'n said we wanted to join up."

"Then that's what I'll do," Elmer said.

"What are talking about?" Jason asked.

"I told you, me 'n Cyr was cousins. We also rode the outlaw trail together for a while. He would vouch for me."

"You two get along, do you?" Jason asked.

"Not particularly. But then, we never did."

Hanson chuckled. "I would think not, considering that you bit off his ear."

"I'm curious. Why did you do that?" Jason asked.

"Because he stole my fried peach pie."

Jason and the others laughed.

"I've got me another idea, but bein' as you're a sheriff 'n all, you're goin' to have to help me."

"I'll do what I can. What do you need?"

Elmer didn't hesitate. "I need you to get a fella I know out of the Texas State Prison."

Jason hesitated, then said, "I'm not sure I'll be able to do that."

"Didn't you say that Jaco and Putt was s'posed to be hung, but they escaped from the prison before the warden could get the rope around their necks?"

"Yes."

"And since the two of 'em has come over to Texas, what with the killin' 'n all, don't you think they're wanted here just as bad?"

"I imagine they are."

"Well, the feller I got in mind is just in there for thievin' 'n such, and I expect his time is most served by now. If you tell the warden that he'll help you get Jaco, he might be willin' to let 'em go. His name is Jim Morley."

Jason frowned. He wasn't big on letting prisoners go. "You know him?"

"Yeah, I know 'im."

"Is he someone you can trust?" Hanson asked.

Elmer stroked his chin for a moment before he answered. "Well, now I'm not too awful sure about that. I think if he believes this will get 'im out of prison a bit earlier, I can trust 'im. The only thing is, I'm not sure he's goin' to be all that set on helpin' me."

"Why not?" Jason asked.

"I was ridin' on both sides of the law for a while. Sometimes I was the outlaw, sometimes I was the law. For a while I was deputyin' up in Tarrant County. I'm the one that brung 'im in."

Shumla

"Who is the proprietor of this establishment?" Wang asked, speaking in Chinese as he stepped into the laundry situated at the outer edge of town.

"I am Kai Mot," an older man said.

Wang wrapped his left hand around his fist, keeping his elbows straight, and made a slight dip of his head. "I am Wang Chow."

Upon seeing the martial arts greeting, Kai Mot's eyes grew wider, and the expression on his face stiffened. "You are a martial arts priest?"

"There are people who would pay a great deal of money to have that information," Wang said. "I have placed my life in your hands."

Kai Mot put his hands together in the position of praying and made a more profound dip of his head than had Wang.

"I am honored by your trust, and you need have no fear of betrayal."

"I thank you for your kindness."

"Why have you come to my humble establishment?"

"I have heard that this is a town of thieves, vandals, and murderers. Is this true?"

Kai Mot nodded. "Yes, it is called, by the round-eyes, an outlaw town."

"And is there an evil man here, named Jaco?"

"Yes. He is the leader, and he is most evil."

"Thank you for the information."

"Pardon me for asking such an injudicious question, *Ji si,* but why have you come to such a place?" Kai Mot asked.

"Recently, Jaco and the evil men who ride with him captured two young American boys. Do you know of this?"

"Yes, I have seen them in the saloon."

That surprised Wang. "You are allowed in the saloon?"

"Not as a customer. I wash the towels and the aprons and the clothes of the *chāngjì* who entertain the men. I go and I leave, but I am never noticed."

"That is good. Have the young Americans been mistreated?"

"They are kept tied, but I have not seen scars or bruises. They were being kept downstairs, but I believe now they are in the room of one of the *chāngjì.* But I have not seen them there, so I do not know which room."

"If you have not seen them, how do you know they are in such a room?"

Kai Mot shrugged. "The *chāngjì* talk as if I am not there. I have heard them say this."

"When do you go to gather the laundry?"

"Every evening at six o'clock."

Finally, Wang asked what he'd come there for. "I ask that you allow me to go tonight."

"Are you going to attempt to rescue the *hái zi qì de rén?*"

"Yes."

Surprised, Kai Mot asked, "Why would you risk your life for American boys?"

"It is a debt of honor," Wang said.

"Yes. I can understand honor."

"Where will I find the articles that are to be brought back to the laundry?"

"In a basket behind the stove."

"I will gather them for you, and have a look around."

Just before six o'clock that evening, Wang pushed through the swinging batwing doors. He made himself "invisible" by keeping his head slightly bowed as if he were unworthy of looking anyone in the face or of being seen. He moved through the saloon, giving everyone plenty of space and heading for the stove which sat in the back corner of the room, cold and empty on the warm night.

He removed all of the laundry, then began carefully folding each piece one at a time before putting it back into the basket. Well aware there were no more than one or two people who even realized that he was there, he was able to fold and watch for several minutes without arousing anyone's suspicion or their notice.

He saw one rather dark-complexioned man sitting at a table with another man whose skin was white as chalk — the albino he had heard mentioned — and a third man. Wang believed, from the authoritative way the dark man was presenting himself, the man doing all the talking must be Jaco.

Wang listened in on the conversation.

"I think we ought to take the boys with us on our next raid," Jaco was saying.

"What for? They'd just get in the way," the third man replied.

"Think about it, Mattoon. A couple kids tied to their horses, riding right smack-dab in the middle of our group? Hell, nobody would want to take a chance on shootin' at us, for fear that they might hit one of the kids."

"Yeah," Mattoon said. "Yeah, I hadn't

thought about that."

Sitting with two men at another table closer to Wang than Jaco, the albino, and the man named Mattoon was one of the bar girls. As Wang studied her, he saw that she, too, was listening to Jaco's words and found them disturbing.

"Did you two hear what Jaco just said?" the girl asked, validating, though no validation was actually needed, that Wang had correctly identified Jaco.

"What did he say?" one of the men asked.

"He just said he's planning on taking those two little boys with him on the next raid to keep people from shooting at you. Do you think he would really do that?"

"He might," spoke the man in the blue shirt.

"Oh, surely not! That would be awful!"

"What's so awful about it? If it'll keep people from shooting at us, I think it would be a pretty good idea."

"Yeah, I do, too," agreed the man wearing a black hat.

"Then you are as awful as he is."

The two men laughed.

"Look, Belle, just because you're keepin' them two boys in your room, that don't mean you're their mama. Hell, you ain't even their big sister," Blue Shirt said.

"Yeah, don't you go lettin' yourself start gettin' feelin's over them two boys, 'cause like as not they're both goin' to wind up dead."

"Not if I can help it," Belle muttered.

"Yeah? Well, more 'n likely if Jaco wants 'em dead, 'n you get in the way, you'll wind up dead, too."

"Larry, Lenny," Jaco called over to Belle's table. "Let's go down to the café 'n get us somethin' for supper."

"All right," Blue Shirt replied.

Both men stood, then Black Hat leaned back down. "Look, I'm tellin' you for your own good, get them two boys out of your mind. They're both goin' to wind up dead, 'n you will, too, if you do somethin' crazy like try and protect 'em or somethin'."

Jaco and several others left the saloon. Belle, wiping tears from her eyes, got up from the table and hurried up the stairs.

Wang picked up the basket and started toward the door, but he kept his eyes on the mirror behind the bar. He could see Belle's reflection, and which door she entered.

Huntsville, Texas

"Now, Sheriff, what can I do for you?" the warden asked when Jason, Duff, and Elmer were admitted to his office in the Texas

398

State Prison.

"You have a prisoner here named Jim Morley. I would like you to release him to my custody," Jason said.

"Jim Morley," the warden said. "Let me see what I have on him." Opening a drawer, he looked through the files, then pulled one out. "He was sentenced to ten years, but he has only served seven. Come back in three years."

"I need him now."

"What do you mean, you need him? Why do you need him?"

"I'm sure you've heard of A. M. Jaco and the Kingdom Come Gang," Jason said.

"Yes, they've been raising hell down in the southwest part of the state."

Jason gave a nod. "That's where I am. I believe Morley can help us put a stop to this gang."

"What makes you think that?"

"Because I'm goin' to get 'im to come with me to join up with the gang," Elmer said, speaking for the first time."

"I can see why they might take someone like Morley. Why would they take you?" the warden asked.

"One of the gang members is my first cousin. He'll vouch for me."

"I don't know," the warden said. "It seems

399

like a pretty far-fetched idea to me."

"Warden, they have my son," Jason said. "My son and another young boy. This is very personal. If you want me to, I'll petition the governor, but that would take time. Too much time, I'm afraid."

"All right. I'll tell you what I'll do. I'll let you meet with Morley, talk to him for a while. If, after you have spoken with him, you still want to do this — and if Morley is agreeable to the terms —"

"We haven't discussed the terms, but if he agrees, I want the remainder of his sentence to be commuted." Jason spoke with authority.

"That's three years!" the warden exclaimed.

"He could get killed doing what I have in mind. He needs some incentive."

"All right," the warden agreed. "Go into my library and wait. I'll have the prisoner brought to you."

Elmer was standing in the corner behind one of the bookcases when, half an hour later, two armed guards brought the prisoner into the library. Morley was handcuffed.

"Take off the handcuffs," Jason ordered.

"This is not a containment area," one of

the guards replied. "It is standard procedure to keep prisoners in wrist restraints when they aren't in a containment area. Besides, it's for your own safety."

"I'm Sheriff Jason Bowles, and I will take personal responsibility for this man. Now, please, take off the restraints."

"Yes, sir." Complying with the request, the guard removed the handcuffs and stepped back.

"Have a chair," Jason invited.

"What's all this about, Sheriff?" Morley asked as he sat down.

Elmer stepped out into the room then. "Hello, Morley. Do you remember me?"

Morley glanced over toward Elmer and immediately, the smile left his face. "Yeah, I remember you." The tone of his voice was little more than a snarl. "You're the one who got me put into prison."

"I'm also the one who is about to get you out of prison," Elmer said, sitting down next to Jason.

The expression on Morley's face turned from hostile to curious. "How are you going to get me out?"

"By offering you a deal," Elmer said.

"What kind of a deal?"

"Have you ever heard of a man named A. M. Jaco?"

"No, I can't say as I have. Who is he?"

"He is one of the most vicious criminals ever to come to Texas," Jason answered. "He has taken over the town of Shumla and has turned it into an outlaw town. He has his own private army of at least twenty men, maybe more, and when they go out on a raid, they sweep through a town like a swarm of locusts, plundering, burning, and killing."

"Especially killing," Elmer added.

"What does all that have to do with this here deal you are offering me?" Morley asked.

Elmer grinned. "You and me are going to join his gang."

CHAPTER THIRTY-FIVE

Shumla

It was nearly midnight when Wang, dressed in black, moved silently down the alley that ran behind the laundry. The blade of his sword caught a beam of moonlight and sent a sliver of silver into the night.

Reaching the back of the saloon, he climbed up the wall, finding foot- and hand-holds where none existed. He could hear muttering sounds coming through some of the windows opened to the warm night. Realizing that they were windows that opened into occupied rooms, he passed by those windows, moving sideways across the back of the building until he reached the window that opened onto the hallway. Using it as his point of entry into the building, he climbed inside.

Even though it was quite late, the saloon was very busy, and from the floor below Wang could hear the sounds of the piano and scattered conversation. A woman's loud shout was followed by a bellow of laughter from both men and women.

The hallway was dimly illuminated by low-burning wall-mounted lanterns, and as Wang moved down the hallway he extinguished the lamps one at a time. The result was a shaft of almost total darkness behind him.

Just ahead of him a door opened and a man stepped out into the hall. Wang moved quickly to step back into the darkness where he completely disappeared, thanks to his black clothing.

"That was good, Pearl. That was real good." Obviously a customer, the man directed his words back into the room from which he had just emerged.

Wang heard a woman's voice reply, low and indistinct, so he had no idea what the woman said.

"Ha! If you say so," the man replied with a little laugh. He closed the door, then looked up the hall, noticing that some of the lamps were out. "Huh. I wonder how that happened." He started toward the darkness, and Wang moved his sword into a thrusting position.

The sword wasn't needed. The man shrugged his shoulders and started back toward the front of the hallway. Wang was glad. He would have killed the man to protect his mission, but he didn't want to kill anyone unless he was forced to.

He left the last two lanterns burning so that the darkness of the hallway would not be noticed from the floor below. When he reached the door of the room he had seen Belle go into earlier, he opened it quietly and stepped inside. By the ambient light of the moon, he saw two boys sleeping in the bed. No one else was there. He walked over to the bed and after lighting the bedside lamp put his hand on Timmy's shoulder and shook him gently.

"Timmy," he said quietly. "Timmy, wake up."

Timmy opened his eyes. "Mr. Wang?" he said in surprise.

The Chinaman nodded. "Come. I will take you back to your father."

Ethan stirred awake then, and seeing Wang standing over the bed, gasped.

"It's all right, Ethan," Timmy said quickly. "This is Mr. Wang. He's my friend."

"What's he doing here?" Ethan whispered.

"He's come to take us home."

It took the boys but a minute to put their boots on, then, admonishing them to be quiet by holding his finger over his lips,

Wang opened the door. He saw no one, so they started toward the open window at the far end of the hallway.

At that moment, two men came out of the same room. "See, Lenny. I told you she'd give us a special deal on account of us bein' brothers. All we had to do was —" he stopped in mid-sentence when he saw Wang with the two boys. "Here, where do you think you're goin' with them two?"

"I think they're tryin' to escape!" Lenny said. "Kill 'em, Larry. Kill 'em all!"

Larry and Lenny Israel went for their guns, but Wang, who was wearing his sword hanging down his back, whipped it over his shoulder and in two rapid thrusts, killed both men before they could fire a shot. It was all quick, and except for the brief conversation between the brothers before it began, it was silent.

Another loud burst of laughter coming up from downstairs gave proof that no one was aware of what had just happened in the hallway above.

"We must move them before they are seen," Wang said quietly.

"Where?" Timmy asked.

"We will drop them through the window."

Wang picked up one of the bodies and draped it over his right shoulder. He draped the other body over his left shoulder. "Get the guns," he said quietly, and Timmy picked up one of the pistols as Ethan picked up the other.

When they reached the back window, Wang dropped the two brothers into the alley below. Then he took Timmy by the hands and lowered him through the window so that he was just a few feet above the ground and let go. Timmy dropped safely to the ground. Wang did the same thing with Ethan, before he dropped down himself.

His first order of business was taking care of the bodies, and he rolled the two brothers into the crawl space under the saloon. Likely they'd be found pretty quickly, but it would give Wang time to get the two boys out of town before they and the gunmen were discovered missing.

Wang lifted the boys into the small, two-wheel cart he'd bought from Kai Mot earlier in the afternoon and covered them with a piece of canvas. Mounting his horse that was attached to the cart, he gave a cluck to his horse, and they started out of town with one of the wheels squeaking loudly.

"Where are they?" Belle demanded.

"Where is who?" Jaco asked, looking up at her.

"You know who I'm talking about. Where are they?"

"Woman, I don't have an idea in hell what you are talking about."

"She's talking about the two boys, Jaco," Sherazade said. "They're not in her room."

"They ain't in the room? Where are they?" Jaco asked.

"That's what we're askin' you," Sherazade said pointedly. "Jaco, have you taken those two boys somewhere? You promised me you wouldn't hurt them. Have you killed them?"

"Puke!" Jaco called.

The man Jaco had appointed sheriff came over to his table. "What do you need?"

"Them two boys is gone. Do you have any idea what happened to them?"

Puke shook his head. "No, I don't have no idea at all."

"Find 'em."

"Find 'em? What do you mean, find 'em? I don't know how to find 'em."

"You're the sheriff, ain't you? Whenever somebody goes missin', it's the sheriff's job to find 'em."

The expression on Puke's face was one of complete confusion. He had no idea what he was supposed to do next."

"I'll help you look for 'em," Mattoon said.

■ ■ ■ ■

Puke, Mattoon, and four others overtook the little cart that Wang was pulling. Wang was slouching in the seat and when the four stopped him, he kept his eyes down.

"Hey, you, Chinaman!" one of the men called to him. "Have you seen two white boys anywhere on this road?"

"Do you want melons?" Wang asked, grabbing the edge of the canvas as if about to lift it. "I have good melons here. You look, I show you."

"No, you ignorant Chinaman, I don't want to look at your melons," Mattoon said. He spoke to the others. "Come on. We're wasting our time here."

Soon after that encounter, Wang told the two boys they could come out from under the canvas.

Eagle Pass

Practically the entire town of Eagle Pass greeted them when Wang rode down East Main Street. By the time he reached the sheriff's office, Jason and Melissa were there to meet them.

Neither Elmer nor Morley nor Justin Craig — the prisoner Morley had recommended — drew so much as a second glance when they rode into town.

When they stepped into the Red Dog, a few of the patrons gave them a casual glance, then looked away.

But for one of the men, the glance was more than casual. "Damn. Elmer Gleason, what are you doing here?"

"You know these three men, Cyr?" Mattoon asked.

"I know that old, ugly one in the middle. There ain't no one nowhere more crooked than him."

"Hello, Cuz," Elmer said. "I see you never found the rest of your ear."

Unconsciously, Cyr put his hand up to his mangled ear. "I ask again, what are you doin' here?"

"We heard you had somethin' good goin' on here, 'n we thought we'd join up," Elmer said, playing the role.

"Yeah? Well you're goin' to have to take that up with Jaco. He's the onliest one who can decide."

"Where is he?"

"Right now he's upstairs, and I don't have no notion of interruptin' a man while he's takin' care of business, if you know what I mean." Cyr grinned.

"Yeah, I think I know what you mean. Come on, boys. Let's get us a beer and wait on Jaco."

The three men bought a beer, complaining about the quarter it cost, then went over to have a seat at one of the tables. Three of the saloon girls sidled up to them with practiced smiles.

Elmer had no idea how old the three women were. They could have been as young as twenty-two or twenty-three, and as old as mid-forties. The dissipation of their profession had taken a heavy toll. "Ladies, we appreciate the attention, we really do, but you're just wastin' your time with us. We ain't got a whole dollar betwixt the three of us." He smiled. "But oncet we get on with Jaco, why, I reckon we'll have some money we can spend."

"Good," one of women said to him specifically. "When that happens, I want you to keep me in mind. All right, old man?"

"Who you callin' an old man?" Elmer asked as if upset by the sobriquet. In truth, his bark was worse than his bite, as given away by the flashing smile in his eyes.

"Ha!" Morley said. "She's got you pegged, Gleason. You are an old man."

"Look who's talking."

"What are we goin' to do if Jaco takes us on?" Morley asked.

"If Duff is goin' to take this town, he's goin' to need to know what he's up ag'in," Elmer said. "I'd say that, over the next few days, we just sort of look around, so's we got somethin' we can tell 'im."

"Here comes Jaco." It was the first time Craig had spoken since the three arrived in town.

"How do you know?" Elmer asked.

"I hear you three men are wantin' —" Seeing Craig, Jaco broke out into a big smile. "Justin Craig. I thought you were in prison."

"And I heerd that you was about to be hung," Craig replied. The two men shook hands.

"I see what you mean. The law may have one idea for us, but we might have somethin' totally different. You with these two, are you?"

"Yeah, this here is Jim Morley 'n this here is Elmer Gleason." Craig pointed to the two men.

"You vouch for them, do you?"

"I can vouch for Morley. Truth to tell, I don't know nothin' about Gleason."

"Well, I've heard of 'im, from Cyr," Jaco said. "And none of it good." He glared at

412

Elmer. "Is it true you're the one that bit off his ear?"

"Yeah," Elmer said.

The glare left his face and Jaco laughed out loud. "Ha! Anybody who would bite off Val Cyr's ear is all right in my book. I'd be happy to have you three boys ride with me."

Chapter Thirty-Six

Elmer spent two days inside Shumla, gathering information he would need in order for Duff to coordinate an attack on the town. He realized that the odds were going to be against Duff. He had only Wang, Jason Bowles, who had temporarily turned his sheriff duties over to his deputy, and Hanson. That was four men against an army of twenty.

Of course, Elmer planned on he, Morley, and Craig also being with Duff. Though that would improve the odds somewhat, they would still be doing battle against a force with more than twice as many men as Duff could muster.

Midway through the second day, the odds grew steeper.

Elmer stepped into the Red Dog. Ever cautious, he glanced around. Four more men were there, but they were townspeople, not part of Jaco's gang. They represented

414

no danger to him.

He was sitting at a table with Belle when Dane and Dingo came into the room, dragging a body — that of Jim Morley. They dragged it all the way over to the table, then dropped it.

Belle got up from the table the moment they approached and moved toward three other girls. All four moved to one side of the room. With shocked expressions on their faces, they watched the drama playing out before them.

"Here, what the hell is this?" Elmer stood up, glaring.

"Did you really think you would get away with it, Gleason?" Dingo asked.

"Get away with what?"

"Craig!" Dingo shouted. "You want to come over here?"

A moment later, Craig came into the center of the saloon. "I told 'em, Gleason. I told 'em ever'thing."

"And you got Morley killed?"

"Yeah, I reckon I did."

"I thought Morley was your friend."

"So is Jaco, only he's got more to offer than Morley did."

"Gleason, Cyr has been tellin' us about you," Dingo said. "He says you 'n him rode together with Quantrill and Anderson.

Good with a gun, are you?"

"I'm all right if I'm close enough to whatever it is that I'm a-shootin' at."

"Do you think you could beat me in a gunfight?"

"Is that what we're goin' to have? A gunfight? I figured you'd probably just shoot me."

Dingo laughed, a high-pitched, insane cackle. "That is what I am a-goin' to do to you, you fool! Do you think that, just because we're goin' to have a gunfight it's goin' to make any difference to you? I'll shoot you down same as if I just walked up to you and held a gun to your head."

"I don't know," Elmer said. "I don't reckon I ever really give it that much thought. But you might be right."

"I might be right? I *might be*? Damn, Gleason, how dumb are you, anyway? You don't really think that you would have a chance ag'in me, do you?"

"Probably not," Elmer agreed.

"You're just goin' to have to deal with it." Again, Dingo laughed. "You're goin' to be shot down like a dog right in front of all these soiled doves." He pointed to the side of the room, glaring at Elmer. "Get up."

"I'll stay where I am."

Dingo grinned. "Don't you think we owe

them a show?"

"Not particularly. If I'm goin' to die, I may as well die comfortable."

Dingo laughed. "That's funny. That's real funny."

"Dingo, you might want to think about this again," Elmer said. "I warn you, it may not turn out quite like you're a-thinkin'."

"You warn me?"

"Yeah."

"First, you say you want to die comfortable, then you warn me. Yes sir, Gleason, you are a real funny man."

"It'll be good for you to die laughin'," Elmer said. "When you show up in hell, laughin', the devil is goin' to be some confused."

"Enough of this!" Dingo shouted. He started for his pistol, but before he even touched the handle, a gun roared from under the table. Slapping his hands over the wound in his chest, he looked at Elmer with a surprised expression on his face. "How? How?"

"I don't have to beat you if I've already got the gun in my hand." Sensing a movement from Dane, Elmer turned his pistol toward him. "You want to die, too?"

Dane threw both hands up in the air.

"Belle, I want you to get Dingo's pistol.

You" — Elmer pointed to one of the other bar girls — "come over here and get Dane's pistol. Bring them to me."

When he had both pistols in hand, Elmer took out the cylinders and dropped them into his pocket. He handed the guns back to the two women. "Drop them over there in that spittoon, would you?"

"You think Jaco is goin' to let you get away?" Dane asked angrily.

"Well, I don't know. I hadn't planned on askin' 'im," Elmer said as he backed toward the door.

Leaving the saloon, he mounted his horse, then untied the reins of six other horses that happened to be tied to the hitching rail. Firing his pistol a couple times scattered the other horses, then, slapping his legs against the side of his horse, he galloped away. He knew it would take several minutes for Jaco and his men to get mounted, and by that time he would be well out of town.

He rode north to throw anyone off who might be following him, then moved into Blanco Creek and took it to the Frio River, where he turned south toward Eagle Pass.

When the residents of Shumla awakened the next morning, they were greeted by printed flyers that had been posted on fences, walls, trees, and windows all over town.

Citizens of Shumla!
Your Time of Delivery is *near.*
The outlaws who have taken over your town will be dealt with.
You are advised to stay in your homes.
<u>Anyone</u> *seen on the street will be a target.*

"Where the hell did these come from?" Jaco demanded angrily when first Cyr, than Mattoon, brought him one of the posters.

"They're posted all over the place, Jaco," Mattoon said. "Hell, there ain't a buildin' in town that don't have one or more of these things posted."

"Who put them out?"

"I don't know, but somebody sure as hell did."

"Get all our men together," Jaco ordered.

Half a mile south of town, Duff, Elmer, Wang, Jason, and Hanson were finishing their breakfast. It was Wang who had sneaked into town to post all the flyers. They had a number of reasons for doing it. One reason was to unnerve Jaco and the men with him. Another was to let the victims of

Shumla, those good citizens who were trapped in the outlaw town by no fault of their own, know that help was coming. And finally, it was a warning to all to stay off the street.

Rarely was a battle ever planned against greater odds. Duff and his friends made five, but there were at least twenty men arrayed against them.

"We aren't at as big a disadvantage as it may appear," Duff said. "When we launch our attack, we will do so with a plan. That means we determine what is about to happen. Jaco and his men can only react to what we do."

"And," Hanson added, "as Euripides says, ten men wisely led are worth a hundred without a head. We are wisely led."

"Wang, I've always heard that Chinamen are good with explosives."

"Indeed they are," Hanson said. "It was the Chinese who invented gunpowder."

"Good. Here are a few sticks of dynamite. Wait until I'm in position, then just toss them out into the middle of the street. Don't blow up any of the buildings. We want to return the town to its citizens. You'll be our artillery."

"You do know what they say about artillery, don't you?" Hanson asked.

"No, but I'm sure you are about to tell us," Jason replied.

"Artillery lends dignity to what would otherwise be an uncouth brawl."

"That's somethin' your friend told you, is it?" Elmer asked.

"My friend?"

"This Youpodees or whatever his name was."

"Euripides," Hanson said with a chuckle. "It is just something he might have said."

"All right. It's time," Duff said. "Elmer, you, Jason, and Cal go to the north end of town. Wait until you hear the first charge go off, then start moving into town. Move cautiously and engage anyone you encounter on the street."

"Where are you going to be, Duff?" Jason asked.

Duff pointed to the railroad water tank. "I'll be up there. Wang, wait about fifteen minutes, then start the fireworks."

Duff rode around to the west side of town and dismounted. Pulling his Creedmoor and sack full of ammunition, he walked across the track to the water tower, then climbed to the top. Just as he had thought, he had a commanding view of the town. He loaded his rifle and waited.

■ ■ ■ ■

The explosion was so loud that it rattled the whiskey bottles behind the bar inside the Red Dog.

"What was that?" Jaco shouted.

"Damned if I know," Cyr replied.

The first explosion was followed by a second.

"Get out there and see what's going on!" Jaco ordered.

Half a dozen men rushed into the street and were taken under fire immediately by Elmer, Jason, and Hanson. The outlaws quickly returned fire and a gun battle ensued.

Several more of Jaco's men came outside to join the battle, and Duff went to work. He began picking off Jaco's men, one at a time. The fact that they were being shot down by someone they couldn't even see had a very unnerving effect.

"Cyr!" Elmer called to his cousin, who was moving down an alley.

Cyr turned and fired, but missed. Elmer returned fire and didn't miss.

"Damn, damn, damn! Killed by my own cousin. Who would a-thought it?"

Blue Putt was next to go down, then Mattoon, then Dane, until finally not one of Jaco's men was left alive.

Elmer, Jason, and Hanson moved down the street until they were standing in front of the saloon.

"Jaco! Jaco, are you in there?" Elmer shouted.

"I'm here," a muffled voice called from inside.

"Come on out here with your hands up."

They heard a woman call out in fear, then a moment later Jaco appeared. He stepped out onto the porch of the saloon, holding his pistol pressed against a woman's head.

"Peggy?" Jason asked, recognizing her and calling her by the name she had been known by in Eagle Pass.

"Now you three fellers drop your guns," Jaco said. " 'Cause if you don't, I'm goin' to shoot this woman."

From his position in the water tower, Duff examined the situation to see if he had a shot. Jaco was holding the woman in front of him in such a way as to completely shield himself. Looking through the sight of his rifle, Duff saw just a sliver of the side of Jaco's head. At least three hundred yards away, the target Jaco presented was no bigger than a fifty-cent piece.

Duff took a deep breath, aimed, let half his breath out, held it, then squeezed the trigger.

Peggy gave a startled cry as the bullet popped by her ear. Blood, brain, and bone detritus exploded from the side of Jaco's head.

Gradually, the citizens of the town began to appear. They walked up and down the street stunned by what had happened. Duff climbed down from the water tower and met his friends in the street. Cleanup began shortly after the people realized their town was free.

After all the bodies were gathered, a delegation of townspeople came to see Duff and his little liberation army in the general store.

"We can't thank you enough for what you done here today," one of the men said. "Thank you for giving us our town back."

Duff nodded. "Hang on to it this time."

Eagle Pass

Six months later, Duff and Megan returned, but it was for a happy event — to attend the wedding of Cal Hanson and Jennie Garrison.

After the wedding when congratulations

were offered and toasts were drunk, Jason asked the question. "When do you think Melissa and I will be going to a wedding in Chugwater?"

Duff and Megan smiled at each other, but neither of them responded to the question.

J. A. JOHNSTONE ON
WILLIAM W. JOHNSTONE
"PRINT THE LEGEND"

William W. Johnstone was born in southern Missouri, the youngest of four children. He was raised with strong moral and family values by his minister father, and tutored by his schoolteacher mother. Despite this, he quit school at age fifteen.

"I have the highest respect for education," he says, "but such is the folly of youth, and wanting to see the world beyond the four walls and the blackboard."

True to this vow, Bill attempted to enlist in the French Foreign Legion ("I saw Gary Cooper in *Beau Geste* when I was a kid and I thought the French Foreign Legion would be fun.") but was rejected, thankfully, for being underage. Instead, he joined a traveling carnival and did all kinds of odd jobs. It was listening to the veteran carny folk, some of whom had been on the circuit since the late 1800s, telling amazing tales about their experiences that planted the storytelling seed in Bill's imagination.

"They were mostly honest people, despite the bad reputation traveling carny shows had back then," Bill remembers. "Of course, there were exceptions. There was one guy named Picky, who got that name because he was a master pickpocket. He could steal a man's socks right off his feet without him knowing. Believe me, Picky got us chased out of more than a few towns."

After a few months of this grueling existence, Bill returned home and finished high school. Next came stints as a deputy sheriff in the Tallulah, Louisiana, Sheriff's Department, followed by a hitch in the U.S. Army. Then he began a career in radio broadcasting at KTLD in Tallulah, which would last sixteen years. It was there that he fine-tuned his storytelling skills. He turned to writing in 1970, but it wouldn't be until 1979 that his first novel, *The Devil's Kiss,* was published. Thus began the full-time writing career of William W. Johnstone. He wrote horror (*The Uninvited*), thrillers (*The Last of the Dog Team*), even a romance novel or two. Then, in February 1983, *Out of the Ashes* was published. Searching for his missing family in a postapocalyptic America, rebel mercenary and patriot Ben Raines is united with the civilians of the Resistance forces and moves to the forefront of a revolution for the nation's future.

Out of the Ashes was a smash. The series would continue for the next twenty years, winning Bill three generations of fans all over the world. The series was often imitated but never duplicated. "We all tried to copy the Ashes series," said one publishing executive, "but Bill's uncanny ability, both then and now, to predict in which direction the political winds were blowing brought a certain immediacy to the table no one else could capture." The Ashes series would end its run with more than thirty-four books and twenty million copies in print, making it one of the most successful men's action series in American book publishing. (The Ashes series also, Bill notes with a touch of pride, got him on the FBI's Watch List for its less than flattering portrayal of spineless politicians and the growing power of big government over our lives, among other things. In that respect, I often find myself saying, "Bill was years ahead of his time.")

Always steps ahead of the political curve, Bill's recent thrillers, written with myself, include *Vengeance Is Mine, Invasion USA, Border War, Jackknife, Remember the Alamo, Home Invasion, Phoenix Rising, The Blood of Patriots, The Bleeding Edge,* and the upcoming *Suicide Mission.*

It is with the western, though, that Bill found his greatest success. His westerns propelled him onto both the *USA Today* and the *New York Times* bestseller lists.

Bill's western series include *Matt Jensen, the Last Mountain Man, Preacher, the First Mountain Man, The Family Jensen, Luke Jensen, Bounty Hunter, Eagles, MacCallister* (an Eagles spin-off), *Sidewinders, The Brothers O'Brien, Sixkiller, Blood Bond, The Last Gunfighter,* and the new series *Flintlock* and *The Trail West.* May 2013 saw the hardcover western *Butch Cassidy: The Lost Years.*

"The Western," Bill says, "is one of the few true art forms that is one hundred percent American. I liken the Western as America's version of England's Arthurian legends, like the Knights of the Round Table, or Robin Hood and his Merry Men. Starting with the 1902 publication of *The Virginian* by Owen Wister, and followed by the greats like Zane Grey, Max Brand, Ernest Haycox, and of course Louis L'Amour, the Western has helped to shape the cultural landscape of America.

"I'm no goggle-eyed college academic, so when my fans ask me why the Western is as popular now as it was a century ago, I don't offer a 200-page thesis. Instead, I can only offer this: The Western is honest. In this great country, which is suffering under the yoke of political correctness, the Western harks back to an era when justice was sure and swift. Steal a man's horse, rustle his cattle, rob a bank, a stagecoach, or a train, you were hunted down and fitted with a hangman's noose. One size fit all.

"Sure, we westerners are prone to a little embellishment and exaggeration and, I admit it, occasionally play a little fast and loose with the facts. But we do so for a very good reason — to enhance the enjoyment of readers.

"It was Owen Wister, in *The Virginian,* who first coined the phrase *'When you call me that, smile.'* Legend has it that Wister actually heard those words spoken by a deputy sheriff in Medicine Bow, Wyoming, when another poker player called him a son of a bitch.

"Did it really happen, or is it one of those myths that have passed down from one generation to the next? I honestly don't know. But there's a line in one of my favorite Westerns of all time, *The Man Who Shot Liberty Valance,* where the newspaper editor tells the young reporter, 'When the truth becomes legend, print the legend.'

"These are the words I live by."

The employees of Thorndike Press hope you have enjoyed this Large Print book. All our Thorndike, Wheeler, and Kennebec Large Print titles are designed for easy reading, and all our books are made to last. Other Thorndike Press Large Print books are available at your library, through selected bookstores, or directly from us.

For information about titles, please call:
800-223-1244

or visit our web site at:

http://gale.cengage.com/thorndike

To share your comments, please write:

Publisher
Thorndike Press
10 Water St., Suite 310
Waterville, ME 04901